A FAMILIAR MISTAKE

NIKKI FRANK

SOUL MATE PUBLISHING

New York

A FAMILIAR MISTAKE

Copyright©2019

NIKKI FRANK

Cover Design by Fiona Jayde

This book is a work of fiction. The names, characters, places, and incidents are the products of the author's imagination or are used fictitiously. Any resemblance to actual events, business establishments, locales, or persons, living or dead, is entirely coincidental.

Published in the United States of America by
Soul Mate Publishing
P.O. Box 24
Macedon, New York, 14502

ISBN: 978-1-68291-895-1
eBook ISBN: 978-1-68291-873-9

www.SoulMatePublishing.com

The publisher does not have any control over and does not assume any responsibility for author or third-party websites or their content.

For Richard

Acknowledgments

While I'd love to claim to be a story-telling superhero, single-handedly saving the world from boredom one action-packed page at a time, I can't—for one huge reason.

I am not alone.

Behind me stands a whole cast of truly amazing people who at every turn reaffirm me in my dreams. So, to my sidekicks:

Joan – Thanks for reading outside your regular genre. I'll convert you to fantasy yet.

My family and friends – Thank you all for your enthusiastic support and numerous questions about when the next book is coming. It's so much easier to write knowing that anticipation awaits my work.

Jessica and Grey – Thanks for your unwavering encouragement.

My editors – Thank you for the team effort, ladies. Theresa, especially, for patiently answering all my questions and polishing down to the detail to make sure the book shines.

Chapter 1

A low cement building sprawled before the tall, shockingly blond young man, holding in its walls an item worth more than his life. One which he must recover or suffer the consequences. He'd arrived early at six-thirty in the morning, hoping the hour would render the building empty. Solitude would make searching easier. Shivering, he pulled his coat tighter around his neck. Early spring in upstate New York wasn't any warmer than home.

Across a parking lot with only a handful of cars stood the main building. When he reached the metal doors with peeling green paint, he paused. Locked. Such a detail wouldn't stop him. He had a deadline breathing down his neck, leaving no time to wait. He reached for the lock, determined to force it open. Luxe jumped. A face appeared on the other side of the square glass window in the door.

A man sporting a prominent bald-spot and a cheerless expression silently undid the lock and wandered off. Heaving a sigh, Luxe put a hand on the door, ready to make this a quick search. Noise behind him called his attention. He knew that sound; it came from his nightmares. He turned and cringed in fear. A thing of terror advanced up the path toward him. Something so frightening it almost made him reconsider his search.

Girls. A group of nearly forty of them, all in their teens, carrying tennis rackets and chattering in their short skirts. He didn't do well with females.

Luxe fought a panicky feeling, as they drew near. He

quickly stepped off the path and out of the way of the door. Standing silently, he hoped they would pass him by and then he could be on his way. One or two sets of eyes glazed over him briefly, but largely he went unacknowledged. Perfect. Once inside, the girls scattered. Luxe let himself into the hall after they'd safely dispersed.

Doors and posters lined a hall brimming with roving teens. Where had all these people come from? Another large group of kids came in the door behind him. The situation had gotten bad. All the teens clogging his path made his job harder, and he didn't have much time left. He'd been expecting an easy extraction. Who knew his search would end up in one of the busiest places in the morning: a high school?

In some ways fortune favored him, being young enough to blend. An office building would have been worse. But still, he didn't need the headache or all the bodies in his way. Sighing, he held out his hand, looked for a clear path, and started down the hall toward his goal.

~ ~ ~

Slamming her car door and breathing deeply of the spring air, Paige Gentry let the joy of being alive permeate every cell. The sweet smell of things growing and coming to life wafted in on the breeze. She took off across the student parking lot, waving to her friends. With only two months until graduation and the arrival of warm weather, nothing could put a damper on her mood. Especially since the best thing to ever happen to her waited right on the other side of graduation.

Her older brother Owen would finish a semester abroad in Barcelona just after school ended for her. He'd agreed to spend four weeks taking her to visit as much of Europe as they could pack in. He'd even helped put pressure on her parents, promising to look after her. They'd finally agreed, as long as her brother traveled with her.

Her backpack currently carried more travel printouts than school work, but she didn't care. Her grades were so good that even if she barely passed the last few tests of the year, she'd still be fine. She'd already completed her senior project and presented it. That major weight had disappeared as of last Friday. She'd responded to her college acceptance letters already. Her future waited at the University of Hawaii. She only had to wait until orientation in August.

Her parents weren't thrilled with her choice, Hawaii being about as far from New York as one could get and stay in the US. But travel called to Paige. Her parents called the urge *wanderlust*. That just sounded . . . no. Parents should never use anything containing the word "lust." Owen called it "the travel bug". He said he'd been bit too, admitting to Paige that he'd stay in Barcelona to finish college if he could afford it.

Their parents ran through the whole gamut of guilt. So many excellent colleges on the east coast, all within commuting distance or at worst an easy flight. Paige's grades were so good, she could have gotten into an Ivy League school. That thought made her pause. There'd been some truth to their argument for going to a prestigious school. She'd been accepted to Brown University, but when she'd seen the cost, she'd tucked the letter away and not told her parents.

The driving desire behind her choice always came back to wanting to see the world. To see white sands and palm tree so unlike her home. She wanted to experience a winter without snow. Besides, from Hawaii she could travel to Asia, Australia, India. Places which took way too long from New York.

She had virtually nothing to do until school let out, leaving her a bit giddy. She could focus on things like prom, which waited a mere three weeks away, without any guilt. Rumor had it that the boy she'd been eyeing for months now, Justin, was finally over his ex and back on the market, just in time for the spring dance. Now to do a little fishing and see if he might be interested in her, too. Paige sighed and shook her brown ponytail. Yes, life was good.

The final bell rang for first period as Paige slipped into her seat. She'd caught Justin at his locker before class and dropped hints about the dance, but they kept getting interrupted. Her dawdling nearly made her late. Despite that, she was determined to let nothing ruin the buzz of her good fortune. Besides, he'd been very friendly—always a good sign.

She glanced dreamily around the classroom, and her gaze fell on a strange figure at the other end of her row of desks. A new boy occupied the last seat. Three things immediately struck her about him. First, what an odd time of year for a senior to join a new school. Second, he looked very cute. The *prop your elbow on the desk, put your chin in your hand and stare*, sort of cute. The last and weirdest thing was that no one else seemed to notice him.

Paige *did*. How could she not? He had blond hair, so light it almost looked silver. Nearly white eyelashes framed blue eyes. He appeared delicate and fine boned with an intelligent face. Even while sitting, she could tell he would be tall.

Deeply-seated curiosity nagged her, but at that moment the teacher called class to attention. However, she made no mention of the new mystery student. So Paige settled for observing. He seemed interested in the room—overly interested. His bright-eyed attention darted across all the corners. Once or twice his glance brushed over her, and Paige gave a little shiver. He never stopped or acknowledged he'd caught her staring. But she had a feeling he perceived more than most people would have.

~ ~ ~

Luxe drummed his fingers on the desk in impatience. After searching the school building, he'd found himself cornered in a classroom when the morning bell rang. Such an inconvenience. The thing he sought was close, and he needed to grab it and go.

To make matters worse, the girl with the brown ponytail kept looking at him. How odd. He ought to be pretty much unnoticeable, which was exactly the way he preferred it. Girls tended to be trouble, and he certainly didn't have time for the inconvenience today.

He fiddled with the underside of the desk, his fingers looking for an outlet for his growing anxiety, when he came across something round and hard and stuck to gum. He wrinkled his nose. Disgusting, but at least he'd found what he needed. Better soiled than lost. Since he'd retrieved his item, he could sit back and relax until it was time to leave.

He listened to the lecture with some amusement. History classes always held some fascination for him. Besides, if he focused on the lesson, maybe the girl over there would stop paying attention to him. She was now making eyes at him, trying to get him to look. She pointed at her book like she wanted to share, since she probably noticed he didn't have one. Nosy girls. They really shouldn't meddle, but inevitably they did. Where he went never mattered; they were *all* the same.

~ ~ ~

As soon as the bell rang, the blond boy bolted from the classroom, leaving Paige disappointed. Thoughts of him scratched at the back of her brain for the next two periods, but she didn't see him again to make her offer. Paige's curiosity about the mystery student completely disappeared when Justin caught her at her locker. She gazed up at him, warmth spreading through her body at the close proximity. Her hands hung in front of her, holding her open backpack. She should have been gathering books, but the pack dangled, forgotten.

Justin's hazel eyes twinkled at her. "Hey, Paige."

Her knees went wobbly, and her imagination ran wild with a storybook invitation to the dance. Maybe her hints had soaked in since this morning and inspired him.

Without warning, she took a collision to her chest, and her body flew backwards. She got out one shriek before connecting with the floor. Something, or rather, someone crushed the air out of her. The new boy sprawled across her, looking confused and fidgety. Justin yanked him off her by the back of his shirt.

"What the hell, man?"

"I'm so, so sorry." The new boy's voice came out in a quiet stammer. He had a faint English accent, which tickled Paige's sensibilities.

Justin held a hand out and helped Paige off the floor. "Do you randomly tackle chicks all the time, or are you just messing with Paige?" he growled at the blond boy.

Paige's stomach soared at the sound of his defense of her. It wasn't the grand invitation she'd been imagining a moment ago, but being rescued by a prince could be nice, too. The new boy tried to get himself out of Justin's grip. His platinum hair was completely disheveled, and he looked nervously through his pockets while his eyes kept sweeping the floor.

"No. I'm sorry, really. I simply glanced behind me. I didn't see her. I swear." His eyes caught Paige's for a moment. "Are you all right?"

"Yeah."

Justin dropped his grip on the thinner boy. "Whatever. Just watch what you're doing. If you hurt Paige, I'll hurt you. That's a promise."

The boy nodded and scurried off down the hallway, his gaze glued to the floor as he went. Justin had kept Paige's hand when he'd pulled her up, and her heart soared. Nothing could spoil this day. Her stomach flip-flopped as Justin closed the distance between them.

"Paige, would you—"

The one-minute warning bell screamed at them from the wall over their heads. She drew her hand back reluctantly. "Tell me at lunch, okay?"

He looked frustrated but agreed and left for his class. Paige went blissfully off to her own. Lunch followed fourth period, so she wouldn't have long to wait.

~ ~ ~

Fourth period started and panic had settled over Luxe. He'd lost his prize. With the halls now clear he could search for the missing item again. He had to find it; he'd run the clock down to the final hour. How could he have been stupid enough to drop something so important?

Luxe crawled the hall on his hands and knees, checking under the lip of the lockers and in the corners, yet his search yielded nothing. The bits of crumpled paper, pen caps, and other tidbits made him sure his item hadn't been swept up while he wasn't looking. So, either someone had picked his item up, or . . .

His breath caught in his throat. He knew where the article had gone. He felt sure. Now, how to get it? If he was correct, the object had ended up in one of the most uncomfortable places imaginable: in the possession of a girl.

~ ~ ~

Paige blushed as she caught sight of Justin waiting by her locker. She'd started down the hall toward him when someone tugged on her sleeve. Turning, she found herself face to face with the mysterious boy.

"Um, Paige, was it? Might I have a moment of your time?"

Paige raised an eyebrow. His voice sounded masculine enough, though rather soft. But his words were stiff and formal. "I'll give you a sec. I've got plans for lunch today."

He glanced up at her locker and Justin. "Yes, of course. Pardon my interruption. I'll be brief. I think I may have dropped something in your bag when we collided earlier. May I see the contents of your bag?"

"No. I'll take a look for you, though. What did you drop?"

He looked nervously at the back of his hand and licked his lips. "I'm nearly out of time. Conducting the search myself would be much more expedient."

Paige scrunched her nose in distaste. He might be good-looking, but she got a weird vibe from him. She had no intention of letting him rummage through her stuff on his own. She pulled the backpack close to her chest.

"No. I don't want you in my bag. You're kinda creeping me out. What could you possibly have dropped you can't tell me about? Maybe I should take my bag to the principal. I don't want to get in trouble for something bad you brought to school."

He glanced at his hand again, his eyes widening. "Paige. I beg of you, please. Let me see your bag."

He reached, and she backed away. On his second snatch, he caught her wrist. Before she could protest, the world plunged into darkness. A roaring like a waterfall surrounded her, and she had the sensation of falling through the darkness.

Chapter 2

Paige crashed onto the ground hard. Pain shot up her spine. A thud came from next to her, and the blond boy scrambled to his feet. Cold and damp air hit her face, smelling like–wet stone? She gawked around her in total shock. She'd ended up on her butt in the middle of a stone hallway. Torches in brackets gave off a flickering yellow light. Hewn stones lined the walls, and a window with no glass gave her a slivered glimpse of gray sky. It looked exactly like a hallway in a medieval castle.

Paige did what any girl in her situation might do. She screamed. The boy jumped on her in a moment, a hand clamped over her mouth, desperately shushing her.

"Please be quiet, Paige. We'll be in ever so much trouble if we're found like this."

"Who are you, and what the hell happened?" she tried to ask through his hand.

He glanced to her left, then right, and over her shoulder. Reaching around, he grabbed her backpack. She yanked it back, sitting on it.

"I really need to see inside." He held his hand out, his palm glowing with a floating green arrow which pointed straight at her.

Her mouth free, she grimaced at him. "Not a chance in hell. You've done something horrible. I can't imagine what or how, but I know this is your fault. The only thing you're allowed to do with me is explain and take me back to my school."

"We can address your requests after I see—"

"No. *Explain.*" She shot him the fiercest expression she could.

"You . . . um . . . ." He heaved a sigh. "There's no easy way to say this. I'm going to list the most important points, and you can ask me what you will from there." He took a deep breath. "My name is Luxe. I'm a warlock. You accidentally got pulled through my portal when the spell timed out."

Paige gave a snorting laugh. "Like hell I believe that," she spat out at him.

"It's true. I swear by my ancestors."

"I suppose that's why you talk all funny, too? Am I supposed to believe you have some sort of warlock accent?"

"Not really. I actually have a very muddled accent due to my propensity for time shifts. However, my family lives here."

"And where exactly are we? I don't know anywhere like this on campus."

"No. This location most certainly would not be at your school. We are in the outer wall of my family's castle."

"Right, your castle. No one lives in castles, unless you want me to believe you're some sort of royalty."

Luxe shook his head. "Many of the nobility live in castles. We're in 1521, after all. Where else would we live?"

Paige scrambled away from him until she hit the unforgiving rock wall. "What? How is that possible? Where did you take me? I want the truth."

He grabbed her bag off the floor, sticking his hand inside. "I *have* been telling you the truth. You're in my family's castle in Cheshire. We're currently in the year 1521, and it's possible by magic." He held his hand out toward her, flicked his fingers, and sent a shower of green sparkles at her.

Paige screamed.

Once again Luxe had a hand over her mouth, dropping her bag. "Please. Please, don't make a sound." He stood pulling her up with him.

She nabbed the backpack and clutched it to her chest.

Keeping her mouth covered, he went along the hall to the next torch bracket. Leaning into the stone he whispered, *"Apertia."*

Paige clung desperately to her sanity as the wall slid open, revealing a staircase winding downward into the dark. He wrangled her inside, and as soon as the wall slid shut behind them, Luxe dropped his hands with a huge sigh.

"I am deeply sorry. I understand your apprehension. However, bringing you with me happened completely by accident. I'll send you back, and you can forget all this ever took place."

"You can do that?" she asked, deeply suspicious. Paige caught a moment of hesitation on his part.

"Sure. I got to your time in the first place, right?"

"You're not going to drop me off somewhere random, are you?" Paige asked. Not that his answer mattered much. This had to be a dream. She must have hit her head when she got knocked over in the hall. Any moment now she would wake up in the nurse's office. "I don't want to be running from dinosaurs while you kick back and assume I'm safe."

"I won't do that." This time his answer came swift and smooth. "I'm really good with time portals."

The way he said it made Paige suspect there were things—supposedly magical things—he wasn't so good at. He made another grab for her pack, and she swatted his hand. He had a seriously creepy obsession with her backpack.

They started down the stairs, Luxe leading the way. She'd expected the stairwell to be dark and cavernous, much like the hall they'd landed in. Instead, light illuminated her way from the most unexpected source— Luxe's hand. It glowed the same shade of green the sparks had been: a brilliant, apple-green. Paige pressed herself against the stone wall of the spiral staircase, fighting the urge to scream again.

She let him get ahead of her, not wanting to get too close to the glowing boy. But as his green light and white-blond hair disappeared around the bend in the staircase, and darkness began to settle over her, she reconsidered. She scrambled down the stairs to catch up with him. The dark might actually be worse, she decided.

They reached the bottom of the stairs, and Luxe opened a heavy wooden door with an iron ring for a handle. Inside, he spoke a single word. *"Illumina."*

Around the room, torches flared to life. The room wasn't anything like what she'd expected. It spread the size of a living room: about twenty-five feet by fifteen feet. Hardwood planks lined the floor, polished, smooth, and glowing in the torch light. These torches let off no smoke, unlike the ones in the first hall.

The furniture appeared mid-century modern, from her time, with clean lines and white leather upholstery. Glass-topped tables held elegant cut-glass jars in various colors. Two of those tables stood along each of the far-end walls. In the center wall, across from the door, a massive built-in bookcase dominated the room, filled to the top with leather-bound books. Some looked incredibly old. In every free space sat artifacts from cultures modern and ancient and from all around the world. Paige stopped, studying a sparkling cat statue. The cat resembled ancient Egyptian artwork, and it appeared to be made of gold.

Luxe beckoned her over to one of the tables. "Okay. I'm going to give you a memory draught and send you home. The potion won't hurt, and you'll remember this as a dream."

He ran a finger across the spines of the books on the table. "Huh . . ." Crossing to one of the bookshelves, he perused the titles there. "Damn it, Atlas," he mumbled to himself.

Paige frowned. Why did he need an atlas?

"My brother must have taken the spell book." He muttered some other things Paige couldn't make out. "That should be everything. I can do this from memory. Yes. The potion shouldn't be an issue."

He pulled the stopper out of a pale-blue, cut-glass bottle in the shape of a tear-drop. When opened, it filled the room with the scent of flowers.

"It's so pretty." Paige gasped. "What's that smell?"

"Forget-me-not."

He rummaged around, checking the contents of other bottles. Finally, he returned to where Paige stood waiting and deposited six more flasks on top of the table. He then opened a cabinet hidden behind a row of books and pulled out a small golden bowl as well as a wooden spoon so dark it looked black. He set them on the table and took the stopper out of one of the vessels. Luxe nipped at his lip with his teeth as he counted drops of a smoky, wheat-colored liquid. Four jars later, a sheen of sweat had broken out on his forehead. He wiped his sleeve across his head and grabbed the last bottle. The mixture in the golden bowl sparkled like a disco-ball.

Luxe stood and held the bowl out to Paige. "All done. Drink up, and I'll get you straight home." His expression didn't match the confidence of his words.

Paige took the bowl hesitantly. Inside the liquid rippled, bubbled, and danced like champagne on caffeine.

At least the stuff smelled good. Paige sniffed deeply, and crazy things ran through her head. Impressions of warm places, companionship. The aroma made her compliant and relaxed. She put the bowl to her lips. A dream couldn't hurt her anyway.

The moment the mixture touched her tongue, her mouth flooded with freezing cold. The room rocked with a soundless explosion which shattered all the glass. The shock wave blew Luxe back against the bookshelf. Only Paige remained in her original spot. Luxe ran back to her and grabbed her shoulders.

"Veratus."

Warm prickles spread all over her body. Luxe now paced the ruined room, shaking his head.

"Damn." He looked over at Paige, his eyes wide. "Damn, damn." He grabbed a handful of his own hair and turned a pleading look on her. "I'm going to be in *so . . . much . . . trouble*."

Paige surveyed the room. "Well, the place is a mess, but just send me home and you can blame it on the cat or something."

"No. You don't understand. Everything has gone terribly wrong. I can't send you home now. Not ever."

"What?" The blood drained from Paige's face. She wanted to wake up. This dream had gone south quickly. "Explain."

"I . . . well . . . you see . . ."

"Oh, for crying out loud. Just spit it out. If something went wrong, fix the mistake. You're a warlock or whatever, right?"

He rubbed at his face a little too hard, leaving red marks down his cheeks. "I am. But . . ."

"But, what?" Paige narrowed her eyes at him.

"I'm only a student. My father's a very accomplished warlock, and my mother's an extremely gifted witch. But

I . . . well, I make a lot of mistakes. I really do have a gift for creating time portals, but some other subjects are more difficult for me."

Paige narrowed her eyes further. "Elaborate," she hissed.

"Um, for example, potion making. It's actually my worst subject."

"And?"

"I may . . . have miscalculated some of the ingredients. I'm not sure which." He grabbed the bottles, reading labels. "Forget-me-not, cat's claw, lotus, negated gingko, wormwood, crushed amber, and purified glacier water. Those should be right."

"Obviously something wasn't. Was the recipe in the book you couldn't find?"

"I think my brother has been borrowing without asking. I seem to be missing several of my spell books."

"So why didn't you go get them back?" she grit out at him. "Or ask your brother, or something?"

"I . . . uh . . . I can't ask. This mistake is really big and if I admit to it, no one is going to let me finish . . . Really they're fairly rudimentary . . . *oh, crap*. I'm going to catch hell . . . But if I die, they'll just send her back . . ." He went chalky on top of his very pale complexion. "There has to be a better way to fix this."

"What *exactly* did you do?"

"I may . . . have turned you into my familiar instead of erasing your memory."

"*What* is a familiar?" Rage prickled all over Paige, and she struggled to keep from shouting at him.

"A familiar is a witch's or warlock's assistant. Their aid, so to speak. The two have a nearly impenetrable bond through mutual magic. The warlock does the spell-work, and the familiar does his bidding." His voice had slipped to a whisper at this point.

"Let me sift through the big-word bullshit and lay this out. You've screwed up and turned me into your magical slave?"

He nodded, keeping his eyes on the floor.

"You said your parents were good with magic. Let's go see if they can break this 'nearly impenetrable' bond." She growled the last three words at him, and he fell back a step.

Luxe's face and neck turned scarlet. "We can't. At least not yet."

"Why?" Paige crept up on him. She'd never attacked anyone before, but she was getting dangerously close to trying.

"Because I'm in the middle of trying to fix another screw-up. A really *big* mistake, and I can't alert my parents to that unless I feel like spending a century as a toad as punishment."

"What could possibly be bigger than this?" Paige snapped.

"Well, a warlock's power is largely drawn from family tradition. The founders of the most prominent magical families found ways to trap their magic and allow successive generations to draw from those powers. My family has nine generations of power to draw from trapped in nine rune-stones. I managed to scatter them by accident while trying out a theory of mine."

He licked his lips nervously. "They've landed all over the world and all over time. That's why I came to your school. One of the rune-stones landed there. I've got to get all the stones back before my parents find out. Once I've got them, and I'm not in trouble, I can ask my parents to help you."

His face brightened for a moment. "But since you're my familiar, you'll have to come with me. Maybe with help I'll get them back faster. Where's your bag?"

Paige ripped open the zippers, tipped her backpack upside-down, and let the contents dump. At this point she really didn't care. Amongst the thuds of her books hitting the floor came a distinct click. A round, flat stone in nondescript brown hit the floor and rolled. Luxe ran after it, trapping the small rock under his foot. He picked the pebble up and flipped it over, relief washing over his face.

"Thank goodness. It's Grandfather Merlin's rune-stone."

"Wait. Grandfather Merlin, as in *the* Merlin?"

"Yes, Miss. The one and only Merlin."

"But how is he your grandfather? Didn't Merlin live like a thousand years ago?"

"Please try to keep up, Paige. Do you or do you not hail from several hundred years in the future? Time means nothing to my family." He took the stone and placed it in an intricately carved box on his work table. "My parents are currently on vacation at the 2048 Olympic Games. Their choices were either that or the coronation party for Emperor Jianwen, the second emperor of the Ming Dynasty. My parents opted for indoor plumbing."

Paige took a moment to process this. "Then how old was Merlin when he died?"

"Almost 986. Warlocks live a long time."

Paige stared at Luxe in shock and then glanced around the room to distract herself. "Why here? Why now? With the inquisition and stuff, seems like too much trouble."

He smiled. "Just the opposite really. Like humans could do anything to a real warlock. The residents of this period are incredibly superstitious. They take their fears out on the peasants, but we're safe.

"Each of the noble magic families claims a bit of history as a home-base. My family runs about an 800-year period of Britain's history. Another family calls ancient

Rome home, and yet another is set up in feudal Japan. The separation gives us the freedom to rule as we see fit."

"How many families are there?"

"Eight noble ones like mine, and a handful of small families in each time period under our protection."

"Protection from what?" Paige asked incredulously. "Aren't you the top of the food chain?"

"Not really, although we're getting close. There are still vampires, demons, and fairy-folk who have magic which rivals ours."

"But I thought those creatures are evil. Well, not the fairies, of course."

Luxe laughed. "Evil is in the eye of the beholder. Except demons. Demons are pretty much evil in a 'gratuitous violence is fun and they won't stop for anything,' sort of way."

Paige shuddered. "Okay. Let's talk about something else." She eyed Luxe carefully. He didn't seem so out of the ordinary. "So, if Grandfather Merlin was nearly a thousand, how old are you?"

"Twenty. Why?" He gave her a surprised look.

"Things are way beyond weird as it is." She tried smoothing down her hair which had nearly come out of its ponytail in all the excitement. "I don't know if I could take it if you turned out to be like 500 years old." She pulled the rubber-band out and re-gathered her hair before putting it back up. "How many more stones do you have left to find?"

"Eight."

"*What*?" Paige shrieked. "I thought you said you were *well into* this task. One of nine isn't well in."

Luxe flushed again. "I . . . I may have painted things a little to the positive side."

"No. You lied," Paige snapped. "You're even dragging me into your problems by suggesting I help. I can't." She shot him a dirty glare. "Do I look like I have magic powers to you?"

"You do now. They come with the familiar contract. Though, I don't know what the link will do for you. The contract is usually sealed between a warlock and an animal."

Paige rubbed her face in exhaustion. "Well, shit. I've always wanted to be a combination slave and pet. Any other good news while we're at it?"

"Um . . . I'm not sure how bad you think this is but . . . you kind of have to obey me."

"Elaborate," she demanded.

"Paige, I want you to do a cartwheel."

"But I don't know—" Invisible hands jerked her arms and legs in the direction she needed to go. The room turned upside-down briefly and then righted. "Holy—"

"Don't worry," Luxe cut in. "I promise not to abuse that power."

Paige's heart dropped into her feet. The implications of being completely at his mercy were terrifying. "You'd better not. Or I'll . . ." Actually, what threat did one make to a warlock? "I'll figure something unpleasant out." Her response got half-drowned out as her stomach growled. "You made me miss lunch." She gave up fighting for pouting. "Got anything to eat around here?"

"We could go to dine with the court."

She glanced down at her jeans, black leather skimmers, and the royal-blue, baby-doll tee with the silver shimmer. "They'd probably burn me for a witch just for my clothing."

"You forget who you're speaking to." Luxe did the finger flick again, sending green sparkles in her direction. He gave them a light blow and whispered, *"Chritudo gratia."*

"What language is that? You keep using it."

"Most of the magical commands my family uses are in Latin. Now, see the results." He flicked his fingers again and a large mirror appeared. The kind with gilt edges, which stood on its own clawed feet.

Paige took one glance at herself and stumbled back. She tripped on the edge of her gown, and Luxe caught her. He was stronger than his wiry build gave away. Setting her back on her feet, he turned her toward the mirror again.

"You'll have to be careful of sudden movements until you've adjusted to the dress," he told her kindly.

The gown was a magnificent piece of art in rich green velvet. An underskirt of cream with intricate gold embroidery peeped through the front panels. More embroidery curled all around the square neckline and open sleeves. A round hood covered in pearls topped her head and hid most of her brown hair with its honey highlights.

"What do you think?"

"I think my car weighs less than this dress," she gasped. "How many layers are there?"

"Five. Or six. I wouldn't know. I don't wear them."

"Anything I should know before dinner? Besides how to walk in this." Her stomach fluttered with both nerves and excitement. She'd wanted to see the world, and now she got to in the wildest possible way.

"Yes. Several things. First, if I bow to someone, you do too. Can you?"

"I've never tried."

"It's just bent knees and a lowered head."

A quick lesson demonstrated she had a definite lack of skill in smoothly bending properly for nobility. Luxe helped her muddle through until he said she could fake well enough.

"Keep your mouth shut. Just smile and nod. Silence won't be obvious, rather appreciated. But your speech pattern will be hard to hide if you talk."

"What about you? You don't sound the way I imagined. You know, like a Shakespearean character."

"I'll be fine. I use an illusion so people around me will notice nothing."

"So why do you sound like you grew up down the road from me? I mean you use different words, and your speech is a bit stiff at times, but overall . . ."

"I spent five years at a boarding school in your time learning about technology. Actually, my visit would have been about thirty-five years after you graduated, but close enough."

"Hey, what's my future like? Did I get married? Have an awesome career? Do I have kids?"

"Nuh-uh. You could really mess up your own fate if you knew. Warlocks can't interfere with our own fate since we're born time-hoppers. There's no chronological progression to disrupt. But you're human. Besides, it's not like I knew you'd be coming back with me. I hardly looked you up when I stayed there."

"Will I be screwing with fate by moving through time with you?"

Luxe shook his head. "You're bound to my magic. It protects you from ruining things the same way it protects me. We can't do much to alter the main course of human events, though some warlocks enjoy playing with the details. There's big punishment from the CoW if you do manage to disrupt the flow of time. A few have carried their exploits that far. Not many though."

"Cow? Like 'moo'?'"

Luxe gave her a look with a wrinkled nose. "No. Chamber of Warlocks. 'CoW.' It's a disciplinary committee which only meets if someone does something so serious a family can't police it on their own. As for your personal fate, we need to keep it intact for when my parents fix you up and send you home. You can go back to the ape-man waiting at your locker like nothing happened."

"That ape-man's name is Justin. He was going to ask me out, but now I'm stuck here instead."

"Yes, dining with Justin must have been a much more thrilling prospect than dining with the infamous King Henry the eighth. I'm sorry I've so seriously downgraded your social experiences."

"I'm eating with the king?" Paige gasped out.

"Yes. Which reminds me. Everything the king says is funny. Laugh. If his music is played, it's inspirational. Look enthralled. If he pays any attention to you at all, find me quickly and we'll leave."

"Why?"

"Do you not read at all? The man has a very definite history of taking lovers. Since I assume you are not interested in a liaison with the king, simply stay out of his way. He also has a very definite habit of squashing those who displease him. I don't want to have to rescue you from London Tower."

Paige turned slowly, not wanting to trip on her skirts again. "You would rescue me?"

"Maybe I should reiterate. We are bonded magically. This is not some contract that says you work in the office with me. Think of us as magic Siamese twins. My power now runs through us both. What hurts you, hurts me."

A tingle ran through Paige's body. "Will you be teaching me magic?"

"Probably. But let's not try just yet."

"Why not?"

"As I said before, this is usually done with an animal. I don't know what the side effects of turning a human into a familiar are. Now, I'll dress for dinner. We must make haste, because one does not keep the King of England waiting."

Chapter 3

Luxe flicked up more sparkles and stepped through them, muttering as he went. He came out of the magic dressed in nearly as many layers as Paige. She stared openly, so he peeked in the mirror. His whole shape had changed. His delicate frame got lost under all the velvet and fur. Only his slim legs in white hose sticking out the bottom indicated he hadn't actually altered his physical form.

He rather liked the fashions of this era on himself. Maybe not the hose, but the rest was quite flattering. He felt so skinny otherwise. Secretly, he would love to have been built burlier, like Paige's ape-man. These clothes covered up the muscles he felt he lacked.

Paige pulled up her skirts, examining them as if trying to count the layers and see what each looked like. He gave a mental sigh and shake of his head. He knew he should have stayed away from her. As always, in his experience, girls were nothing but trouble. And here he was, in the worst trouble he could possibly get into, stuck with her until his parents could fix his mess.

That made him shudder, too. Even if they did get the rune-stones back, his parents were going to be livid about what happened with Paige. His father never held much understanding for his mistakes. Well, he *was* Merlin's son, and he'd been a quick study himself. It stood to reason he expected the same of Luxe.

Luxe assumed only his talent with time portals kept his father from putting him in a tower and pretending he didn't exist. All witches and warlocks used portals throughout adulthood, but Luxe had run off to the gladiatorial games at the Coliseum at the age of five. Not only had he gotten in trouble for time hopping without an adult, but his mother was beside herself since she'd forbidden him from seeing his first disemboweling until his ninth birthday.

As punishment, she'd forced him to care for his grandmother's pet dragon for a decade, a nasty little pot-bellied thing. The creature's drool burned his skin, and it singed things when it farted. He'd gotten lucky when the dragon picked a fight with his older brother's wyvern. The larger dragon had eaten the beast.

His brother had been, and probably always would be, the apple of his parent's eye. Atlas was a proper warlock in all respects. He worked flawless spells. He kept a show-quality dragon. And he came with excess muscle and good looks to boot. Despite only turning thirty-three a short time ago, Atlas had first thrilled their father by wooing and winning a witch with shining talent. Then he'd thrilled their mother by fathering a set of twins who Luxe's mom swore were the cutest witches ever born.

Luxe found his seven-year-old nieces to be more trouble than they were worth. Certainly, they had talent, and undeniably, they were cute. Both sported blond ringlets and huge, brown doe-eyes. But more often than not, those looks were used to cover up some mischief, and they'd already learned they could blame him.

Luxe's own reputation preceded him, and his parents seemed inclined to believe that any mistakes were his fault. It went to show that girls were trouble at any age. Though he did wonder why he always attracted the most troublesome sorts.

Paige snorted with laughter, dragging him back from his wandering thoughts. "Do you have any idea how stupid and impractical these clothes are?"

"Clothing is all about attractiveness, and attractiveness is subjective," he answered, feeling sage. "Is a bikini always a good idea?"

"For some people, no." Paige continued giggling. "But if we're talking about attraction, nothing says 'let's get it on' like one-hundred-fifty pounds of heavy-duty fabric. 'Hold on another forty-five minutes, honey. Let me get off three more skirts and you can see my legs.' Guess there's no equivalent of a quickie in this era."

Luxe snickered and let his eyes twinkle, then held out his arm for her to take. "Since no one here is looking for a quickie, I guess we ought to be all right. Shall we away to dinner, madam?"

She looked at his arm blankly, and he reached over, taking her hand and placing it on his arm above his elbow. He led her to the bookcase. Placing his hand on the leather spines of the books, he spoke softly to them. As he did so, a doorway opened, not behind the books but straight through them.

"We're going in there?" Paige balked at the dark doorway.

"Trust me," Luxe reassured her. "Windsor Castle is a two-day journey by horse, but we have a portal into our family's quarters within the castle."

"Just who are your family at court?"

"My father has himself set up as an Earl. High enough to go where we want, but not claiming a direct link to the throne."

"Oh. Are you? You know, linked to the throne?"

"Not of any human government. We had a warlock king, once. All eight noble families are descendants of his. But he left no laws governing inheritance. Human rules don't apply. Warlock status has to do with the level of power you can wield. The noble houses nearly destroyed themselves before they called an end to the violence and set our system up the way it is now, with each house governing a time."

He placed a free hand on top of hers, smiling reassuringly at her. At least he hoped. Who knew how his expression came off to her, because who knew how girl's minds worked. Before stepping in he paused frowning at her. Her twenty-first century English wouldn't serve for conversation. Unfortunately, the solution terrified him.

Luxe stood in front of the doorway frantically trying to remember the spell to let her speak Early Modern English. The last thing he wanted to do was screw up another spell while putting it on her.

"Luxe? Dinner?"

"I'm trying to concentrate." He hadn't meant to snap, but women were so infuriating. You couldn't do anything right around one. This was too much trouble. He'd give the spell a whirl and hope it worked. Luxe grabbed her shoulders and held her still.

"Donum vetus Latina sermonis." He pressed his lips to hers for a moment before she shoved him back.

"What the hell?"

Luxe's cheeks blazed. "I only gave you the gift of speech," he answered. "It's, ah . . . well, the spell was made with a real familiar in mind. You know. It's not a big deal to kiss your cat."

"And if I want to speak normal again?" She still sounded irritated.

"The spell is easy to get rid of. But we'll worry about that later."

"The way you say that makes me nervous. Your track record isn't stellar. I'm still waiting for your parents to take one spell off."

"No. Really." Luxe's cheeks flamed. "All you . . . all you have to do is give the new language back the same way I gave it to you."

"Oh." Paige fell silent.

Holding up his free hand, he let it glow with his apple-green magic. His hand lit the doorway and what looked like a tunnel lined with black satin. He pulled her along with him. The journey to London took them four steps down the satin hallway. Then they stood in a room very similar to the one they'd left. Except in this one, a fire snapped cheerily in the massive fireplace. A huge four poster bed with red velvet curtains dominated the center of the room. Incredible tapestries embroidered with brilliantly colored scenes of hunts involving mythical beasts covered all the walls.

"Where are we?" Paige asked, staring around them, wonder etched on her face.

"My parent's bedchamber. But come, time runs short."

~ ~ ~

Luxe led her out of the bedroom and through a maze of hallways. When they arrived at the great hall Paige gasped in awe. The massive room had a soaring ceiling supported by huge wooden beams. People, in clothes much like she and Luxe wore, milled around chatting with one another. The whole scene gave her the impression of looking at a living kaleidoscope, dresses and finery in every conceivable color. Over all that twinkled more jewels than the flagship Tiffany's.

The banquet hall was long but rather narrow. At the far end from where they'd entered stood a raised dais on which sat a table and two thrones. At right angles from the main table, two long tables ran the length of the room on either side.

Luxe gave her fingers a gentle touch. "We'll be sitting over on the left side. All the children of the nobility are seated on that side."

"Anyone I would know from my history books?" she hissed back at him.

"Ah." He gave a chuckle. "Well, for the time being things are fairly stable. 1521 is before Henry started to turn things on its head. But over there, the young lady in the peach-colored gown. That's Mary Boleyn, Anne Boleyn's sister. She'll be Henry's mistress by next year."

"Mistress, really?" Paige wrinkled her nose. "She looks like she's twelve."

"Thirteen, actually. But married already." He pointed to a gangly looking young man nearer to the dais. "Her husband, William Carey, is a page."

"At thirteen?" She clapped a hand over her mouth. Keeping her voice low, she went on. "She's so young."

Luxe looked her over. "You are how old?"

"Eighteen."

"Yes, well, in this era you would most likely be married with children already. The only noble women your age left unmarried are ones whose families are still brokering the marriage deal. Thirteen is particularly young, but by sixteen most women are settled."

A sudden fanfare of trumpets changed the mood of the room instantly. The gathered nobility snapped to attention as a man and woman walked through the doors of the hall. Paige stared, mentally comparing the king and queen to the images she remembered from portraits in her history books. The paintings had nothing on the original subjects. Queen Catherine was a formidable looking woman, her face full of fierce pride and distinction. She looked far prettier and younger than the history books made her out to be.

King Henry frightened her. He was certainly good-looking, though already starting to go to seed. The first traces of his coming fat lingering on his jawline. But any attractiveness he might have held had spoiled, because to her, he looked like a bully. Paige compared him to the over-complimented star quarterback: a guy who would torment those around him simply to build himself up. Unlike any modern bully, this one held power over life and death for an entire country.

The king and queen seated themselves, and the rest of the court scrambled to their seats as well. Musicians struck up a trilling song, and benches scraped as courtiers sat and resumed their conversations. Another fanfare announced the arrival of the first course. More servants than Paige could count carried weighted trays of food, first to Henry's table and then to the others. The adults at the right-hand table were served first. Luxe poked her under the table. Looking down, he'd offered her a silver spoon and a matching knife.

"You bring your own silverware," he hissed.

She leaned over, so only he could hear her. "Where's the fork?"

He gave a snort of laughter. "Forks are considered barbaric."

"Oh sure, a thirteen-year-old wife, no problem. But proper utensils, heaven forbid."

"It is what it is. You could adjust if you had to."

She gave him a pointed look. "But your parents are going to fix this, so I don't have to. Right?"

He looked a little pale, but maybe it was the flickering candlelight. "Of course."

A dish of meat and a tray of bread were set on the table in front of them. The others around them, all young nobles of similar age, began helping themselves. Luxe put a bit on her plate for her before serving himself.

Paige sniffed discretely at the lumps of meat in its own juices and the hunk of wheat bread. "What is this?" she whispered.

"Mutton," he answered.

She wrinkled her nose.

"Just try it."

She used her bread as the others at the table were doing to scoop up some of the meat and took a taste. "Bland. It tastes like a barnyard."

Luxe shrugged. "I'll eat yours. You want your bread?"

"The bread's fine. Seems like bread is bread, whenever."

"That's true." He swapped their plates. "Don't worry. There's another course as well as a dessert course. You'll find something to eat."

A fanfare proceeded the next course, and Paige found herself staring at a tureen of something which looked like vegetable stew, which Luxe called pottage, more bread, and pasties or little meat-filled pies. She enjoyed this course much more. By the time the servers set the dessert course on the table she was already pleasantly full. But the confections called to her. Each one looked like a work of art, sculpted marchpane, candied fruits, and sweet breads.

She nibbled at a marchpane shaped like a pear when Luxe jumped to his feet and a solid body took his place.

"The marchpane is nowhere near as sweet as you."

Paige looked up and fear thrilled though her body. King Henry himself sat in Luxe's spot smiling at her, as if his presence ought to be cause for jubilation. Not knowing what else to do, she dropped her face to the floor and let her blush run wild. She'd never been so uncomfortable in her entire life. But then again, she'd never had a killer flirt with her before.

"Thank you, your Majesty," she mumbled. Maybe he would go away.

"I have an eye trained to see only the finest objects of beauty. My eye has chosen to rest upon you. Yet I have not seen you at court before now. To what, or whom shall I give thanks for this pleasure?"

"The pleasure is all mine." Paige gasped, her brain whirling on how to avoid conversation without pissing off this most volatile man.

"She is a friend of my family, Majesty," Luxe added, to Paige's great relief.

King Henry looked up at Luxe. For a moment, Luxe might have been a large mushroom popping up out of the floor for all the delight on Henry's face. Slowly recognition dawned on the king's face. "You are the son of William Talbot, young master . . .?"

"Henry, your Excellency. After your illustrious self."

A small smile turned one corner of Henry's mouth. "Yes, yes. I recall. Please excuse me while I dance with the . . . ?"

"The Lady Margaret Paige," Luxe answered.

King Henry stood, taking Paige's hand and pulling her along. She looked desperately at Luxe, who simply shot her a warning glance. King Henry led her out into the very center of the room. The musicians had been playing the whole time but they fell silent, instruments at the ready. The servants made a mad scramble to pull the dining tables off to the sides of the hall so others could join the dance.

"Do you know the Pavane?" King Henry asked.

"I'm sorry, your Majesty. I was raised . . . overseas. I don't know any of the English dances." Henry frowned at her, and Paige tried desperately to salvage the moment. "Perhaps your Majesty can teach me? I hear you are a wonderful dancer and a patient teacher."

The compliments turned his mood on a dime. "So much is true. I would be happy to teach a beautiful woman, such as yourself, anything in which you might lack . . . experience."

Paige tried not to make a face. Henry was thirty if she'd done her mental math right, way too old for her. Yet here he stood, throwing out suggestive phrases like a boy her own age. But then she remembered the poor little teen who would be his mistress in a year and fought the gag reflex.

Henry had their fingertips touching as she tried to keep up with the dance. For the first time that night, she welcomed her huge skirts. No one could see the mess she made of the steps. After nearly an eternity, the dance ended. Henry took her hand, leading her over to a window seat. He huffed into one corner and gestured she might sit as well.

Leaning toward her, he asked, "What do you think of the English court, my pretty miss? How do we compare to wherever you are from?"

"There is absolutely no comparison," she answered honestly. "I've never seen anything like your court. It's completely overwhelming."

Henry must have assumed these were meant as compliments, because a huge smile spread across his face. "Now, my dear Lady Paige. Do tell me where you are from. I wish to know what poor kingdom measures up so small in comparison. As well, I cannot place your accent. It is not French, nor Spanish, nor Italian. Seems you are a mystery. I insist you tell."

Paige gulped. He'd definitely issued an order, but Luxe hadn't given her a cover story. What could she say without screwing things up? Finally, she settled on the truth. Columbus had already discovered America after all. Maybe coming from overseas could be plausible enough.

"I'm from the new world."

Henry frowned at her. "As discovered by the Spanish lapdog Columbus?"

Paige nodded, and Henry threw back his head, roaring in laughter. "Madam, I do so enjoy a good jest, and that is ripe for certain."

He turned glancing back at the queen who stared frigidly at Paige. Henry cocked his head and lifted Paige's hand to his lips, kissing the back of it. "I have enjoyed your company tonight. I will seek you out again. I promise." In one swift motion, he rose to his feet and started toward the dais, courtiers parting in front of him like a slipstream on a boat.

Luxe materialized at her side. "I couldn't get close enough to listen in. What did you say to make him laugh so hard?"

"He ordered me to tell him where I come from. He said my accent wasn't from most of the European countries I know exist in this time. So rather than guessing wrong, I said I came from the new world. He thought I was joking."

"It's good he did. They've only explored the Caribbean so far. He has no idea North America exists and even if he did, upstate New York is still held by, as yet, undiscovered tribes."

"Well, what was I supposed to tell him? Huh? I just danced with a man who hacked off the heads of his wives so he could take new ones. Oh, and he promised to seek out my company again. So as soon as we can politely leave, let's do so."

Luxe stepped close enough he brushed against her skirts. He spoke quietly again. "I wouldn't worry. Once he leaves he's usually done for the night. You should be safe. But it's best not to discuss such things here. Save your complaints for back in Cheshire."

Paige stifled a yawn. "How long do the after-dinner parties go?"

"Hours. But once the queen retires, and she usually

does so early, we can politely leave, as well. Until then, would you like to dance?"

Paige shook her head. "No thanks. With all the layers, it's a million degrees inside my dress. Is there anywhere to cool off?"

He smiled and offered his arm. "Shall we stroll in the rose garden?"

She took his arm with a giggle. "I never in my wildest dreams thought a guy would ask for a 'stroll in the rose garden.' It sounds like a line from a movie."

Outside, the cool spring air dampened Paige's face. She wished she could take the stupid hood off her head and shake her hair out. The rose garden turned out to be a set of moist and slightly slick stone paths along which roses grew. But of course, nothing bloomed this early in the year. Only sap and pollen perfumed the night breeze. Paige let out a sigh.

"The air is even better here than at home. It's like you can smell the color green. And maybe a bit of midnight-blue. Not inside the dance hall though. With the food and perfumes, I didn't notice at first. But once everyone got dancing, I have to say, I'm grateful for deodorant."

She gave his sleeve a little tug and leaned closer. "Where are we going next, and when do we leave?"

He stopped and pulled her into a little stone alcove which might have been a gate at one time, but now the hedges grew through the center. He tucked his arms around her and leaned his face near her ear. To anyone walking by on the path they might look like lovers embracing, but the proximity gave Luxe the freedom to speak softly.

"I don't know where we're going until I track another stone. That I can do before bed this evening, but creating the portal once I've found the location will take a little longer. The spell is very delicate because I have to set a recall timer. That's how you ended up back here with me in the first place. Leaving a portal hanging open is dangerous. So, the spell is like your modern airline tickets. The portal allows me through at a specified time, then closes for safety's sake. When the preset time arrives, it re-opens and brings me home. Then I can't get stranded without the means of creating a portal in some random time."

"Oh." Paige gave a little shiver.

The night had grown chilly now that the heat of fear and dancing were both gone. Time travel with Luxe scared her a bit. After all, he'd lost the rune-stones in the first place, then managed to turn her into his familiar by mistake. What if he screwed this up?

He ran his hands briskly over her arms. "How thoughtless of me. You must be chilled. Shall we return?"

"No. Please, I don't want to go back to the dance. King Henry terrifies me."

He gave her a quick pat on the arm. "I meant leaving for home. Don't worry about the King. I won't let you get into real trouble. Remember, we're bonded. What hurts you, hurts me and vice versa."

Paige eyed him. "Do you mean like if you get a paper cut I get one to? Because I'd really hate to think I'm going to suffer through your food poisoning or some such."

He vigorously shook his head. "No one would want a familiar if the bond worked that way. Imagine how a warlock would look each time his cat got into a fight! It's more like a warning beacon. You or I will know if the other is in mortal danger. Then we'd save the other, because breaking the bond by letting the other die is supposed to be very painful. We're not supposed to interfere in the course of human events, but if you were going to be harmed, I'd have no choice."

A bubble of anger lodged in Paige's chest. "Oh, that's good to know."

"Why are you upset?" He looked completely bewildered.

"You'll drag me into dangerous situations in an unfamiliar time, and you'll only save me because it would be uncomfortable for *you* to ignore my distress? Worse still, I'm always supposed to save your butt?"

He jerked back looking even more baffled. "No . . . well, yes, but . . . I mean . . . I'm lost."

Paige put a hand on her face, rubbing at her frustration. "I really want to tear into you. But it's not really your comment which has me so pissed."

"You're upset?"

"*Yes*." She glared him down. "You've screwed up my entire life. Nothing is the way it's supposed to be right now, and I'm *very upset* about that." She let out a huge sigh. "Please, let's go. I need some alone time. I need to think."

Chapter 4

Luxe looked over at Paige's sleeping body. They were back in his private workroom at the castle in Cheshire. She'd fallen asleep on the white leather sofa. He didn't really want to take her to one of the bedrooms. The family servants were human and had no idea their castle lords were warlocks. Paige would never blend in properly. Besides, the main bedrooms offered his brother the chance to pop in. Or worse, prying eyes might report her appearance to his parents.

He'd tracked the next rune-stone and begun working on the portal, setting it for their return. Three days ought to be enough. He really disliked their destination and wanted to spend as little time there as possible. One last flourish with the crystal he had been using to draw the scrolling runes that charged the spell, and he'd finished. The portal would pull them through at six o'clock tomorrow morning. Luxe knew their destination would be too hot if they went any later. He looked around with a yawn. Of course, Paige occupied the only surface worth sleeping on, and the wood floors were hard and uncomfortable.

He would sneak out and go back to his room for the night. She'd never know. Anyway, even if she did wake up and come looking for him, she could only get as far as the door at the top of the spiral stairs on her own. Since she didn't know how to use magic, she'd never get through the wall. He stepped out of the stairway and into the outer hallway, shivering. With no glass in the windows, cold air filled the hall.

"Luxe."

Luxe cringed. He knew that dulcet voice. It belonged to his older brother, Atlas.

"What?" he answered, his voice short. They didn't need to play pretend; they both knew they disliked each other.

"I wondered if you were done with the rune-stones yet? I've got something I'd like to use them for. You can't possibly need them for anything which takes this long."

"You'll simply have to wait. I'm not done." Luxe hoped the darkness would hide his shiver.

Atlas leaned casually against the wall. "Enjoy them while you can, little brother. Once they belong to me, you can kiss your experiments goodbye. You'll never handle a rune-stone again." He covered an exaggerated yawn. "You're simply not worthy." He stood and started to walk off, then stopped and looked over his shoulder. "You should have let Cleo keep you. I certainly don't want you in this family, you're an embarrassment."

Atlas walked away, his shoulders providing a large silhouette in the torchlight. Gulping, Luxe opted to return to his workroom. A female frightened him far less than Atlas, and that was saying something.

He didn't have long before things with Atlas would come to a head. As soon as he reached his majority at twenty-one, he and Atlas would duel for the stones. The looming fight terrified him. Atlas was stronger physically and could wield magic much better. But since inheritance was based on power, the heir to the stones would be the child with the most power: the one who won the duel.

Dueling held plenty of danger. Lots of witches and warlocks got hurt doing it. On occasion, the weaker one died. He really hoped Atlas would stop short of that. He'd rather lose access to the stones than die. In most families, they shared their heirlooms, the title of keeper being merely a formality. But this wasn't the only occasion Atlas had threatened to cut him off.

Setting aside thoughts of his brother, Luxe set to finding a place to sleep. He'd need the rest before his task tomorrow. This mission held no room for error. If he ended up face to face with his fears on this one, the consequences could be disastrous. He tried sleeping in a chair which matched the white leather and stainless steel of the couch. But after turning several times with no comfort in sight, he flicked green sparkles at it and turned the chair into a squashy recliner. He kicked up the foot rest. No need to even set an alarm. The portal would pull them through automatically. Though the encounter with Atlas left him restless for quite a while, Luxe finally managed to fall asleep.

~ ~ ~

The roaring noise and falling sensation ended abruptly as Paige connected hard with shifting earth. Heat slammed against her body like a physical force, searing her skin. Where on earth had they ended up? This place blazed like standing too close to an open oven. A breeze tugged at her clothes and while it carried strange new scents: flowers, spicy wood, and the smell of hot rocks, the breeze carried no refreshment. She rubbed her hair in confusion. The last thing she remembered, she'd fallen asleep on the couch in Luxe's workroom. But now they were in a vast, golden desert.

Luxe stood up next to her, brushing himself off. Beneath her butt slightly dusty, golden sand burned Paige's exposed skin. Paige mopped her forehead against profuse sweat. She still wore a couple of the Tudor-style petticoats.

"Where are we?" she snapped, letting loose her irritation at the abrupt awakening.

"1284 B.C. Ancient Egypt, at the height of the reign of King Ramesses II."

Luxe pulled her to her feet, thankfully saying nothing about the fact her hands were slick with sweat. Flicking his fingers and sending green sparkles in her direction, he muttered a few words, and Paige shrieked. He'd dressed her in a gown of mesh-beads with nothing underneath, and she scrambled to cover herself.

Luxe flushed and apologized. "That's an Egyptian dress but not what I aimed for. I'm sorry. The beaded faience dress was worn at . . ."

"Don't give me a world history lesson in fashion," she yelled at him. "Just *fix* it."

He tried again with more sparkles and this time dressed her in a diaphanous gown of linen. The fabric was so fine it practically floated and so thin it hinted at the curves of her body, backlit by the sun. Gold bracelets jangled at her wrists and her hair flopped over her shoulder in a long braid.

Luxe smiled. "You look lovely."

Paige flushed a little. "This seems a bit . . ."

"Scant?" Luxe asked. Paige nodded. "You disliked the plight of women in my home time, but you'll find the lives of women here quite liberated in comparison. Particularly noble women, which you will be traveling as. One thing the Egyptians are not afraid of is the female physique. Enjoy it. Women in many other desert societies wear full robes."

While he spoke, he'd magicked himself a soft kilt of linen. The bleached fabric made his skin shine a creamy peach which glowed in the harsh desert sunlight. Paige blushed for his get-up as well. Shirtless, his muscle stood out on his thin frame, enough to define his upper arms, and leave the impression of his abs and the thin V leading down into his kilt.

Usually, she liked more bulk, but she had to admit, he had a nice body. Maybe Ancient Egyptian clothes weren't so bad. And they were far more comfortable than the court dress from the sixteenth century.

"Where do we start looking from here?" she asked.

She couldn't imagine their destination, since at this moment they were surrounded by sand and glaring rock. What if this *was* their destination? How would they ever find a rock like the one which had been in her backpack in a location like this? Pebbles covered everything around them.

Luxe held out his palm and spoke to the air. *"Invenerunt lapidem."*

A green glow formed over his palm, forming moving symbols and a hand which looked like a compass dial. The hand came to a rest, pointing off to his left.

"We go this way." Luxe strode off in the direction the compass had pointed.

Paige stumbled through the sand after him. "Why didn't I see any of this glowing at the school if this is how you search?"

"Humans can't. You see the magic now because of our bond."

She stumbled over her skirts and swore, gathering them up in one hand. "So, this bond, what exactly is it good for? I mean, for me. Or for you, if I'm not actually any help." She slammed a toe into a rock hidden by the sand and swore again. "Good God, can't you just spell us out of here? You know, *'factus stellio'* or some other Latin crap." She had an odd tingling sensation but ignored it and continued to complain. "Why couldn't you have lost the stones in a comfortable place? Like Hawaii? A hotel suite in Paris? *What?"*

Luxe had turned and stared oddly at her. He stepped closer and she gasped. "Luxe. What the hell happened?

You're *huge*." He bent and carefully lifted her, the astonishment on his face turning to open amusement.

"I'm not huge. It's you." He conjured up a mirror, angling it so she could see.

Paige peered into the mirror and a small brown lizard with bluish fringe at its throat stared back at her. "Ha, ha. Very funny, Luxe. Let's . . ." She fell silent. The lizard's mouth matched her words. Paige let out a scream. "I hate lizards. What did you do? Change me back."

Luxe laughed. "I did nothing. You did this to yourself. I have no idea how you managed to guess the words for turning yourself into a lizard. But good work. At least we know the link is strong enough for you to use my magic."

"How is anything about this good?" she sobbed. "Just get me back to normal."

He held her near his nose. "If it helps any, I think you make a cute lizard." He threw a few sparkles at her. "Factus humana."

The tingling sensation returned. Paige reverted to full-size and, embarrassingly, sat in Luxe's arms. He was definitely stronger than he looked. She squirmed, and he set her down.

"Everything better?" His voice and expression still suggested laughter at her expense.

She glared at him.

"Well, this way then. And let's keep all grumbling in English so we don't do any more inadvertent spells, shall we?"

They trudged on, heat baking her alive. Paige presumed the desert had no end, and she might be better off crawling under a rock and waiting for the inevitable. Ahead of her, Luxe stopped at the top of a small rise, and Paige told herself if the other side held nothing but more desert, she would quit. However, once on top, a very different and remarkable landscape revealed itself.

Luxe reached for her hand, pulling her up the rest of the way. "Just where I thought we might be. There's the temple of Hathor."

Below them and toward what Paige assumed must be the Nile, a complex of stunning buildings rose from the golden sands. The massive tawny temples soared above tall palms planted in ordered gardens. It looked more inviting than Paige could put into words.

"That's good," Luxe murmured to himself. "The Absko family controls this period, and they have family members in many of the temples. If we're lucky, we might get some help." He hesitated a moment and focused on Paige, speaking louder. "But don't tell them anything about why we're here. Let me think of an excuse so this doesn't get back to my parents, all right?"

Without waiting for an answer, he began scrambling down the hill toward the Nile. He stopped as they reached the edge of the papyrus reeds swaying over both their heads in the breeze. Something rustled in the reeds, and Paige froze. Images of Nile crocodiles, desert bandits, and other horrors ran through her head. The next moment, someone small with trailing black hair flung themselves out of the reeds with a shriek, straight at Luxe's chest.

He grunted as the person hit. Then, to Paige's shock, the attacker pulled Luxe's head down and kissed him passionately. Paige startled, then hot irritation ran through her. Detaching himself from the woman, Luxe stepped back, smoothing out his platinum blond hair.

"Good to see you, too, Cleo." His tone was in direct opposition to his words.

Cleo looked Paige over. Her face wrinkled, and her nose turned up as if Paige were a smelly dog. "*What* is that?"

"This is Paige. My familiar."

Cleo gasped. Then an impish grin spread across her face, and she wagged a finger at him. "You naughty boy." Her voice purred, and she ran her fingers across his bare chest, leaning into him. "See, I'm not the only one who causes trouble. Going and making a familiar out of a human. I can't think of a family who sanctions that. Unless the Boanerges family is now actively practicing black magic."

Luxe had taken two more steps back and each time Cleo cut the distance, putting herself back on his chest. Paige got more annoyed each time she tried. Clearly, he didn't want her hanging onto him. The girl should take a hint.

"Turning her wasn't deliberate," Luxe fumbled. "I mixed up something in a memory erasing potion."

Cleo shook her head. "Luxe, Luxe, Luxe. That's not a mistake. The potions have two entirely different ingredients."

Her voice was completely patronizing, and a wave of rage washed over Paige, but not in Luxe's defense. If Cleo meant what she hinted at Paige's current situation had been the result of an obvious error. If Luxe hadn't simply added the wrong amount, then she was less the victim of an accident and more of ineptitude. Luxe stared at Cleo, eyes wide, shock written on his face.

"Which . . . which ones?"

"You switched the powdered locust for powdered lotus," Cleo answered promptly. "And you messed up cat's claw, the toenail, with cat's claw, the plant."

"I drank toenails," Paige shrieked.

"Silence, um . . . whatever you are," Cleo ordered. She turned her attention back to Luxe. "You really are hopeless at potion making."

"I'm not a *whatever*," Paige snapped. "I'm a human. And I deserve to be treated like—"

Luxe shook his head to stop her, but it was too late. Cleo tipped her head back giving a cruel laugh.

"You want to be treated like what? An equal? I've got news for you, honey, you're not even close. Humans are inferior to us in every conceivable way. And to top it off, you're not even really human anymore. But you're not a witch, and it's debatable if you even qualify as a familiar since you're not an animal." Luxe grabbed at Cleo's arm, but Cleo shook him off and got in Paige's face. "If you think you can snag him by binding yourself to him this way, you're wrong. He'll never see you as anything but a burden. Luxe is mine."

"I'm not yours, Cleo." Luxe sighed. "We've been over this before. You'll just have to wait for some other cradle to rob. And leave Paige alone. This whole mess is my fault. She wasn't trying to snag anything. How could she contribute to my mistake? She's human. Besides, I'm not going to leave her this way. I've got some things to finish up while my parents are on vacation. When they get back I'll have them break the familiar's spell and send her home."

Cleo laughed and patted Luxe on the head. "You sweet little boy. You really think they can fix this? The only way to get rid of a familiar is to kill it. But I can help you with that if you'd like." She shot a look through narrowed eyes at Paige.

Luxe swatted her hand away. "That won't be necessary. The only help I need is information. I need to know what defenses your family set up to guard the sacred pool and how to get around them. I lost something by accident, and I've unfortunately located the item there."

She gave a giggle. "Oh, no. That's not the kind of information I can give you. But for the right price, I'll escort you in."

Luxe went even paler than his normally pale peach. "What sort of price?"

"Oh, I know you're just a little boy. I'll make sure you can afford my help." She stalked him like a cat stalks its prey, lithe in her linen gown. "Tonight is the festival of Bast. Come as my date, and stay the night at my place. I'll take you to the pool in the morning if you play nice."

"I can't stay the night with you. You're an acolyte at the temple. They would never allow a man to stay over. And wherever I stay, Paige stays."

A pout marred Cleo's pretty face. "Fine." She tossed her black braids, making beads in them clink together. "You guys can stay in my rooms at the family villa across the Nile. But I'll be staying with you." Her expression grew sly. "I'll take you there now. But you'll spend the afternoon with me for the favor." She narrowed onyx eyes at him. "And you're here as my boy-toy. No fooling around, no deal."

Luxe nodded his head, looking defeated. Cleo squealed in joy and linked her arm through his, leading him through the rushes, toward the river. Paige pushed along behind them, grumbling as reeds snapped back in her face and scratched at her arms. They arrived at the edge of the softly lapping Nile, it's green-brown expanse glittering in the sun. A small skiff had been tied off at the shore, and Luxe followed Cleo into the boat.

Paige hurried to join them, sure Cleo would leave her behind if she got half a chance. The mud at the river's edge smelled slightly fishy in the heat and Paige held her breath as she leaned over the skiff to rinse her sandals off. Cleo wiggled her fingers at the boat, sending orange sparkles its direction. The boat took off on its own accord for the far side of the Nile.

Chapter 5

Luxe let his head droop for the duration of the ride to the far bank. Once he felt sure Cleo would behave and let Paige in the boat, he had nothing to do but wait for the inevitable. Hopefully Paige would be all right by herself for the next couple of days. Cleo wasn't going to give him the opportunity to be alone with her and certainly wasn't going to let Paige tag along to whatever she had planned for him.

Ultimately, the unpleasantness of being Cleo's boy-toy for a couple days would be worth it to recover the stone. Though if Cleo knew how desperate his situation was, her price might have been much higher. Thank goodness that she'd been distracted by her joy at seeing him again. That brought up thoughts of the last time he'd seen Cleo. Luxe shuddered. She'd been the one to solidify his aversion to women.

Once again, he cursed his luck with females. Cleo had selected him for attention over his brother, who should have been equally young in her estimation. And Luxe had to admit, Atlas was infinitely more attractive than himself. If only Atlas had been subjected to her last scheme . . . Any way he looked at it, the next three days were going to suck.

~ ~ ~

Paige surveyed the opposite bank with curiosity. Sprawling villas surrounded by lush gardens lined the river's edge. Their boat headed toward a small jetty, sticking out of one of the gardens. Once the boat had been secured, Cleo pulled Luxe along without sparing a backwards glance at Paige. Cleo marched Luxe through the gardens and chatted at him, though he didn't really seem interested. But Cleo moved fast and knew her way around. Paige quickly fell behind.

She called to the pair, and Luxe glanced behind him. His expression showed worry, and he struggled, but somehow Cleo managed to keep a hold on him while pulling him forward. They took a turn around some flowering bushes, and by the time Paige rounded the same bushes they were nowhere to be seen.

Hot tears stung her eyes at the injustice. She dropped onto a bench beneath the flowering bush and let the anger wash through her. She hated Cleo. She was furious with Luxe, too. The tears weren't going to go away, so she pulled her knees up and tucked her face onto them. On the off-chance Cleo and Luxe came back for her, she would never give that witch the pleasure of seeing her cry.

"Are you all right?" The words were accompanied by a light touch on her shoulder. A male she didn't know had spoken them, and her head jerked up in alarm.

A young-ish looking individual, she supposed in his mid to late twenties, stood over her looking concerned. He was gorgeous. His skin shone a deep bronze. He had wavy, black hair and kind black eyes. Muscle stood out all over his sculpturesque body. Since he wore a kilt, she could see enough to have her blushing furiously. His air of concern deepened, and it dawned on her that she'd forgotten to respond.

"I'm lost," she stammered. "And how did you know I speak English? Isn't this ancient Egypt?"

"It is Egypt, but you don't have the coloring of an Egyptian. And the people living here don't consider themselves ancient. That confirms my suspicions. You do not belong here. How did you end up in my family's private gardens?"

He sat on the bench beside her, and she stayed curled around her knees. She didn't know or trust this man.

"Where are you from?"

His voice held nothing but curiosity. Maybe she could tell him a little. "Cleo brought Luxe and I here from across the river and then left me here."

He looked up sharply. "Luxe is here? Are you family of his?"

"Not really." A flush of embarrassment crept across her cheeks. Cleo's words concerning her state in limbo still rang in her ears. What if this man considered her some sort of subhuman creature as well?

"A consort perhaps?" he guessed. "A witch in the care of his family?"

Since he'd never even mentioned *human*, she assumed warlock-kind didn't take them time hopping very often. That made her feel worse. She couldn't stand it if all of the witches and warlocks thought she was a freak. Another wave of anger toward Luxe washed over her.

Paige dropped her face back onto her knees. "Imahumanandhisfamiliar," she mumbled hurriedly.

"What was that?" His voice came soft and close, inflaming the heat on her cheeks.

"I'm a human and his familiar." She over-enunciated every word this time.

The man gave a yelp. "Does his family know? Why did he do that? We don't use humans as familiars."

"He turned me by accident." She sighed into her knees. "His parents are on vacation. He said he'd tell them when they got back so they could fix the mistake for him." She sat up and her braid flopped over her shoulder.

The man sucked a little air in through his teeth. Paige pulled the strap of her gown back up onto her shoulder, since it had slipped. His eyes wandered from the top of her head to the tips of her toes where he paused.

"You're injured."

She looked down at her feet. Her toe had a nasty open gash. The skin must have split when she'd tripped over the rock in the desert. Blood and sand had formed a gross-looking clot, and under it fresh blood still oozed. She suddenly felt a bit faint. She didn't do well with blood. The world swayed, and strong arms caught her. The man lifted her, carrying her toward the villa.

"I'm Nesu, Cleo's younger brother. And you are?"

"Paige. Paige Gentry."

"Welcome to my family's villa, Paige. I promise the hospitality is better than whatever my sister offered you. She has a thing for younger men, so if she thought you might interrupt her time with Luxe, she would not welcome your presence." He raised an eyebrow. "Would you? I mean, interrupt."

"*No.*" She blurted that a bit fast and caught Nesu swallowing a laugh. "No. I only met him yesterday, and he dragged me back in time and now I'm his familiar. I'm not really impressed, to tell the truth."

Paige tried to not focus on the fact that Nesu was still carrying her. Or that he walked like he carried a basket of laundry and not a full-sized human. But she couldn't ignore the touch of his arms, and a blush crept across her cheeks.

The next smile Nesu gave her was *very* warm. "I assure you, not all warlocks are so . . . inept. Please don't judge us all by Luxe."

Supreme embarrassment rolled over Paige. "You don't need to carry me," she mumbled. "Where are we going anyway?"

"I'm taking you to my workroom. There's no need for you to limp along after me. The villa is quite large.

I'll have you fixed up in no time. If you like my service, you can do me the favor of attending the festival with me tonight. You have a story I would love to hear. Specifically, how you ended up here. Please tell me about yourself, as well, when exactly are you from, etc."

"I'm from 2025. I live just outside Albany, New York. I'm supposed to be finishing up my senior year in high school right now." Bitterness crept into her voice. "I was moments away from being asked to prom by the guy I've wanted to date. My brother and I were supposed to explore Europe in a couple months. Then Luxe randomly appeared in class two days ago, and everything fell apart. I got sucked through a time portal, and when he tried to send me home and do a memory charm, I got stuck as his familiar instead."

She heaved a breath and Nesu stared at her with open amusement. "Anything else you'd like to explain? Like what you're doing here perhaps?"

"Luxe needed something. *I'm* only here because I'm stuck with him."

"Ah, I see."

They had arrived in a vast room under shady stone columns and a cool roof. Vibrant frescos graced all the walls, and linen curtains trembled in the slight breeze running throughout the villa. Urns with plants growing out of them stood in the corners of the room, but other than that, the room resembled Luxe's workroom: full of books, tables with glass vials and strange instruments, as well as relics from around the world.

Nesu set her gently on a divan with clawed feet and the heads of beasts carved on the curled ends. He gathered up several things Paige didn't recognize, along with a few strips of linen, and then sat at her feet. He washed her foot, and though his hands were gentle, she couldn't help but flinch as he tried to clean the grit out of the cut.

An intoxicating smell of flowers filled the air around them as Nesu popped the cork on a pale-violet glass vial. Paige observed with fascination as he poured three drops on her toe. The potion tingled and made a sizzling noise as the pain disappeared, and the skin healed before her eyes.

"That's so cool." She wiggled her toes. "I didn't know your magic could do such neat stuff."

"I am capable of much which would impress you."

His voice took on a provocative tone, and Paige found herself blushing again. Time for a change of subjects.

"What's Cleo's . . . *thing* . . . with Luxe anyway?" she asked.

"That's a long story," Nesu said, by way of dodging.

"Luxe never said when we were going back, but I heard Cleo tell him they would take care of business tomorrow and he agreed. So, I'm assuming I have time." She lounged back on the divan and looked expectantly at him.

~ ~ ~

Luxe fought with Cleo, trying to get back to Paige. Paige might be causing him trouble, but Cleo was a disaster. Between the two, he'd gladly choose Paige. He'd hoped to find Renni, a cousin of Cleo's. Even her brother Nesu would have been preferable. As soon as she'd managed to give Paige the slip, Cleo took to guiding him through the villa by way of a hand to his backside. Every time he tried to dodge, she returned to his side in seconds.

"People might think you were disinclined to women the way you run off." Cleo giggled. "Don't be a naughty boy any more than you already have. You agreed to play today."

Luxe didn't look at her or raise his head to take his gaze from the floor. He secretly hoped if he played dead for a while, she might lose interest and go find someone with more energy. Not that such tactics had worked in the past, but he really didn't have any other ideas.

He hoped someone reliable would find Paige. He'd know if anyone tried to hurt her, and he'd insist on tracing her under such circumstances. But since Cleo held the key to getting his rune-stone back tomorrow, he didn't want to rock the boat unless absolutely necessary.

Cleo pushed him into her bedchamber. A bed of carved ebony with curtains of linen stood on a dais in the center of the room. The tiles on the floor made a mosaic water garden which met the walls upon which frescos of papyrus and waterfowl completed a room-wide scene. Under other circumstances, he might have enjoyed spending time in such a lovely room. But really, he thought, maybe London Tower wasn't so bad after all.

~ ~ ~

"May I?" Nesu made to join Paige on the divan where she lounged.

She nodded and scooted her feet aside for him to sit. He went around the room closing all the curtains first, until the light in the room grew dim. Then, instead of sitting in the space she'd created, he lay beside her. She opened her mouth to protest when he held his hands aloft and let orange sparkles create a sort of sphere. A picture began to form in the sphere, like watching TV—if TV came from inside a big, Chinese lantern.

"Cleo has a thing for younger warlocks," Nesu started. "This has caused problems for many people. The most major incident happened about a hundred years ago. Cleo was a little over 200 when she met a young warlock from the Antonius family on a time hop. According to my sister, they met on a seaside holiday in Alexandria."

A picture of a magnificent city on the water formed in Nesu's sphere. Alleys lined with colossal lion statues and glistening obelisks stabbed at the sky. The images were so real Paige could almost smell the salt air. The sphere held a vision of Cleo and a young man with brown ringlets and a clearly Roman nose, frolicking on the beach.

"Cleo and Marcus became deeply involved in a love affair. Of course, that didn't sit well with his parents, since he was only eighteen at the time. Nor did their affair sit well with ours. My father, Pashet, has been trying to convince my sister to marry ever since she became a young adult. The problem is she keeps getting older, but her taste in men doesn't. When both sets of parents insisted they desist with the affair, she kicked up a huge ruckus. She got the human governments at the time involved and created such a mess the 'CoW' nearly sanctioned her.

"Marcus' parents sent him to the far edges of their time span, the Roman Empire. Since Rome spread into Britannia at the time, he ended up meeting Luxe's parents. By the time Cleo managed to sneak away to visit him, he'd grown too old for her tastes, but the son of his new friends was fresh meat. That's how she met Luxe, about four years ago.

"Cleo planned to hijack Luxe under the guise of being his 'tutor,' so she could have 'fun' at her leisure. Unluckily for her, the one thing Luxe is good at is time portals. He doesn't even need much supplies for them anymore, and that's pushing it even for a several-hundred-year old warlock, most times. Cleo ran off with him to Ancient Babylonia, but Luxe bolted home on the first night, and his parents had her banished from their time district. She's been waiting for him to go wandering ever since."

He let his hands fall and Paige lay, staring at the spot where the orange sphere had played a visual of all the events as Nesu talked about them. She'd been so absorbed in the method, the words were just starting to hit home.

"Wait." She shook her head. "So . . . Cleo and Marcus . . . *Oh My God.* They're Cleopatra and Mark Antony."

He gave a chuckle. "You've heard about them in your time, too? Yes, Cleopatra and Marcus Antonius. I see her infamy knows no bounds. Not that the Pendragons can say much, their family meddled by sending in Arthur to end the civil wars in ancient Britain. Of course, the humans weren't ready to quit fighting. The peace didn't last long, so they didn't bother after the first try, but . . ."

Paige shook her head in disbelief. "By Arthur, you mean Arthur Pendragon, *the* King Arthur?"

Nesu nodded.

"He's a relative of Luxe's?"

Nesu nodded again. "His great-great-grandfather, I think. But I'm surprised you didn't guess, what with magical swords and enchantresses and a last name like Pendragon. Could King Arthur really be human?"

"Luxe never told me his last name. Wow, you warlocks really hide in plain sight, don't you?"

Nesu laughed and tightened his grip. When had his hand ended up on her thigh? He must have let it drop there. She reached to remove his hand, and he caught hers. Again, she wriggled her fingers to get away. A small part of her didn't mind. He was good-looking enough, and his attention flattered her, anyway.

"I don't know you," she protested as her fingers slipped free of his.

"What would you like to know?" His question came as a whisper, given so close his breath stirred the fine hair around her ear.

"Well, how old are you? Cleo's got to be over three hundred now, I know you said you were younger but that leaves an awful lot of years still."

He propped himself up on one elbow and let his eyes twinkle at her. "I'm two-hundred-eighty-seven. Cleo is three-hundred-thirty-four, but don't tell her I told you. You know how sensitive women are about their age."

"You both look damn good for your age. I have to say."

"Thanks." His voice grew husky, and he leaned toward her.

She gave a little scoot back. "Why don't you tell me about this Festival or whatever it is you want to take me to."

He rolled onto his back and flipped a hand in the air, lazily. "Oh, it's a religious ceremony. You know, sacramental wine, a feast, sacred dances, processions."

Paige nodded with relief. This sounded safe enough. Maybe even educational. She smiled back at Nesu. "Okay, I'll go."

He gave her a sleek grin. "If we're going out I'll just give you the gift of speaking Egyptian. To make you more comfortable.

He leaned in saying softly, "*Donum Aegyptia sermonis.*"

If someone could caress another's lips with theirs that's what Nesu did. Paige might have protested the length of time he lingered, except for the fluttering in her stomach. This man knew what he was doing, and he did it well.

"Can I wear this?" She gasped when he pulled back.

"No." His answer had a purring quality to it. "I'll get you an appropriate gown before we leave, but may I add something first?"

"What?"

"You'd look lovely if you let me henna a few parts. I'll start with your feet."

Chapter 6

Luxe spent most of the day dodging Cleo in her own rooms. Quite a feat if he gave himself credit. So far, she'd only managed to land a few random kisses. After lunch, he succeeded in keeping her off him by offering to get her ready for the party. He made sure as he laced beads onto her braids and applied kohl to her eyes that he let his hands linger long enough to satisfy her clause of flirting. He wasn't sure how he would avoid her at the festival. The logistics of dodging her there promised to be particularly problematic. Though, he still had an hour or so to worry over a solution. At least Paige would be safe at the villa. He hoped she wasn't still stuck in the garden.

Done changing her sheath, Cleo came prancing across the room and took Luxe's hand, lacing her fingers through his. "Come on, the family barge is waiting to take us down river to the temple grounds."

Without waiting for him to respond, she darted from the room, pulling him behind her. Her litter waited at the front gates to the villa to take them to the wharf. Luxe climbed up beside her. He'd never get used to riding on the backs of men. He found it a bit distasteful. But when in Rome . . .

Inside, with nowhere to run, he spent fifteen minutes smacking her hands away. She giggled and dodged, clearly not deterred. She finally managed to settle on his lap. He would have tossed her off, but the litter was perched rather precariously. He didn't want to shift around the weight inside too abruptly.

"I wonder about you." She rubbed his shoulders. "Do you feel nothing? You're a young man. This has no strings attached. Surely such an offer is appealing to you."

"If I didn't know how predatory and temperamental you can get, it might be. But you don't want a one-night stand. You want a boy-toy for a few decades until I outgrow your tastes. I'm not interested."

"Why not?" She ran her tongue across his lips, and he flinched.

He shook his head and ducked to hide his face. Hopefully she would find some other, more willing diversion at the festival to take some of the heat. It would almost be worth getting a wife to keep her off—almost. Being with her like this amounted to playing with fire. He could come up with at least a dozen ways she might try to keep him captive, even a few that could circumvent the automated time hop back home. And of course, having left no indication of where he'd gone, his parents would never know to search for him here. Being a twenty-year old man and hoping his parents could rescue him from the clutches of a woman depressed him.

~ ~ ~

Paige emerged from the cabin of the barge to find the blistering sun beating down on the deck. Not that the heat mattered as much, because her cheeks had been flaming since Nesu had done her henna. He'd started with her feet and then did her hands, arms, and her breasts, then moved around her navel and down her thighs. He'd insisted such decoration was customary, even showing her a scroll of artwork with party goers in thin linen gowns. When she looked closer, she realized they did indeed have henna in those places.

The gown disturbed her most. It cut below the breasts, and the whole bottom was so shear that the outlines of her body were visible in the mirror he provided. The dark drawings on her skin showed easily through the fabric, both beautiful and far too revealing. The dress left her so uncomfortable that she'd refused to uncross her arms until Nesu relented and gave her a wide collar to wear. Woven with brightly colored beads in intricate patterns, it fell just low enough to cover the most important parts exposed by the dress.

Nesu stepped out of the cabin behind her, brushing his hands lightly across her shoulders. "Be careful of your fair skin here. You have another hour or two before you will cease to burn." He bent and brushed his lips across her shoulder. "Such beautiful skin it is. Like cream and berries." He straightened up. "Shall I introduce you to some people so you feel less alone?"

He led her across the boat to where several people stood along the rail, three men and two women. Much to Paige's relief the women were dressed like her—minus the collar. Strangely, the men had no more trouble keeping their eyes on the faces of their female companions than men at home did.

All five listened politely as she told her story again. Looks of pity crossed a couple faces, but nothing unpleasant like Cleo. One of the men Nesu introduced as his cousin, Renni. The others were more distant relations. When she'd finished her story, they went back to talking about things she didn't understand. Since she had no hope of keeping up with the conversation, Paige focused on the world going by.

Mostly the boat drifted passed miles of farmland dotted with modest, mud houses. Every so often they would pass by a small town. The first of these gave Paige a shock. The barge passed close enough to land to allow the people on shore and the people on the boat to yell at each other. The shouting must have been good-natured, because everyone smiled. Though Paige couldn't tell for sure, seeing as they all spoke Egyptian. Then, to her shock, everyone on the boat threw their skirts up over their heads and flashed those on the shore.

Paige stumbled back into Nesu. "What are they doing?" she gasped.

"It's tradition." He sounded amused. "We're nearing the temple. Would you like a glass of palm wine?"

"I don't . . . I'm not old enough." Paige hesitated. "I'm only eighteen."

At this Nesu laughed outright. "There is no drinking age here. Everyone, teenagers and up will be having some tonight. The wine is also part of the traditions."

Paige doubted these traditions as they passed another town and all the skirts went up again. Nesu pressed the wine into her hand and she tried a sip, out of curiosity. The wine tasted surprisingly smooth and sweet. The alcohol only bit a little as she swallowed.

"It's good."

"You can have as much as you like," Nesu told her with a smile. "When we reach the temple, you can try the pomegranate wine as well. It's thicker and more tart."

Paige took the second glass he offered her. "There can't be much alcohol in this. I can hardly taste any." She put the glass to her lips.

"*Paige.*"

Little sparks shot through her body, and she wheeled around to find Luxe. He stalked across the barge toward her, a mix of anger and worry on his face. Cleo followed, hot on his heels and scowling at her.

Luxe ran his eyes over her, and a faint blush tinged his cheeks. "What happened to you? Why are you here? I counted on you being safe at the villa."

"Safe at the villa? Where you abandoned me?" she

shrieked at him. "You were hoping I was still alone and scared to death in that garden while you partied?"

"No. I . . ." Luxe looked unsettled and flustered. "Cleo wouldn't let me go back for you, but I knew someone would find you."

"Well, someone did." She slipped her arm around Nesu's waist. "Nesu fixed my toe and told me all about *you*." She narrowed her eyes at Cleo. "You should be ashamed at your age. Then Nesu invited me to the festival and helped me get ready. He even put my henna on all by himself. No guy at my school could, that's for sure." She took another swallow of wine.

Nesu shot her a gleeful look before undoing the back of the beaded collar. He kissed her shoulder blade as he lifted the jewelry away. "A work of art, if I say so myself."

The spots of color on Luxe's cheeks blazed. He reached for Paige's hand. "You need to come back inside and stay there tonight. I really don't think you're ready for this."

"It's just a religious festival. I think I can handle myself." Paige pulled her hand back, finished her second glass, and handed the cup back to Nesu.

Luxe's eyes went wide. "Is that what Nesu told you?" He sounded slightly panicky.

Paige had a moment of worry. "Yeah. Isn't that what this is?"

"Yes and no."

Luxe put a hand between her shoulder blades and pushed her toward the front rail of the boat. Cleo followed issuing protests.

"Do you know anything about the goddess Bast?" he asked. "She's the cat goddess of warfare, and she is appeased by a festival of drunken abandon. Tonight, the entire kingdom of Egypt has license to go completely wild. Anything goes."

They had reached the front of the boat, and the grounds of the temple loomed as their boat approached. Somewhere in her mind, she knew she ought to be focused on the impressive temple, its columns and carvings, statues and gardens. But what looked like an ancient rave drew her attention. The party looked exactly like what she saw on shows about Spring Break in Mexico—minus the electric lights and music. Though, floating across the water, music drifted softly amongst the screams and laughter. Fingers traced lightly across her shoulder, and Nesu pulled her sideways, away from Luxe and back into his arms.

"You won't mind if I borrow your familiar tonight?" he asked, though it wasn't really a question. "You know, whatever bargain you were desperate enough to sell yourself to Cleo over won't hold up if you don't amuse her tonight."

~ ~ ~

Luxe looked at Cleo a few steps away for a moment. He took in Paige, sipping a new glass of wine. And last glanced at Nesu. He shot Cleo a commanding look, he hoped, then pulled Nesu away, off to the side.

"I'd actually hoped to have run into you first," he said quietly. "I need a guide to the bottom of your sacred pool tomorrow. I lost something there, and I have to get it back. Cleo said she'd guide me in exchange for being with her tonight."

"You know she's just hoping to get you drunk enough to bind you in some way."

"I know. I hoped to be slick enough to avoid trouble."

Nesu shook his head. "She won't give you an easy out like a time portal this time. No, you're neither good enough nor old enough to get out of this one. You're screwed." His eyes narrowed. "Unless . . ."

"Unless what?"

"Give me your familiar. Just transfer the contract. I can't believe you lucked out like that. Only you could bumble your way into such a fantastic deal. She'll do anything you order, and all you have to do when they catch you is claim your ineptitude." His grin turned a bit wicked. "What have you ordered her to do so far?"

"Nothing." Luxe scowled at Nesu. "I'm not going to either. What you suggest is beyond wrong." He crossed his arms. "I'm not turning her over to you. I'd rather take my chances dodging Cleo."

Nesu clapped a hand on his shoulder and gave him a genuine smile. "Good man. You passed my test. Had you tossed her under the bus, I'd have done the same to you." He looked over Luxe's shoulder at his sister. "Cleo, deal's off. I'll help Luxe without trying to steal his honor. If you come after him, I'll tell Mom and Dad."

Cleo stalked off for the far side of the boat, and Luxe heaved a sigh of relief. "What do I owe you?"

"Nothing, kid." Nesu chuckled. "I like your honor. But I would like to finish my date with Paige. You're cool with that? I promise to play no dirtier than I would with anyone else."

"What glass is she on?" Luxe asked.

"Her third." Nesu shrugged.

"You know, where she's from, they don't drink at her age. She has no idea of her limits."

Nesu gave a wolfish grin. "I know that, but so do the boys in her time. She's either aware enough to watch herself here, or I'm not doing anything which wouldn't happen to her at home. I'm not feeling guilty."

Luxe rolled his eyes. "Fine. But I'm not turning her over like she's a jacket you want to borrow. Let me ask her what she wants. If she says yes, I won't interfere. You have my promise."

Luxe slipped up beside her. "Paige?" She looked at him with glassy eyes. "Do you really want to go to this party? Do you really want to spend the evening with Nesu?"

"Sure." Her answer slurred a little. "He's really nice to me. He even gave me the wine." She sloshed the remnants of her glass at him. "It's yummy, and you can hardly tell there's alcohol." She gave the empty glass a slightly disappointed look. "It'd take tons of these to get drunk."

He took the glass from her. "I think you've had tons," he muttered. He suddenly had an idea. Nesu was right. She would do anything he ordered. He leaned over and whispered in her ear, "You will *not* sleep with Nesu tonight. If he tries to make you, you will call for me."

He straightened up and looked over at Nesu and gave him a thumbs-up. The boat had docked during their discussion, and Nesu now took Paige down the ramp to the party. Luxe followed them, arms crossed. He wasn't sure he completely trusted Nesu.

The way Nesu had dressed her up, Paige looked stunning. She'd even made Luxe's stomach give a small flip-flop when he'd seen her. He chalked that up to the henna on her bare top. Just because he considered women more trouble than they were worth (and this whole day was a fabulous illustration of that) didn't mean he didn't enjoy looking.

Luxe spent his night dodging overly exuberant partygoers and trying to keep tabs on Paige. Nesu kept the wine flowing, and Paige never turned down a glass. But as his hands wandered, she ducked and dodged and spun around him. Luxe congratulated himself on the success of his order.

The night grew late, and the party began to fall into the inevitable result of wine plus abandon. From around them came the sounds of lovers enjoying themselves. The last of the revelers danced with nearly the same amount of freeness as those hidden. Luxe tried to find anywhere to look which didn't embarrass him. Suddenly, Nesu dumped Paige on his lap.

"You're in charge of the little prude," Nesu griped. "I've hit my limit. I'm going to find a more adventurous partner. I'll see you in the morning. One hour before dawn, if you want to live through this crazy escapade of yours." Nesu stalked off.

Paige gave a rolling giggle from his lap. "I'm a prude."

Luxe sighed in exasperation. Of course, she would be completely drunk. Girls were always trouble. How was he supposed to get her back to the barge in this state? Carrying her through the crowd of revelers would be terribly difficult. He tried setting her on her feet. She took two steps and fell sideways. Luxe caught her and swung her up into his arms again. Looks like he didn't have much choice. He started down the path toward the wharf, and Paige snaked her arms around his neck to hold on.

"You said I couldn't sleep with him, and I didn't." She sounded pleased with herself in a drunken way. Then she shoved her nose on the nape of his neck. "But you didn't say anything about you." She ran her tongue up to his ear, and Luxe shivered.

Yes, girls were definitely trouble.

She kissed his neck, shoulders and chest, and wherever she could get at him, making it hard for Luxe to concentrate on the path in the dark. He stumbled, and she squealed, tightening her grip on his neck. The sudden pain helped Luxe regain a hold on reality. He tried to readjust her, but she twisted and pressed her lips to his. The kiss held all the heat and abandon of the alcohol she'd consumed. She twisted her fingers into his hair and pulled. For a moment, he let the kiss happen, the raw emotions taking over his brain like Novocain. They were still both bare-chested. The draw toward her rushed over his body near irresistibly.

He set her on her feet and let her pull him close. He had virtually no physical experience with women. Most of which came from the time when he had been sixteen and Cleo ran off with him. The whole ordeal had been so unpleasant that he'd worked hard to keep women at arms-length, both physically and emotionally.

Then came this Paige creature. She forced him to keep her close because of the familiar contract. Then she threw herself on him when he only wanted to take care of the mess she'd made of herself. Why? Why did she have to feel so much better touching him than Cleo had? How did she manage to make *any* space in his iron clad guard? Maybe she *was* a witch and didn't know it. How else could she make him kiss her like this?

Like he liked it.

Luxe still puzzled over how to get away when Paige turned and threw up at his feet. Fabulous—spell broken.

Luxe wrinkled his nose as she vomited again and again. Once she'd finished voiding the drinks, she burst into tears, leaving Luxe completely lost. What did one do with a crying female? And what on Earth was she crying about? He would simply pretend this wasn't happening.

He took her shoulders and pushed her down the path from behind. He managed to get her up onto the barge. Someone, Cleo probably, had locked the door to the cabin. Luxe looked around for somewhere to stash Paige. He found a suitable spot at the back of the boat, near the rail.

Luxe wiggled his fingers and muttered the words to create a bed. His green sparkles left behind a soft pad of foam. He made the mat low enough she wouldn't tip over the edge of the rail if she tried to crawl around in the night. He laid her down and as an afterthought changed her dress, which she soiled beside the river. He had just gotten up to leave when Paige heaved, ruining both the bed and the new clothes. Luxe sighed and picked her up, helping her to the rail to finish. He smoothed back the loose hair which had come out of her braids, an unaccustomed flutter of sympathy tickling him.

She resorted to sobbing again. What could possibly be so wrong? He changed her clothes a second time and magicked the bed clean. When he tried to lay her down she clung to his neck, tears still in her eyes.

"Don't leave me." Her voice held desperation and pleading. "You left me. I felt so scared. All alone in a new time." She gave a shudder, and guilt prickled Luxe. "I don't wanna new time. I just wanna go home."

She slumped against his shoulder and gave a sleepy sigh. He resisted the urge to push her away and run. Instead, he set her on the mat and made to leave. A sick sounding hiccup stopped him. What if she threw up in her sleep? She could asphyxiate and die. He didn't want that. Curling at the very edge of the mat, as far away from her as possible, Luxe closed his eyes and tried to sleep.

Chapter 7

A knock like a gunshot woke Paige. She felt several things simultaneously, all of which sent her head and stomach spinning. First, to her horror, Luxe scrambled off her bed at the same noise which woke her. What had she done? She didn't remember anything of the previous night. The last thing she remembered, Luxe asked if she really wanted to go to the party.

Nausea nearly overwhelmed her. She hurried to her feet and heaved over the edge of the boat. Also, her stomach grew heavy as if rocks had settled in the bottom, a sensation which had nothing to do with the wine. Her situation caused the discomfort. She had really been hoping to wake and find this all a dream. Would she wake to this disappointment every morning from here on out?

Gentle hands pulled her up and pressed a glass into her hands. "Drink," Luxe told her. "It's a hangover cure."

She glared at him, and he gave her a dirty look in return.

"I didn't make the potion. Nesu did."

"I feel bad for making you so sick," Nesu added. Had he been standing there all along?

She swallowed the mint-green concoction. The liquid burned all the way down to her stomach. But as soon as it reached the trouble spot, a cooling sensation spread across her gut. All the nausea disappeared, and the world stopped moving, except for the gentle rocking of the boat. Finally, she could take in the details around her. She'd woken before dawn, the world still glowing a dark blue. No one else seemed to be awake, and the wharf vaguely took shape in the dawning light. The pier and shoreline were dotted with revelers sleeping where they had collapsed.

"Come on. We're wasting time." Nesu led them to a small boat tied off to the side of the barge. They climbed a rope ladder down, Nesu helping her into the boat. "Keep your hands in the boat. The crocodiles are still active now."

He wiggled his fingers, and his orange sparkles cause the boat to surge forward across the deep green Nile. Little droplets of spray hit her face as they navigated back up the river at a speed which rivaled motor boats at home. The horizon now shone with a line of pale buttercup yellow. The air still smelled fresh as it blew on Paige's face, warm enough to be comfortable and not yet blazing with the day's heat. Maybe the Absko family ended up better off than the Pendragons by having control of this period. The word *monster* caught her attention. Luxe and Nesu were deep in a serious conversation involving a beast.

"Ammit tends to be at her most drowsy this time of morning. But she'll be sleeping on the bottom. So, we're going to have to tangle with her. That's where you need someone from our family. Only Abskos are allowed in the sacred pool. Only an Absko can make Ammit submit."

"What's Ammit?" Paige wasn't sure she wanted to know.

"Our family guardian. One of several. All the noble warlock families have them. The Pendragons tend to keep dragons. As if that wasn't easy enough to figure out. Our guardians have ties to the Nile. Ammit is part crocodile, part hippo, part lion, and all temper."

"Sounds perfect. So, you've gotta go swimming with that?" Paige crossed her fingers and hoped she wasn't required to go, too.

"Sadly, yes." Nesu looked at Luxe. "Are you sure this is really necessary?"

Luxe turned red. "Yeah. I have to get this back."

"All right." Nesu didn't look convinced, but the boat slowed as they came into a pool formed by a curve in the bank of the Nile. "Paige can wait on the shore where it's safe. We'll take the boat out over the center of the pool and start tracking your item from in the water." He turned to Paige, trying to appear reassuring. "There aren't any hippos or crocodiles here, since Ammit keeps everything out. If she comes for you, you're pretty much lunch, but you'll be as safe as you can get at the water's edge."

The boat gave a soft thump as it hit the muddy bank, and Luxe helped her out. "Sit tight. I'll be back. I promise." He squeezed her hand. "This time I won't leave you for long."

She blinked at him. How had he known her fear so accurately? They pushed the boat back out to the center of the pool. Two splashes and they were gone.

As the water smoothed, icy claws tightened around her chest. She was alone—again. Terror prickled her all over, and she fought to control her breathing. What if he didn't come back? What if she got stuck here forever? Her imagination had just started to get the better of her when a line of ripples moved across the pool toward where Luxe and Nesu had disappeared. A new terror gripped her.

~ ~ ~

Luxe hit the water. The river held a deceptive chill for being in the middle of the desert. Opening his eyes, he found himself in a murky world where the early morning sunlight shimmered against floating silt. He hoped Paige would be all right until he got back. He held his hand out in front of him, the green compass glowing against his skin. It pointed to the bottom, between the shore and where he floated. Hopefully the pool wasn't too deep. Something yanked at his foot and pain so sharp that colored stars burst in front of his eyes laced through his leg.

Dozens of thoughts ran through his mind. Surprisingly, at the forefront was a deep concern for Paige. What would happen to her? He wished he'd had a chance to make up to her for all his mistakes, or at least to apologize.

He caught a lung-full of air as he broke the surface. Not that the oxygen brought any relief as he currently flew through the sky. His descent brought him down, straight into gaping crocodilian jaws. Screaming echoed from the riverbank, and a jet of orange light knocked him far enough to the side that he missed the jaws but not the claws. Four searing stripes were carved into his back. He held his scream as he hit the water. A massive weight came down on top of him.

~ ~ ~

The ripples disappeared, and Paige held her breath. Did that mean something good, or had things just gotten worse? A tight pull jolted the familiar's bond. A moment later the creature broke the surface, tossing Luxe like a dog toy high up into the air. She screamed as the monster opened its mouth to catch him. Nesu broke the surface and sent a jet of orange light at Luxe, which knocked him into the water instead of Ammit's jaws. But Ammit raked her claws across Luxe's back on his way down. Paige screamed again as blood rained from his back only to mix with the pool as he hit the water. Ammit leapt, coming down on top of Luxe.

In her lunge, Ammit disturbed the bottom of the pool, and a wave of water and mud washed over Paige. Something hard hit her knee, and she fished around in the mud, finally pulling up a small oval stone with a rune carved on one side. This one was sidewalk gray. Thanks to her connection as a familiar, she could feel the power buzzing in this stone. They had what they needed. Or she did, but without some serious help, Luxe would never know that.

She began to think frantically. Even Nesu had no luck out-magicking the creature, and it belonged to his family. There had to be a way though. Suddenly she had an idea. If only she knew the words for what she wanted to do! She'd taken Spanish in high school. All romantic languages were born from Latin. Maybe she could get close enough with some Spanish. She remembered the word for meat. Now, how to make *carne* sound Latin?

She also pulled up a very embarrassing memory of her and her best friend going through her older brother's drawers once at a sleepover. After many jokes about the contents of the drawer and a trip to the internet, they had discovered the name on the small foil wrapper meant *big*. At the time, the translation had sent them into fits of laughter. Now she hoped the knowledge might save Luxe's life.

Putting the two together, she gripped the stone and blurted out, *"Magnum Carnis."*

To her joy, a steak about two-feet across appeared in her hands. She repeated the command several more times until she staggered under the weight of the stack of steaks. Using one foot, she splashed the water, hoping to get the creature's attention. The third time she splashed, reptilian eyes broke the surface and focused on her. Fear clawed at her mind, screaming for her to run away, but she fought it and raised one of the steaks in her hand. The blood dripped down her arm and into the water.

The creature still hadn't moved, but she definitely had its attention. She tossed the steak like a Frisbee, as far out into the water as she could. The eyes disappeared below the surface and so did the steak a moment later. She tossed the next one out and looked frantically around the pool.

A moment later Nesu surfaced on the far side with a limp Luxe in his arms. They were steadily making their way toward the shore. Paige just had to keep Ammit entertained for a couple minutes more.

She tossed a third steak out. This one vanished far too close to the shore for her liking. She backed out of the water and stood on dry shore to toss the fourth steak. Only two more, but now Nesu stood in waist deep water, tugging Luxe's body on shore. Paige tossed out the last two steaks and ran for Nesu.

Nesu pulled Luxe all the way out of the water and held his hand out above the surface. "*Tranquillum,*" he shouted, as Paige skidded to her knees at Luxe's side.

"Is he dead?" she gasped, breathless with fear and running.

"No. But he's not in good shape. Our boat's destroyed, and we're a good three miles from my workroom."

Luxe interrupted by coughing and then throwing up a copious amount of river water. He let out a cry as he flopped to his back. "Paige? How did you stop Ammit? How did Nesu get the chance to get me out of the water? I didn't get what we came for. I need to go back."

"Shh . . ." Paige smoothed his hair back. "I used your magic." She took his hand and pressed the small stone into his palm. "I made steaks and fed them to Ammit until you were safe."

"I don't think you're going to get whatever you're looking for." Nesu glanced back at the still pool. "I've rarely seen Ammit in such a temper. Whatever's in there is hers now."

Luxe tried to sit up, the effort causing his back to arch as he groaned in pain. "It's okay," he gritted through his teeth. "I need my stuff, but not at that expense. I'll live without it."

Obviously, they weren't going to tell Nesu about the stone. At least she hadn't said anything. Her relief quickly faded as the mud beneath Luxe turned red.

"He's losing a lot of blood." The world spun but she ordered herself to pull it together. Nesu couldn't take care of both of them if she passed out.

Nesu stood, pulling Luxe's arm over his shoulder, ignoring Luxe's screams. "We'll find a boat to borrow, and I can get him patched up in my workshop."

Paige snuck a peek at Luxe's back and nearly blacked out. The four red gashes ran from one shoulder to his opposite hip, each oozing steadily. The blood stained the back of his white kilt pink. She bit her lip and started tearing strips of linen off the bottom of her dress.

"Hold him still," she ordered Nesu. "He can't go like this." She wrapped the first strip around his wounds and tied it off. "I took a first aid course this year so I could waive my PE credits. This ought to help, I hope."

She got all four gashes bound, figuring the pressure would be better than nothing. Though her dress had been muddy, if Nesu fixed Luxe's wounds with magic, infection wasn't much of a worry in the next hour. She slung Luxe's other arm over her shoulder and plucked the stone from his hand before he passed out and dropped it. Her dress today had a tight band of linen beneath the bust and she tucked the pebble in there for safe keeping.

Luxe tipped his head sideways until it touched hers. "Thanks. For saving me."

He'd barely said the words when his head hit her shoulder as dead weight, and suddenly his whole body felt twice as heavy. She staggered under his weight.

"Help get him up over my shoulder," Nesu grunted.

They managed to get him draped over Nesu's back, and luckily, they didn't have to go far before they found a boat. Nesu loaded Luxe onto the boat, and once Paige had settled in, he used magic to propel the boat toward his family's villa.

Together, they lugged Luxe across the tiled floors and laid him out on his stomach on the divan in Nesu's workroom. Nesu cleaned the wounds, which were already red and puffy, then pulled out his vial of purple potion. Again, the potion hitting and the skin sealing itself amazed Paige. In seconds his skin went back to its normal peach color. Luxe gave a sigh of relief and a slight snore.

Nesu stood and held out his hand to Paige, nodding toward the door. Once they'd left the room he spoke softly. "Did you enjoy yourself last night?"

Paige flushed. Was he referring to Luxe scrambling out of her bed this morning? "I'm not really sure. I don't remember anything after we arrived at the temple."

"That's too bad." He gave her a sideways smile. "I used my best moves on you, and you resisted them all. But have no fear. Luxe stood up for your honor. He made an excellent nanny." Nesu took her hands in his. "I would like a second shot. Would you join me for lunch?"

Paige's stomach growled, making the decision for her.

"I'll take that as a yes," Nesu said with a laugh. He kissed the back of her hands. "You are welcome in my time whenever you please. I do hope you'll return for a purely social visit at some point. I am sorry you'll have to leave disappointed." He pulled her along his body, his voice suddenly husky. "Well, Luxe will. I never disappoint, and *we* still have time."

"You seem to have some of your sister's tendencies. You're more than two hundred years older than me." Paige wiggled until he left space between them.

"Ah, no. You're by far the youngest woman I've ever felt attracted to. You are so many delightfully forbidden things. So young, a human, a familiar. And yet you are wonderful in so many ways. You've been a part of this world for only two days, yet you stood up to Ammit and saved your master."

"He's not my master," she snapped.

"Sorry, it's the common vernacular." He gave her a grin. "You follow your values. Rare in any time. All in all, I'm impressed and genuinely sad you will be leaving."

He bent to kiss her, and Paige let him, even tipping her face to meet his. "I'd have liked more time to get to know you, too." She flipped a lock of his hair. "But if Luxe fixes things the way he should, I'll end up back in my own time with no memory of this."

He ran a hand up her back. "Even more reason to take advantage of the time we have."

She shook her head. "Maybe . . . well, no that's stupid. There really aren't any maybes with this. Sleeping together can't happen. I'm not into one-night deals, and this can't be anything but."

He pecked a kiss on her cheek. "Just as I said, holding to your values. Now let's get lunch, and we'll see if I can't change your mind."

~ ~ ~

Luxe groaned and sat up, his back completely stiff. He'd been sleeping, curved in the wrong direction on a divan. What had happened? He sorted his memories. Ammit. Paige, coming to his rescue, binding his cuts and finding the rune-stone. How had he gotten so lucky?

On his own, or with a different creature as a familiar, he'd have been eaten for sure. For one moment, he toyed with the idea of keeping Paige around before shoving the thought away. Retaining her broke more rules than he cared to think about, and it would mean she'd be with him until he died. That was too much like a wi . . . a wif . . . He couldn't even apply the word to himself.

If he kept her, she would age with him until he died. Then she would get the extra years dumped on her at once. Familiars were usually mortal animals; the heavy burden of years meant they turned to dust at their master's passing. If he lived eight or nine hundred years, she would be no different.

Though thanks to her, he now had the chance. He looked around the room for her, but he'd been left alone. He scowled. Nesu had better play nice today.

Groaning and stretching, he stood and made himself a new kilt, then cleaned himself. He stank of mud, river water, and blood. Fresh and stretched, he took off, searching for Paige. He followed laughter and stopped as he reached the garden. Nesu and Paige were side by side on a divan in the shade. Paige giggled as Nesu showed her stories in his orange sphere. Every so often Nesu would touch her tenderly. Luxe didn't need much experience to see how smitten Nesu was. His attentions weren't lust, unlike the night before; this was . . . they were . . . unsettling.

Luxe paced the outer reaches of the garden. This was wrong. She was human. And so young. She . . . well, being with her just wasn't right. He stopped pacing. He would have to interrupt. Things couldn't go on like this. He turned and stalked back toward their divan, pulling up short. Now they were kissing. Not a chaste peck, but slow luxurious kisses while Nesu played with her hair.

Something growled in Luxe's chest. He ought to rescue Paige. Nesu shouldn't mistreat his familiar this way. She ran her hand up Nesu's arm, fingering the muscles as she went. Luxe turned and went swiftly back to the divan in Nesu's workroom. He threw himself onto it and crossed his arms, scowling at no one.

He seethed at Nesu. The man ought to know better. Paige should be off-limits for so many reasons. He fumed at Paige, too. What was she thinking? She'd just met the guy. Even his own emotions steamed him. Why get so worked up? Why did he even care?

He crossed his arms and jammed himself further into the divan. They would get his parents to break the connection and send her home. He wanted to be rid of her, he told himself. He simply had to wait until all the rune-stones were back in his possession. Then he could face his parents. He *had* to be rid of Paige. Girls were nothing but trouble.

Uninvited, the image of Paige with her low-cut dress and henna appeared in his mind. Excitement welled up in his stomach before almost immediately dissolving from the image of her on the divan engrossed in Nesu's kisses. *No*. Her choices *didn't* matter to him. She could kiss Ammit if she took the notion. Her romantic activities were absolutely none of his concern. Nope, not his business. He would put her out of his mind. When he saw her again, everything would be the same as before. Everything would be normal.

"Oh good, you're awake." Nesu's voice came from behind the divan.

"*Luxe*." Paige rushed around and squeezed herself onto the edge of the divan. "I was so worried. You lost so much bluh . . ." She went a little pale as she choked on the word. "Blood. I mean you lost so much. I thought Ammit would eat you for sure."

"I'm okay. Thanks, uh, thanks to you." The conflicting desires to both hug her and to run screaming from the room left him completely awkward. So, he sat very still in that one spot like a cornered animal deciding which way to run.

"Nesu gave me a communication crystal." She happily

stuffed her hand under his nose to show him the small, glowing orange crystal. "I told him you had a few more things to gather up before we went back to your home. He said I could call him if I got in a jam."

Luxe bit back half a dozen sarcastic comments. He had the sneaking suspicion Nesu gave her the crystal so he could contact her again himself.

"Thank you for the offer of help." Luxe tried to sound superior. "But I doubt we'll be needing you."

He'd meant to close down Nesu, but instead the older man chuckled. "Maybe not with Paige helping you, you won't. But in case she's not enough, keep the crystal. By the way, when is your time portal home?"

"Noon tomorrow."

"Well then," Nesu eyed Paige who now poked around the tables full of vials, "looks like we've got to make the most of the time."

Nesu led Paige out with a promise of a tour around the villa, telling Luxe over his shoulder to find dinner in the kitchen whenever he wanted. For moment, Luxe considered tackling him. He got a thrill of hope when Paige ran back and grabbed his hand. She pressed the rune-stone into his palm and then hurried back to the waiting Nesu.

Once they were gone, Luxe took his first good look at the rune-stone. This one had belonged to his Great-Grandmother Morgana. Two down, seven to go. He glanced around the workroom and decided that if Nesu could run off with his familiar, then he could help himself to Nesu's supplies. Besides, using that time to track the next stone would keep his imagination from running wild. He had no idea what had come over him, this strange fluctuation regarding his familiar, but he seriously needed to get it in check.

Luxe rummaged through the supplies and found what he needed. He mixed the foamy, cream-colored mixture, took a swallow, and closed his eyes. The potion pulled on his mind as pictures of locations began to form. From these pictures, he could discern where the stone called to him from. Colors whirled and began to solidify. His eyes flashed open. He knew where they needed to go.

Chapter 8

Paige woke feeling like a princess. Nesu had shown her around the villa and left her alone with the slaves in the magnificent bathes. There the girls had washed her up and rubbed her down with scented oils, massaging until she felt like putty. She'd been tucked in on a down bed and she didn't even remember the girls leaving.

Nesu woke her by rubbing gently at her cheek. She smiled at him. He rewarded her with a soft kiss to her upturned lips.

"Good morning," he purred, his voice as warm as down. "Egypt never had a tradition of angels, but I think your arrival may have changed that."

She blushed and waved away the compliment. Nesu had been showering her with attention since yesterday. He was *very* smooth. Not getting suckered into doing too much with him took real effort. In only a few hours, she and Luxe would leave, putting hundreds or maybe even thousands of years between them.

But oh . . . he ran a hand along her thigh, his fingers tracing gentle designs along the fading henna. He had such a good touch. Paige closed her eyes and stretched under his hands, letting them wander at will.

"Ahem."

Luxe stood in the doorway to her room, staring at the ceiling, his face very red. A blush raged across her face, as well. Nesu had traced the design to a rather compromising location and seemed in no hurry to remove his hand. Paige swatted him off and looked at the floor herself, her cheeks uncomfortably hot.

"Did you need something, Luxe?" Nesu kept his voice smooth, completely unruffled.

How could he possibly not be embarrassed?

"I, uh . . ." Luxe's voice cracked. "I came looking for Paige."

"Indeed. It seems you found her." Nesu's voice pushed amused now. "As you can see, she is busy at the moment. I will have her back to you by noon."

Paige still couldn't meet the eyes of either of them. How could Nesu think they'd pick up where they'd left off, so easily? She'd gotten way too uncomfortable for more romancing.

"No. I mean . . . I . . ." Luxe had dropped his face into a hand, muffling his words. "I wanted to talk to her. It's kind of important."

"So is this. My time is far more limited than yours." Nesu stood and walked to the door, where he leaned and whispered something to Luxe which caused him to make a choking noise and turn an even deeper shade of red. "I'll be back in a few minutes with your breakfast." He winked at Paige and left.

Paige wanted to hide. Anywhere. She wished Luxe wasn't so self-conscious. His discomfort made things worse for her. What was his deal anyway? He acted like he'd never seen someone make out before. Okay, so Nesu had been copping a feel. But they were only boobs; her dress the other night had bared everything. Her and Nesu shouldn't be such a source of embarrassment for Luxe, and by proxy, for her as well.

But no. Luxe stood mute in the doorway, staring at the ceiling. How did he constantly end up in the way? First with Justin, and now Nesu. Luxe had superb timing. This seemed to be the correct thing to focus on, because once she'd found irritation, she could look at him.

"Spit it out, Luxe," she snapped.

He shuffled his feet and answered without moving his eyes from the ceiling. "I found our next stop. Do you want to go home first, or go straight there?"

"What home?" Now she really felt snappish. "Yours or mine? And if we're going back to mine, what's the point? I'm just going to get sucked back with you in a few days anyway."

Luxe appeared completely pitiful. "I'm sorry," he whispered. "I didn't think . . . I meant my family's castle." He looked up at her, his face now so red it moved toward purple. "As my familiar, it's your home now, too."

"No, Luxe. That's not home. This is not a vacation, nor some romp we decided to take together. You're on business, and I'm being dragged in your wake." Hot tears gathered in her eyes. "For the first time since this started, Nesu offered a distraction. I'm not his magical slave, and he's been treating me like a princess. I've never been this pampered. I've got like three hours until you start dragging me around again." The tears leaked up and out. "I just wanted to forget." She sobbed.

Luxe stepped back like he'd been slapped. "Do you want—"

"Go away, Luxe." She rubbed the tears from her eyes. "I'll be ready at noon. I don't care if the next stop is Hell. It's all pretty much the same to me, so just do what you need to do, and I'll go along. Not like I have any other choice."

Guilt niggled Paige at the look on Luxe's face as he left. But only mild guilt. Everything she'd said had been sitting on her chest anyway. She really didn't want Luxe to start acting like this adventure was okay with her, or worse, that she'd agree to it. Maybe if he went out of his way to pamper her a little, make up for his mistakes, she might be more inclined to forgiveness.

Instead, he'd treated her like baggage, and sometimes she swore he looked at her as if being there was her fault. He'd left her to traipse through the desert before abandoning her in the garden. Then she'd had to save his butt at the sacred pool after he'd promised her he wouldn't leave her alone again. How much more alone could she get if he got eaten?

Nesu poked his head back in, and Paige tried to smile at him. She'd gotten herself so worked up that fooling around held no interest right now. Damn Luxe. Now instead of getting lost in Nesu's arms, she was going to sit and seethe . . . Okay . . . maybe not.

Nesu sat down behind her and massaged her shoulders. "I could hear you yelling at Luxe from down the hall. What did he say to get you so worked up?"

"Nothing. He doesn't seem to get I'm not a willing participant in this mess. Ahhh . . ."

His hands worked up her neck and into her hair.

"Let's not talk about that," she whispered.

"Hmm . . ." He kissed the back of her neck. "I couldn't agree more."

~ ~ ~

Luxe paced Nesu's workroom. Finding Paige had not gone at all the way he'd hoped. He'd sought her out to ask if she wanted to go straight to Rome. He could tweak the portal to drop them there. He'd promised himself all the muddled feelings were only the result of his near-death experience. Interacting with Paige ought to be no problem since he had no issue other than being overwrought.

Then he'd walked in on . . . Nesu had his hand . . .

The whole situation had made talking to her *so* awkward, which probably led to Paige lashing out at him. But her tone had hurt. She'd sounded so angry. It wasn't like he'd meant to do this to her. Now he was simply trying to make the best of a crappy situation.

Girls.

He gave a little growl. Of course *she* would have to dwell on the negative. So like a female to make the situation worse. She had to go looking all pretty and kissable and . . . *wait*. What the hell? No. No. That wasn't right. She was a complication. Trouble. All women were. Why would she be any different?

Well, she *had* saved his life.

Luxe walked over to the wall and thumped his forehead against the plaster. Why? Why had Paige gotten dumped on him and complicated his life? Was this some sort of divine retribution for fooling with the rune-stones in the first place? If so, the punishment worked. His insides were in turmoil, and he'd gone halfway to crazy. He heaved a couple of deep breaths. What was he supposed to do when they were alone now? He wasn't sure he could look her in the face without seeing . . . things he didn't want to see.

They would go straight to Rome. She hadn't acted all too comfortable in his home time. Perhaps spending a little more time away would make her happier. He used his green crystal to draw a set of symbols on a blank space of wall. Flicking sparkles at the symbols, they began to shimmer in iridescent colors. He then used the crystal to rewrite one of the symbols and muttered a spell for closing. The symbols vanished and satisfaction settled over Luxe for a moment. Now what should he do with himself? There were still two hours until . . .

A naughty smile spread across his face. He didn't have to sit around waiting for her to finish making out with

Nesu. He scribbled on the wall again and made another modification. Now in five minutes, they'd be on their way—ready or not.

~ ~ ~

Paige gave in. Nesu's back massage put her back in a relaxed and happy state, and she let his hands wander freely. She speculated with herself as to how far she would let this go. Part of her didn't care anymore. She caught the back of his neck as he bent lower, so she could kiss him. Something jerked at her. Then the world went black, and she fell. She hit the ground hard and screamed. Long enough and loud enough to cover the fall, the pain, and the fury.

She jumped to her feet and slugged Luxe in the shoulder. He flinched. But when she swung a second time he dodged.

"Why did you hit me?" He rubbed at his shoulder.

"Why did I hit you?" she shrieked in return. Paige hitched up the shoulder of her gown. She wouldn't give Luxe any viewing pleasure. "I punched you for jerking me away from what I was doing."

"You were doing Nesu?" Luxe snickered.

"No. I . . . that's not . . . *argh*." She reached out to slap him and he dodged again. "I was getting a back rub. Trying to relax. We should have had over an hour. What did you do, Luxe?"

Luxe snorted. "Right. He was rubbing your back."

"God damn it, Luxe. Grow up. What do you care anyway?"

"I care because he manhandled my familiar. Not to mention you forced me to sit there waiting while you fooled around. If you wanna get home for real, we should collect the stones."

"He wasn't manhandling me. You know what, no, we're not having this conversation. I'm *not* a familiar. It's a technicality. I'm a person. An adult. I'm perfectly capable of making my own decisions on these things. I don't need you to chaperone."

Luxe stared at her with spite on his face. "You *do too* need a chaperone," he hissed. "If I hadn't given you an order as my familiar the night of the festival, you would have slept with him. You were so drunk you would have slept with anyone. You even tried to get me in the sack, but I didn't think you really wanted to. I kept you from making a fool of yourself."

Paige put her hands to her mouth. "I don't remember any of that."

"Because you'd had more than six glasses of the palm wine. That's the stuff the commoners drink to get drunk. Not to mention I had to clean you up twice because you threw up all over everything. Then spent the most uncomfortable night ever, half-off your mattress in case you puked again. I didn't want you to choke on it."

Relief flooded Paige. "You mean we didn't . . ."

"No. I didn't let you do anything with anyone. You're really upset about everything that's happened. Destroying yourself to kill the pain would be counter-productive. Not to mention, how is that going to sit with you later? Or worse, what if you destroy your body? How will that go over when I try to send you back to your old life? There are things I can't explain away with a memory charm."

"You . . . really thought so far ahead for me? I mean, about me? You care that much?"

"Yeah. I guess. You're my familiar. You're kind of my responsibility."

Paige rubbed her head. "Just stop, Luxe. I feel like a stray cat you picked up when you talk like that. Thank you, though. For the other things. I guess your motivation doesn't really matter. You're right. I don't really want to self-destruct." She looked around at the tawny countryside. They were on coarse grass beside a cobbled road. "Where are we? When are we?"

"We're in Rome. The next stone is here. It's 80 A.D. Now all we have to do is track the rune-stone down." Luxe sent green sparkles over each of their clothes, and Paige's Egyptian gown transformed into a long dress. "It's a *stola*," he told her as she picked at the folds of the garment. "Careful, if you pull the pins loose, it'll fall away."

She stopped picking and looked him over. He wore a calf-length toga, draped several times and tossed over one arm. The white toga with his white-blond hair made him resemble a model for a renaissance master's angel. He held out a long piece of blue cloth.

"A respectable lady doesn't go out without a *palla*. I'll put it on properly for you."

"Why didn't this come with the clothes?" Paige asked as Luxe draped the woolen wrap over her left shoulder.

"You picking at the pins reminded me. The magic only brings what I think of. But this will cover the pins and help you keep everything proper."

"Oh. It's too bad we have to cover the pins. They're beautiful."

"They're my mother's favorite when we visit. She's really the only reference for women's fashions I have. But she loves the gold filigree and garnets. You probably noticed the garnet eyes on the snake bangles you were wearing in Egypt."

"Wait, those were real?" Paige yelped.

"Of course. Now let me do your hair." Luxe spun her around so he stood behind her. He blew on her hair.

"What are you doing?"

"I blew the magic across your hair. I'm not good at

braiding by hand. But you're all set and looking the height of fashion for Rome of this era."

Paige patted the mass of intricate braids and felt the little pins in her hair, too. "Are all these real, as well? What if I lose one? I can't afford these."

He gave her an impish grin. "The Absko family has fourteen family heirlooms while we only have nine. I believe theirs are scarabs, but that might be a rumor. All the families are pretty secret about the appearance of their heirlooms. Not about the number, though. The rank of each house depends on the number. But . . ." He drawled the word out for effect. "We never told anyone that Grandfather Merlin succeeded in creating the philosophers stone. If we need more gold, we'll just make it."

"Um, maybe I'm mixed up on my legends, but doesn't the philosopher's stone make you immortal? You said Merlin's dead."

"We don't know if the stone works like that." Luxe had a dodgy look.

"You don't have to tell me if this is another family secret. But you're going to give me a memory potion anyway."

"It's not that." Luxe ruffled his hair uncomfortably. "The elixir of immortality is kinda why I lost the rune-stones. See, Grandpa Merlin didn't die very long ago, and he'd only begun to play with the stone and learn how to use it. Simply making the stone took his whole life."

"The gold is easy. Touch the stone to any metal, and it turns to gold. He thought the immortality worked the same way. He touched the stone to himself. Well, you know how that worked out for him. Now my parents have to try to figure out the elixir of life without him. They thought maybe the elixir's a potion. But all the rats they tested it on died. That's the problem—magical objects can be used in so many ways. I tried experimenting with the philosopher's stone while my parents were away."

Luxe hung his head and looked at the paving stones. "I thought if I could figure the elixir out before they got back, then maybe they'd . . . oh, never mind."

"What, Luxe?" Paige poked at his arm.

"They kind of think I'm a failure," he admitted in a whisper. "I'm a descendant of Merlin. Yet, aside from the time portals, I excel at nothing. Unlike my brother, who father loves because he can do all sorts of magic." Luxe's voice went bitter.

"I see. You wanted redemption in their eyes." Luxe nodded, and Paige patted his shoulder. "So how did you lose the rune-stones if you were working with the other stone?"

"Bad luck. I borrowed the rune-stones to amplify my power. I hoped the power boost would make the experiments more successful. Instead, when the potion exploded, it blew all the rune-stones away. Luckily the philosopher's stone survived, still in the caldron."

Luxe held his palm out and the green, sparkling compass appeared again. The dial whirled before pointing directly at the center of the city in the valley below. He shook his hand to get rid of the dial.

"All right, off to the city center." He offered her his arm.

Paige hesitated. The sprawling city of ancient Rome daunted her, and she didn't want to be separated. Slipping her hand around his arm for a good grip, she fell into step beside him. They walked down the cobbled street, and the day's heat shone off the stones and heated the bottom of her dress. She missed the light linen sheaths from Egypt already.

Even though her stola was made of cotton, her palla wrap was wool, so soon enough she began to drip with sweat. At the start of their walk, she smelled only dust and hot stones, but as they got into the city, she could smell hot and sweaty people. She really hoped the smell wasn't coming from her. How completely humiliating, to push through the city while stinking of sweat.

As they reached the bottom of the hill, she realized her own scent wouldn't matter. They were now in a press of people, and everyone stank from being in the heat of the day. Someone jostled her from behind and apologized rapidly in what Paige now recognized as Latin.

"What did they say?" she asked Luxe.

"They said to hurry up. The afternoon games will start soon." He shook his head. "Of all the luck. The stone landed in Rome's city center during the inaugural games of the Colosseum. It's going to be a madhouse down there right now." He ducked his head and swore. "I just can't catch a break."

Paige squeezed his arm. "It'll be fine. Maybe the crowds are better."

He looked at her like she'd gone nuts.

"No really. Whatever we're doing won't be as noticeable with all the people milling around."

Luxe brightened up. "You might have a point there. You're such a big help. What would I do without you?"

"Curl up your toes and die?" Paige muttered. "And speaking of dying, I'm going to if I don't get something to drink."

Luxe led her over to a street vendor serving drinks and bought her one. Paige took a sip and smiled.

"That's good. What is it?" As she spoke the vendor shot her a dirty look and shooed them off. "What's his problem?"

"You're speaking like a foreigner and wearing the dress of a high-class woman. It's against the law for foreigners to wear Roman clothes. We need to fix that."

"By changing my clothes?" Paige asked hopefully.

"No, by changing your language."

Paige opened her mouth to say something but lost the words as Luxe pulled her off down a side alley. If it weren't for the smell of the garbage in the alley, the location might have been better than out on the street. The buildings shaded the space and cooled the air. And here, only Luxe pressed close to her.

Chapter 9

Luxe stood in the shade frantically trying to get up the guts to give her Latin. She needed the language to function but working the spell meant kissing her again. Not to mention she was pressed against him in the narrow alley, and he found the proximity very distracting. He could smell the lotus oil Nesu had used on her that morning, and while beautiful, it was also disturbing.

"Luxe? What are we . . ."

He touched a finger to her lips, and his cheeks colored. Her lips were soft, and he had to resist the urge to run his finger across them. He let his head fall back against the stone wall behind him and knocked it a couple times. He seriously had to get a handle on this. These feelings were totally unwelcome and completely inappropriate given who and what she was. Besides, they were entirely unreturned, based on the way she'd been with Nesu and the way she'd yelled at him.

"Luxe? Is everything all right?"

"Donum latini sermonis." He pressed his lips to hers for a moment fighting the desire to linger.

"Vere? Rersus?" Paige scowled at him.

Luxe's cheeks blazed. "You needed a new language," he answered in Latin.

She didn't answer, nor did she lose the scowl. The quiet beat at Luxe's ears. He jammed his fingers into the coarse stone of the wall behind him hoping the pain would bring him back to his senses. He'd liked casting the speech spell far too much.

"Luxe. The rune-stone."

"Yeah. Okay. Let's go."

They slid back out of the narrow alley, but no one seemed to notice. The press of people had begun to lighten. Everyone still in the streets was heading in the same direction. The Colosseum.

The arena loomed large over all the common buildings, making it easy to find. Paige and Luxe joined the crowd. He kept a tight hold on her hand. He'd promised not to leave her alone again, and he didn't intend on losing her. She was mad enough already. Besides, he didn't have the time to track both her and the stone.

Holding the free palm in front of him again, he sighed when the hands pointed straight at the Colosseum. Thankfully, as they got closer, the hand pointed toward the back of the building. Unfortunately, the only thing back there was the entrance to the slave quarters and the gates through which the animals were brought in. He couldn't take Paige to such a dangerous location. Instead, he took her to a public entrance and found her a seat fitting for an upper-class matron.

"You'll be safe here," he whispered into her ear. "The stone is in the slave's quarters or the gladiator's quarters. Not a good place for a woman, if you follow me."

She nodded and looked at him with frightened eyes.

He patted her head. "I'll be back. This isn't like last time. There are no monsters here. I just need to keep you safe this time. But if you're worried, you have your communication crystal, right?"

"Yeah." She patted the fabric between her busts.

"If for some reason I'm wrong, and I'm in imminent danger, you can call Nesu." The name tasted like dirt in his mouth. "But I'll come back. You have my word. This one should be easy. Like at your school." He gave her hand a squeeze and left her to watch the games.

Hopefully she wouldn't pass out or anything. Her modern sense of entertainment was so vastly different. The video games and movies from her era were nothing compared to seeing a real person disemboweled by a wild animal.

Luxe stopped in a dark corner and switched his toga for the short tunic of a working man, then stepped back out into the light and made for the workers' entrance. A set of cool stone stairs took him underground, beneath the Colosseum. The stench of men and animals hit him like a stone wall. He kept the shimmering green compass up and deliberately didn't look at anyone. This lifestyle drew in a large number of unsavory types. There would be many demons and vampires pretending to be humans here, hoping for their cut of the carnage.

The underground was a labyrinth, and he worried how to find his way out. All around him men yelled, animals cried, and whips cracked. The thought that most of them would be dead by the end of the day made him shudder. The Romans enjoyed bloodshed nearly as much as a demon. In fact, a good number of the successful gladiators were demons. The disguise gave them license to kill as they pleased.

The Antonius family ruled this time period. Like other ruling warlock families, they did what they could to keep the local demons and vampires in check. Here, at least, such creatures had a legal outlet for their habits.

The compass led him to a wooden platform in a stone shaft. He crawled on and found the stone jammed in a crack at the back. He flipped the small black stone, Bronwynn's rune shining up at him. With a sigh of relief, he secured the stone against his chest with a leather strap and flopped back with a sigh. Three down. Now, to find Paige before she panicked.

The floor beneath him started to move upward, and fear bloomed in his chest. Daylight shone down through cracks around the overhead sliding door. They were sending him into the arena. Panic roared in his ears, fueled by terror. Despite the futility, he clawed at the walls as the platform rose. The stone shaft completely boxed him in while transporting him to the ring above—he'd gotten stuck in a "damned if you do, damned if you don't" situation.

He had his magic of course. But if he broke through the platform, soldiers waited below to ensure anyone destined to enter the ring did so. He be faced with fighting a host of burly men in close quarters, or worse, demons. He might be able to handle two, but the hypogeum housed far more demons than that.

Above, a pack of wild animals might await him, or a demon gladiator, or they could try to run him down with a chariot. Either place he did magic here would have witnesses and any family would issue punishment for a public display large enough to get him out of trouble. He'd never dealt much with the Antonius family. He had no idea what sort of mercy they would be willing to grant if he had to fight.

The trap door opened. He'd run out of time and fate chose for him. The roaring of the crowd beat him as sunlight temporarily blinded him. He could smell the blood-soaked sand before it came into view. The platform jerked to a stop, and the movement knocked Luxe to his knees. Clanking announced another gate opening behind him. The noise of the crowd reached a fever-pitch. Luxe twisted. A hulking man lumbered toward him.

Shit. A demon. The red gleam of his eyes reached Luxe all the way across the arena.

"I can smell you, little warlock," the demon sneered. "You ended up in the wrong place. I never get to eat your kind, but out here no one is going to stop me . . ."

His words cut off as a knife lodged itself in his throat. Luxe snapped his fingers creating another round of green sparkles and ordered them into a second weapon. This time a sword. The demon laughed and pulled the knife from his throat.

"You've gotta do better than that if you wanna kill an immortal, kid." He reached behind him with both hands and pulled two swords from the sheathes on his back. "Give it your best shot. I love to play with my food."

For the first time ever, Luxe thanked his brother for being ten years older and a bully. His father insisted they go all out in fights, but Atlas would never have held back anyway. Luxe had learned to hold his own against a larger and more skilled opponent early on. Unfortunately, the demon was indeed immortal, or nearly so, making this trickier than fighting another warlock. The only way to kill him would be to immobilize him and then set his body ablaze with holy fire. Luckily that only involved prayers and no ingredients. But how to immobilize this beast?

The demon gladiator whirled his swords, and the metal whistled through the air, chilling Luxe. The demon's blade arced around, and steel rang as it met Luxe's sword. Luxe rolled away from the swing of the demon's other blade. He used the momentum to kick the monster's feet out from beneath him and rammed his sword through its chest. He threw his whole weight onto the sword, driving it through the demon's body and into the dirt.

"*Sanctus ignus,*" he screamed. "*Beatus ignus, Incendent bestiam. Feret ducite eum ad infernum unde venisset.*" The demon caught fire and in a brief moment burned up. "That's right, you cocky piece of shit," Luxe yelled at the scorch mark on the ground. "Never judge a warlock by his size."

The crowd thundered and applauded. Luxe stood and stabbed the air above his head with his sword. The crowd roared even harder.

He heard a collective gasp, and then a hush fell over the crowd.

Luxe's high evaporated like water in a desert. He looked around him, and his heart sank. That's right. No one killed a prize gladiator and got away with accolades. Now stalking lions surrounded him.

His mind raced as fast as his heart. He had no hope if he tried to use his sword. He'd have to use a spell. He knew dozens, but which would counter so many lions at once? Only magic big enough to land him in trouble came to mind. One of the lions made a low snarl, and Luxe decided he'd rather face the Antonius family.

~ ~ ~

Paige had already seen enough bloodshed to last the rest of her life when the trap door opened, and a platinum-blond youth rose out of the ground into the center of the arena. This poor guy didn't stand a chance. He had slim legs and arms sticking out of his short tunic. His doom walked in with the gladiator, whose arms were the size of the youth's thighs. The gladiator was swarthy and had more dark body-hair than anyone ought to be allowed to have. It gave him a rather bestial appearance.

When the knife appeared out of nowhere in the youth's hand, Paige recognized him as Luxe. She gave a little scream and bit her lip. Then, against all odds, Luxe took down the larger man in a few swift moves. She'd never seen anyone move so fast. Clearly, she hadn't been giving Luxe enough credit.

The crowd had screamed its approval when the gladiator went up in flames and left nothing more than a scorch mark on the sand. She jumped to her feet, screaming with them. Wild elation ran through her. Luxe might drive her crazy, but she didn't want him dead. He'd started to grow on her, like a pair of shoes with an unsure fit. Each time she tried them out, she liked them a little better.

Her elation got brutally squashed under the paws of six lions, who entered the arena crouched and ready to hunt. She could almost taste the fear he must be feeling. She bit her lip again and tasted blood. Even the best swordsman wouldn't stand a chance, but then again, that was probably the point. Only a couple people had left the arena alive since she'd been watching, and they had both been badly injured.

She followed along as he paused, sizing the lions up. She sat too far away to make out his expression, but he straightened his shoulders and jut his chin forward. He slowly pushed both hands away from his chest in a yoga-like move. Once they were fully extended he slapped them together and a burst of green sparkles created by the slap exploded in front of him. She'd never seen him use so much magic. Wasn't using so much a bad thing? He drew back his head and blew the sparkles, spinning in a circle until they surrounded him. One more clap and the sparks ignited and formed a giant cobra.

Paige gasped. The snake had to be more than forty-feet long. The body stood as tall as Luxe's knees. She covered her mouth and stifled a scream. How could Luxe even make something so appalling? Besides, he'd used blatant magic. Even those around her could see. They gasped and pointed at the mammoth reptile. Didn't he say doing this would get him punished?

Luxe moved his mouth, presumably to order the snake. One by one, it ate each of the lions. As the last lion disappeared, the snake burst apart in a shower of green sparkles and vanished. The entire stadium fell silent for a moment, then thunderous applause erupted. Even from where she sat, Luxe obviously did not share the crowd's elation. She pushed her way through the sweat-soaked throng toward the stairs below. When she'd finally reached the lowest edge above the arena, the wall fell in a drop one-story to the sand below. She stopped at the rail and looked desperately at Luxe. What happened now?

She didn't have to wait long to find out. Mere moments after she reached the rail, the gates around the arena opened and centurions in full armor marched out. They stopped in front of Luxe and made the echoing announcement of his arrest and immediate trial. The lead soldier took Luxe's arm and started to lead him away. Paige shook her head. No. This couldn't happen. She didn't want to be left alone again.

"Luxe," she screamed. "Luxe. *Luxe.*"

Her screams had no effect. He couldn't hear her over the crowds. He scanned the spectators, searching for her. She waved her arms and screamed his name again. She kept waving until they had marched him through the open door and the heavy iron gates slammed shut behind them. The clang triggered her tears.

She could hardly breathe. Once again, she'd ended up completely on her own in an unknown time. Only this time her situation had become exponentially worse than before. Because last time she'd known that Cleo planned to keep Luxe somewhere in the villa complex, and his life hadn't been on the line. This time no Nesu would come wandering through the garden and rescue her. Wait . . . Nesu. The crystal.

Paige elbowed people out of her way until she got through the crowds and out into the nearly deserted streets outside. In a private corner, she pulled the crystal out and held it tight in her hand as she thought Nesu's name and the words *help me*. The crystal grew hot in her hand. But the hope the heat brought dissipated when Nesu failed to materialize. She fought to control her fear as she leaned against the magnificent marble wall of the Colosseum. The stone cooled her back, though the sun beat down on her front. The inside had been shaded by massive awnings, but out here the heat was relentless.

"Need help, little lady?"

Paige spun, hoping to see Nesu. Instead, a man much like the gladiator stood behind her, his form dark, massive, and hairy. He leered at her, and fear ran through her like wildfire. His eyes were a glowing red.

"No. I'm fine," she gasped. She started inching along the wall trying to get away.

He slammed a hand on the wall beside her head. "You ain't going' anywhere, pretty thing. You smell like magic, and I'm hungry." Paige whimpered and tried to duck under his arm. He caught her in a painful grip and pinned her to the wall. "Let's play a bit before dinner."

Maybe, since he knew about magic anyway, she might use it against him. She knew Latin now after all.

"Release me," she ordered.

The man gave a growling laugh. "You've never met a demon, have ya sweetie? Piddly little spells won't work on me." He grabbed her dress and pulled her until she could smell the stench of decay on his breath. "Unless you can pull some top-level shit like the kid in the stadium, you haven't got a prayer."

"She can't, but I can." Nesu stood beside them looking furious. "Eating anyone in a warlock's household is against the law." He gave the man a wicked smile and cocked his head. "And I'm divine justice, dirtbag."

Nesu moved like lightening. He struck the man in the temple with the hilt of a knife. The demon hit the ground, and Nesu jumped on him instantly, ramming knives through both shoulders. He cleared off the pinned demon.

"Sanctus ignus," he growled. *"Beatus ignus, Incendent bestiam. Feret ducite eum ad infernum unde venisset."* Nesu snorted at the scorch mark. "And good riddance." He held a hand out to Paige. "Are you okay?"

Paige looked between him and the scorch mark and burst into tears. Nesu made a noise halfway between a snort and a laugh. "Well, I told you to call if you were in trouble, and you sure took me at my word. Though I'm surprised you didn't even make it to the next day. Where's Luxe during all this anyway?"

Paige rubbed her face dry and rushed through the story as best she knew. "I still have no idea how he ended up in the arena in the first place. Where did they take him?" Nesu wore a deep scowl, and she didn't like what his expression implied.

Finally, he sighed and rubbed at his face. "I can't believe that's the spell he chose to use on the lions. He could've put them to sleep or something less flashy." He quickly changed into Roman clothing, took Paige's hand, and started leading her through the city. "He's gotten himself in trouble with the local ruling family for doing blatant magic. The Antonius family is hard-nosed. He's going to need an advocate. I guess that'll have to be me."

"You'd do that for Luxe?"

He shot her an exasperated look. "Seems a shame to waste our efforts in saving his butt yesterday only to let them execute him today. Besides, you're bound to him, and having a human familiar is unprecedented. Who knows what would happen to you if they killed him." He stopped short for a moment. "Though he's going to have to be my familiar for a few decades to repay his debt to me."

"You wouldn't really make him your familiar, would you?"

"No, you silly girl." He took off again, dragging her along. "We keep telling you, that's not something we do.

Though I would settle for him butting out while I got in a full date with you. I think we'd enjoy ourselves if he could mind his own business for a couple hours."

They ran on in silence, Paige heaving for breath after being made to run in the heat while wearing a woolen shawl. She had just hit a point where she'd rather lay face down on the cobbles than keep going when Nesu stopped.

"This is the place." He led her up a staircase and between soaring marble columns. Inside the shady recesses of the cool, stone building loomed a door, guarded by two young men. They moved to cover the doorway as Paige and Nesu approached.

"These proceedings are closed to the public," they said in unison.

"We're not the public. I'm Nesu Absko, advocate for the accused. This is the accused's partner. Please let us pass."

The guards had already started to shuffle aside at the mention of Nesu's name. They walked through into a dim hallway.

"Wow, Nesu. How important are you?" Paige wondered aloud.

Nesu gave a small laugh. "In my own family, not very. There are several others more powerful than me. It's my family as a whole which holds the power. The Absko family is ranked second of the eight noble families."

"How about the family here?"

"The Antonius family is ranked fifth of eight, right after the Pendragons. That's why the guards didn't ask any questions. They rank too low to protest."

"I guess I made the right friends," Paige said.

Nesu frowned. "We'll see. Getting into the proceedings and influencing them are two entirely different things. And I'm telling you right now, keep your mouth shut and let me handle this. If you have anything to comment on, tell me, and I'll bring your concern up at the appropriate time."

Paige nibbled her lip as Nesu muttered guesses about the location of the proceeding. She really hoped they weren't too late. He burst into the main room at the end of the hall, a grand set of double doors marking it as important. He'd guessed correctly, and inside, Luxe stood in front of a long table. His hands were behind him in shackles, his head down, penitent. At the table sat five people: three witches and two warlocks. All were austere, with varying amounts of gray in their hair. The looks they gave her and Nesu made Paige swallow hard.

"I'm Nesu Absko and I'm here to advocate for the accused."

Luxe's head jerked up, shock on his face and then relief as his eyes landed on Paige. She gave him a small smile and a thumbs-up.

One of the witches looked Nesu over carefully. She was extremely petite and had an angular face with a sharp nose. "So, you're Senetmut's son? She and I were dear friends back in the day. I hope you are more responsible than your sister. What a shame, how Senetmut let any child of hers behave in such a disgraceful manner."

Nesu shrugged. "My sister was two hundred. I think there's a point at which every parent must cut the cord and let their children suffer their own mistakes."

The witch gave a sniff. "Perhaps. Though, I hear you wouldn't know. Too bad you couldn't even keep a wife. Looks like the Absko family is going to have a rank drop in a generation or two. Seeing as neither you nor your sister decided heirs were necessary. You won't stay young forever, you know." She patted her curls and tipped her nose up. "Now, what do you have to do with this troublemaking youngster? He's not even part of your family."

If Nesu felt anger at the witch's lecture, he didn't show it. He answered as smoothly as if she'd been discussing the weather with him.

"The boy is my responsibility right now. Sad story, really. The poor sap wandered away from the safety of his family, and my sister got a hold of him."

He poked Paige in the shoulder. "This one helped me find him. But don't bother asking her anything, she's in way over her head. Someone in the Pendragon's time has been a naughty boy and here she is, half-warlock, half-human and half-witted. Evidently the Pendragon's took her in to study with Luxe. When he wandered off, she went with him, and my sister abandoned the poor girl in my garden. She spent the better part of yesterday lost before I happened across her. My sister dragged the boy off to her lair. I don't think I need to remind this family what happens then. Anyway, I planned to return them both home, but he was so traumatized he ran as soon as he got outside my sister's rooms."

He sighed and gave Luxe a very parental look. "Turns out the kid is pretty good at time portals but evidently not landings. I tracked him here, but he'd overshot any good landing zone and came out in the underbelly of the Colosseum. Things just rolled from there."

The witch looked like she'd bitten into something sour. She chewed her tongue for a moment before speaking again. "I understand what you're getting at, but the circumstances still don't excuse blatant magic in a public arena."

"Oh now, Madam Antonius." Nesu's voice soothed and flattered. "He was already panicked. Then to get attacked by a demon . . . By the time the lions got to him, he had no hope of thinking clearly. Besides, the poor kid's only twenty. A warlock with two hundred years on him might still panic. Surely we can turn him over to his parents for punishment? I'll even escort him home myself if it would make the Antonius family feel better. If you doubt me, you can make the portal."

Madam Antonius waved the other four members together. They bent their heads and spoke too quietly for Paige to hear. After what seemed like forever, they all sat up and Madam Antonius folded her tiny, bony hands on top of the table.

"I've been overruled. You may return the boy to his parents for punishment. But if I find out he only gets a slap on the wrist, he won't be welcome back in my time, nor will any of the Pendragons."

"Oh, I have no doubt," Nesu shot Luxe a dirty look, "once Luxe's parents find out what he's been up to, he's in for a world of hurt. My own parents have left my sister in the garden as a mushroom for a week as punishment, followed by house arrest until she's married. I would imagine that will seem tame in comparison to what Luxe is bound to get."

One of the warlocks had finished a portal and Madam Antonius waved a hand at it. "Get out of here before I change my mind."

Chapter 10

Nesu grabbed Paige by the hand and Luxe by the scruff of his neck and hauled them both into the portal. All three went in at one time, and Rome disappeared. This time strong arms caught Paige before she hit the ground. Nesu kissed the tip of her nose and set her on her feet. She looked around. They'd arrived in the garden of one of the English castles.

"We need to get inside before anyone sees us." Luxe urged them toward a small door in the wall of the castle.

"Hold up, little buddy." Nesu caught the back of his tunic. "I've saved your butt twice now. You owe me an explanation at the very least. What the heck are you doing messing around in other people's timelines?"

"Inside. In my workroom, please," he hissed, his eyes pleading.

Nesu nodded, and Luxe blew green sparkles over everyone, dressing them in proper court attire. Leading them inside the door, he took them down a short stone stair and through a hidden passageway. It dumped them out in front of the heavy wooden door Paige recognized as the door to Luxe's workroom. Once inside, Luxe looked at the two and gestured at the white, ultra-modern sofa. He instead chose to pace around the room. Paige worried about Luxe. He'd turned a strange sort of gray.

"I can't tell you," he started, and Nesu crossed his arms obviously upset. Luxe stopped pacing and faced the older man. "No, you don't understand. I'm trying to fix a mistake I made which could get me punished *so* badly.

Like they might bury me to my neck and leave me there. Permanently."

Nesu leaned back against the sofa. "I'm not leaving without a good reason why I'm sticking my neck out for you. I came because Paige called. I stayed because she looked desperate. But you've got me lying to family heads. I need more than *my parents are gonna kill me.* 'Cause I'm starting to wonder if maybe they should."

It occurred to Paige during this lecture that Nesu was plenty old enough to be a parent himself. She shook her head. Age was impossible to judge with the warlocks and witches. The witch from Luxe's trial looked sixtyish in human years, but Paige had no idea what that equated to in warlock years. Especially since Luxe looked his actual age, and Nesu was almost three hundred but didn't look a day over thirty. Regardless, she suddenly wondered if maybe sticking with someone a little closer to her own age might be wiser. Especially since the witch had been goading Nesu about settling down with a family. She'd never even thought about kids.

Luxe's skin went a chalky-white which, with his pale hair, made him appear bleached. "I . . ." He kept speaking, but his voice trailed off into a faint whisper.

"Oh, for Pete's sake, Luxe." Paige snapped. "I'll do it." She turned to speak directly to Nesu. "He lost his family heirlooms all over time, and he's trying to get them back. That's how he met me. He came looking for one at my school, and I got dragged back here with him by accident."

Nesu sucked air in through his teeth in a sharp whistle. "Damn, kid. Your parents are gonna murder you and bury the pieces in different centuries. I mean your dad and I did some stupid shit together when we were kids but nothing which tops this."

"You were friends with his dad?" Paige said. She grew more uncomfortable as the conversation went on. When no comparisons were being made, forgetting about his age had been easy. Having him talk about being buddies with Luxe's dad made things seem ridiculous.

"Yes, you sound surprised. The eight families interact a lot, especially the youths. If you don't, you end up with no friends. Like Luxe here."

"Hey," Luxe protested. "There *are* no others right now. Maybe if you'd had kids. But I see you've been working on a plan for that. Why have your own when you can adopt?" He jammed a finger in Paige's direction.

Paige threw up her hands. "Leave me out of this. I'm struggling with the fact that I now feel like I spent the last two days making out with one of my dad's buddies."

"Paige, age isn't the same for warlocks," Nesu soothed.

"No, it's not. Because if you were human, you'd have been hanging out with my great-great-grandfather. Or maybe even one more great. Any way you look at it, our age difference kinda makes you a dirty old man and me your pop-tart."

"Huh?"

Luxe snickered. "It's twenty-first century slang, meaning you have tendencies toward young girls. The male equivalent of your sister. Only an old man wouldn't know that."

"That's it," Nesu snapped. "Where are your parents?"

Luxe dropped to his knees at Nesu's feet. "Please, *no*. What do you want for your silence?"

Nesu's eyes wandered over to Paige, and she jumped up off the sofa. "Absolutely not. I'm not a bargaining chip. Luxe, you're not whoring me out because you owe Nesu. And Nesu," she crossed her arms and glared at him, "I'm appalled, with as young as everyone regards Luxe, you'd stoop to blackmailing him. Warlock-kind seems to still regard him as a kid. Do you really blackmail kids against their mistakes? Especially with as hard as he's working to fix this? Retrieving them has almost killed him twice. He's never once passed the blame. He's never even asked for help. Most of the kids I know are completely incapable of owning their mistakes and fixing them that way. As an adult, you should be happy to encourage that. Don't you think?"

"Paige, my dear. You shame me." He took her hand and kissed the back. "You're right. I shouldn't pick on children."

"You shouldn't hit on them either," Luxe snarked at him.

Nesu dropped her hand. "I don't have time to argue with boys who have yet to grow facial hair. For Paige's sake, I'll let my favors thus far be just that, favors. She's right. I should be more encouraging in your quest to fix your mistakes. So, here's the deal. You have how many more?"

"Six," Luxe mumbled.

"You have one month to gather the rest. That gives you a little over four days apiece. At the end of one month, I expect you to report all this to your parents with or without the heirlooms. I want verification of your punishment. I'll report the punishment to the Antonius family for you. You are clearly going to take enough to satisfy even Madam Antonius."

"What's in it for you?" Luxe asked suspiciously.

"Absolutely nothing." Nesu shrugged. "Other than the pleasure of having made Paige's acquaintance. I'll be the adult here. I don't require payment from kids, and I do admire your persistence. But Luxe, teach the girl a few spells for her own protection and give her a dagger or something. She can strap it to her thigh. But while you were off getting yourself arrested, she nearly ended up as demon chow. Luckily, she called me in time."

Nesu stood and drew Paige to her feet. He pulled her in against his chest and brushed a hand across her cheek. "Age means nothing like you think it does. My sister is in trouble because she messed with human history over a young man and keeps coming back for more. You are quite different for me. I genuinely like you. You'd not be a toy, but rather my princess." He leaned in taking her earlobe between his teeth making her shudder. Then whispered, "Call for pleasure instead of work sometime, okay. And I'll still bail you out if it's dire." He ran his tongue up her ear and took a step back. "Luxe, a portal home if you please. I have to go water my poor sister."

Luxe drew a portal on the wall, and Nesu blew a kiss at Paige as he stepped through and vanished.

~ ~ ~

Luxe heaved a sigh of relief. He still had time to fix this before his parents found out. Paige stared curiously at the wall where the portal had been.

"When he says he has to water his sister?" Paige asked.

Luxe raised an eyebrow. "She's a mushroom now. She likes it moist."

"His parents really did that to her?" Paige sounded shocked.

"Yes. Don't parents in your era punish their children?'

"Yeah, but not by turning them into fungus."

"Well, they couldn't anyway. They're only human," Luxe reassured. "It's not like becoming a mushroom hurt her. She gets all the food and water she needs from the soil. It's more symbolic, to remind her she behaved no better than a fungus. Warlock parents are like human parents, punish to get the point across but don't actually hurt the kid. Warlocks just have a lot more creative punishments available to them"

"I guess so. But isn't three hundred a little old to have your parents punish you?"

"Not in a family matter. Just like humans, warlock parents stop smacking our hands for stealing cookies before dinner when we're in our early teens. But since we stay with our families for life, if you do something to hurt the family, they'll still dish out punishment. Would your parents punish you if you wrecked their car when you were forty?"

"Probably. But not the same way as when I was a kid."

"Exactly. My brother has seven-year-old twins. No one in the family would dream of turning them into a mushroom for a week. But Cleo's a big girl, and she knew what she was doing when she tried to run off with me."

"Do you really stay with your whole family for life?"

"Of course. It's why I wanted to get inside so badly. My brother, Atlas, is wandering around the castle somewhere. But each warlock has their own workspace, and we're pretty good about privacy. You never know if someone has a delicate spell ripening or some such wizardry."

Paige nodded. Luxe fell silent, thinking about the events in the arena. As much as he'd been sure he'd receive some deeply unpleasant punishment, he'd only felt fear for Paige. He'd promised to come back to her, and once again he'd let her down. Not to mention Nesu had to save her from a demon. He was a crappy master for a familiar. He should probably apologize. But how exactly did one do that to a girl?

"Paige." Luxe started toward her.

Should he take her hands and gaze at her sincerely or remain distant? Or hug her? Getting on his knees seemed a bit excessive. She stared at him, and now the words wouldn't come. What horrible things female creatures did to him. She didn't need magic. She could freeze him and render him mute with one look.

"Did you need something, Luxe? 'Cause if not, I'm exhausted, and I have no idea how you're not dead on your feet. I think we ought to head to bed."

Luxe squirmed. The way she'd put that sounded like they might be heading to the same bed. What a horrifying thought. The only female he'd stayed the night with was Cleo, but of course she hadn't been interested in sleeping. He'd fooled around with a couple of human girls in high school, before the Cleo incident, but certainly not for the night. Worse, Paige was his familiar. What if he touched something accidentally? What if *she* touched something accidentally? He shook his head. No need to even go there. No possible way she meant sleeping in the same bed. He needed to try again for that apology.

"Paige, I'm sorry," he blurted. Well, that had sounded dumb. But now that he'd gotten the initial words out, speaking came easier. "I really feel awful. I told you you'd be all right and that I'd come back for you. Then I go and leave you alone, and you got into trouble. I'm so sorry I wasn't there to help."

"Leaving me wasn't your fault this time. It's not like you meant to get arrested. Did you?"

"No. Of course not. The whole time they were carting me away, you were all I could think of. I knew I'd be punished, but that disturbed me less than the thought of breaking my promise to you, again."

Paige stepped up in front of him and put a hand on his arm. "Okay, Luxe. I get it. Apology accepted. We don't even have to talk about today anymore. I'm glad you didn't get hurt in the arena. I had no idea you could do that kind of stuff. The magic was . . . impressive."

Luxe's arm went hot under Paige's hand. "Thanks." His voice sounded lower and thicker than normal. "Creating a snake is simple. I only wish I could have told you not to worry about me."

She'd left her hand on his arm, and now all sorts of wild images ran through Luxe's head. Holding her, hugging her. Kissing her—no. He had a job to do. He needed to be focused on that and not the length of her lashes, which were long and curled slightly upwards. He closed his eyes and drew a deep breath. Paige was a human, and he needed to return her to her own time.

He opened his eyes. Paige swayed in front of him, her eyes nearly closed. Luxe caught her as she tipped. She hadn't been kidding when she said how tired she felt. He scooped her up. She would be difficult to carry this way. The dress made her bulky, and it nearly doubled her weight. To get to the most appropriate spare room, he'd have to carry her three flights up and halfway across the castle, next to his own bedroom. As Paige slumped against his shoulder in a dead weight, he knew he'd never make it that far.

Out of desperation, Luxe wiggled his fingers and used the sparkles to turn his couch into a bed. He laid Paige on top and created more sparkles to change her clothes. The crisp, white nightgown came to her ankles. Appropriate, should anyone happen to see her. He started to tuck her in, and she shook her head sleepily.

"I need to wash my face." Her words came out thick with sleep.

He magicked up a warm wash cloth and tried to press it into her hand, but she was too asleep. Instead, he found himself wondering if he ought to do the scrubbing for her. Touching her face wouldn't hurt anything, would it? Just to do her a favor, of course.

And such a luxurious favor for his recreant feelings. They roiled to the surface and drove him to gently trace her cheekbones with the cloth. He ran it along her lips indulging himself in the memory of the kiss he'd given her so she could speak Latin. He could have let that kiss linger for hours. Maybe just one more. He caught himself leaning toward her and jerked upright. He got up abruptly to leave when Paige caught his cloak.

"Please don't go," she mumbled sleepily. "I'm afraid I'm gonna have nightmares after today. And I can't stand the thought of being alone. Bad things happen when you leave."

He looked around the room. It wasn't very large, and he might break something if he tried to stuff in another full-sized bed.

"Paige, I don't think there's space."

She started to wiggle to the far side of the bed. "'M sorry," she slurred in sleep. "I hog s'mtimes." Her mouth drooped open on the last word, and she gave a little snuffle.

Luxe stood, staring at the bed and Paige in total shock. Had she invited him to sleep with her? He mulled over every word she'd spoken and her wiggle to the far side of the bed. He couldn't interpret her request to mean anything else but that. He created a nightshirt for himself and stood there. The nightgown and nightshirt couldn't possibly put enough material between the two of them. There ought to be more of a barrier. Hesitantly, he climbed in, staying as far to the side as humanly possible. He blew a bunch of green sparkles around the room, and the torches went out, leaving the flickering light of the dying fire.

"Luxe?" Paige stretched out a hand without even opening her eyes. When it made contact with shoulder, she left her fingers gripping his shirt.

Luxe lay there, never wanting to move again. Sleep took a very long time to overtake him despite his physical weariness. But sleep he did, an inexplicable warmth coating him all over.

"*Luxe!*"

The heart-wrenching scream sent Luxe flying from under the covers. Paige still slept, tangled in the sheets. A sheen of sweat stood out on her forehead even in the low light from the embers. She moaned and tossed. Luxe scrambled across the bed and took her shoulders.

"Paige. Wake up. It's only a dream. Paige."

She opened her eyes, took one look at him, and burst into tears. She wrapped her arms around him, pressing her face to his chest and sobbing. Only individual words made it to his ears.

"Alone . . . demon, scared. Eaten, Luxe, gone!"

He scooped her up and hugged her without thinking. "Shh . . . I'm here. You're safe, and you're not alone."

He reached down and stroked her hair the way he would calm a horse. She squeezed him tighter and jammed her face into his chest until it hurt.

"You only had a dream," he reassured her. "It's over. Would you like to talk? I'll listen."

She shook her head against his chest. "Hold me."

He tightened his grip on her, and she snuggled in. Tentatively, he lay back down. She didn't resist, but rather twisted herself so they were spooned together and tucked her head under his chin. Surely the thudding of his heart would wake her. But somehow it must have only been so loud to him. The tension left her, and she relaxed back into his body, asleep.

Luxe gave up and let his imagination run wild. He pressed himself along her body until his bare toes found hers. He ran his foot up her foot and ankle, enjoying the sensation of his skin on hers. Even on her feet, her skin felt like silk. Burying his face in her hair, he drank her in. She smelled like dust and very faintly like the lotus from that morning. A morning which seemed worlds away. Even with all the time travel he did, he had a hard time wrapping his head around the mere hours since . . . His heart sank. Since she'd been in Nesu's arms.

He tucked his face into her shoulder. "I'm as good as those other guys, you know. You don't have to have Nesu or that kid at your school. I can be that. I can take better care of you. I *will*, and you'll see. Before this is over, you'll be looking to me to protect you from everything, not just from your imagination."

He fought a wave of self-pity and looked for sleep instead. As the blackness took over, he let his breathing match hers and gave one last snuggle into the back of her neck.

Luxe floated on the edge of sleep, not wanting to wake. It had been hours since he'd curled up with Paige, and they'd probably already missed breakfast. The castle residents ate early. He tightened his eyes against the morning. Just a few more minutes. Hair tickled Luxe's nose. Without thinking he inhaled deeply, smiling at Paige's smell.

"Did you sniff me?" Paige's question jerked Luxe back to reality.

"No." His face quickly colored. "Yes, but . . . it's just you smell like dust from yesterday," he finished lamely.

He really had to get a handle on this crush. Being able to use that word surprised him. A strange slippery sensation entered his stomach and squirmed within him. He'd never had a crush before.

He hated Cleo, and the two girls he'd fooled around with in high school had sought *him* out. Hormones had done the rest. He'd been a little guilty afterwards that he'd felt nothing for either of them. But he figured they'd made all the moves, and he'd told them he wasn't particularly interested. If they insisted on pushing forward from there, any hard feelings between them weren't his fault. As always, they had proven to be typically difficult females, telling all the girls in his class how callous he'd acted.

Rumors, he could live with. He only had to stay there for a couple years after all.

With Paige, his feelings were particular to her situation. She caused him trouble in a whole different way, and this crush only added to the layered cake of issues with her. She was unattainable for so many reasons. It surprised him how much more attractive that made her. Like he could prove something by getting her interest. But he had to quash this feeling. They had work to do. His sentiments would only make things awkward.

"Great," Paige grumbled climbing from the bed. "I'm sorry I stink. I don't suppose they have a proper shower in the castle?"

Luxe's heart sank. He hadn't meant to imply she stank. Looks like things were going to be awkward despite his efforts.

"Sorry, no showers. We bathe. Want me to make a bath for you?"

"Nesu suggested teaching me magic. Why don't you show me?"

Oh, yes, of course. If Nesu said so, let's do that. Luxe let the complaints slide freely through his head. Followed by thoughts on what color mushroom Nesu would make if he opted to turn him into a fungus, too. "If you'd like. It's going to require a lesson. Are you okay with the wait?"

Paige nodded. "Hurry up, though. I wouldn't want to gross you out any further."

"You didn't," Luxe gritted out. Why was she so stubborn? "I merely made an observation." He sent green sparkles at the bed, turning it back into the sofa. "Sit, please."

Paige sat and Luxe paced, trying to think of the best way to explain something which came as second nature to a warlock. He clasped his hands behind his back and tried to appear his most knowledgeable.

"There are three ways to get most of the material things you might want as a warlock. You can do a transformation: turn something into what you want. This works best if the items are of a similar use, like turning my couch into the bed. You can summon something. This involves pulling something from elsewhere in the world. Usually we use this method for large items like the car, or for victuals. Or you can conjure something, create it from scratch with magic. I tend to reserve this for things which are a little less tangible. Following?"

"Maybe. But I'm not sure I like this. Are all the clothes you've been switching us into coming from someone else's closet?"

"It's not like we stole them." Luxe sounded defensive. "My parents keep a stocked closet, and the magic takes care of fitting the garment to you. Once you're done with the item, the piece goes back where you got it from. I guess you could say the method is a combination of summoning and transformation. But the thing about using those two methods is that they involve no potion ingredients. You can use those anywhere, anytime, as long as you know the spell.

"Conjuring involves ingredients, which means you need access to a workroom. Oh, and don't conjure food. If the ingredients are even slightly off, you could be stuck in the bathroom for an ungodly amount of time."

"Okay. Let's try something then," Paige said eagerly.

"*Partum a bale.* That's your spell for a bath. You also need to be able to see what you want in your mind. The clearer the picture, the better the spell will work. And you have to want it. Half-hearted spell-work makes half-baked results. While you work on that, I'll track today's stone."

Chapter 11

Paige went to the far side of the room to practice in private. She took a deep breath and muttered the words he'd taught her. Nothing happened. How unfair of Luxe! Here she assumed they'd been getting along well. She'd even been comforted by him last night. She'd figured they were on their way to being friends. Which, given that they still had six stones to get, would be a good thing for them both. Then he had to go complain about her smell.

She understood she wasn't in a good state. After everything that had happened yesterday, who would be? But still she didn't complain about him. He'd had a sort of pungent man-odor about him, and yet she'd said nothing.

Now that her brain wasn't half-asleep, she also doubted Nesu's timeline for the stone collection. His stipulations, by her math, meant as many as five weeks could pass before she got sent home. And what if things ran longer? Or worse, what if Luxe's parents couldn't undo the spell, and she got stuck here forever? Maybe Luxe could come live in her time for a while so she could finish school and go to college at least. But the trip around Europe would be awkward if she had to drag him around, too. How would she explain that to her brother?

Her second attempt to get a tub went as miserably as the first. She'd grabbed a bowl off one of the tables in an attempt to transform it, but Luxe had said she'd need to concentrate, and her mind threatened to overflow at any moment. One more try. A sharp yelp from behind her caught her attention. Luxe rushed across the room toward her, pulling up short, and giving her a strange smile.

"I found the stone. We're headed to Omi Province in the Sengoku period, 1553."

Paige blinked at him, lost.

"That's in Japan," he elaborated, then frowned as he looked her over. "Aren't you ready?"

"No. I haven't made a proper bath yet." She pointed at the bowl which still looked like a bowl but at least she'd filled it with steaming water.

Luxe shook his head. "We should get going on this." He tossed her a wet washcloth and turned around. "Just rinse and we'll worry about a bath later."

Now irritated, Paige grabbed the washcloth. She dropped the top half of her nightgown and began rubbing herself with it. He must have put some scented oils on the cloth because she smelled like lilacs now.

"What about you?" Her temper wanted Luxe to suffer with her. "I'm not the only one who smells."

Luxe turned. Paige squealed. And he turned back, the whole of his neck red.

"Sorry. I didn't realize."

"How did you not realize? You gave me a cloth and told me to rinse. What? Was I supposed to reach up under the nightgown or wash through the cotton?"

"Neither. I'm sorry." He gave his face a rub. "Don't worry about me. I cleaned up with magic."

Paige threw the washcloth into the back of his head. "Why didn't you say we could do that in the first place?" she shrieked.

He held his hands up in surrender. "You said you wanted a bath."

"I said I wanted a shower. Why else would I want one, except to be clean?"

"How would I know?" Luxe had turned again. "Girls like to hang out in baths and showers. I thought maybe you wanted to relax."

Paige yanked her top back up. "Nothing about anything with you is relaxing. Forget teaching me for right now. Just clean me up and dress me appropriately for sixteenth century Japan. And next time, lose some of the stones in modern times. I'd love a real shower and a toilet which flushes."

Luxe made green sparkles and blew them over her. Immediately she felt clean and dry. She still smelled like lilacs though. If she wasn't so worked up, she might have found it a pleasant scent.

Paige took in her new garb. Luxe dressed her in a light blue kimono, tied at her waist with a red cord. Luxe had on loose pants in the same light blue and a cream-colored shirt with wide sleeves. They were belted in the middle with an obi like hers. They both wore reed sandals. Comfortable they might be, but she still liked the linen gown from Egypt best.

He held a hand out to her. "Shall we?"

She took the offered hand with a grim smile. "Yup. Let's get this over with."

"That's the spirit." He drew the portal on the wall and led them both through.

Paige landed hard on her butt. She'd barely gotten a look at the forest she'd ended up in when Luxe landed on top of her. He lay, sprawled over her body.

"Shh . . ." he hissed, then whispered, *"Nos peribunt."*

His green sparkles tickled her nose as they fell across her face. She sneezed.

"Get off me," she snapped.

A whiz and a thunk followed her indiscrete protest. She glanced up at a throwing star lodged in the tree trunk near her head. She opened her mouth to scream, but Luxe clamped a hand over it and shook his head. He ducked her head and pressed it against the ground with his arms covering her.

Paige tried hard to control her breathing. Anything which scared Luxe this much couldn't be good. They lay there for a very long time. After a while, even the adrenaline wasn't helping ease the weight of his body anymore. Just when she wasn't sure she could take their position any longer, he rolled to the side and heaved a sigh.

"What was that?" Paige whispered, afraid to raise her voice.

"*Shinobi*. You'd call them ninja. This land belongs to Rokkaku Yoshikata. What they're doing out here is beyond me. He shouldn't be in a military engagement right now."

"Ninja?" Her voice came out as a squeak. "How did we get away?"

"I made us invisible. But they can still hear us. That's why you nearly got sliced for griping. It's also why I waited until they were long gone." He stood and helped her to her feet. *"Invenerunt lapidem."* The green compass glowed on his palm.

While Luxe focused on the compass, Paige took the opportunity to peer around. They stood in the middle of uninterrupted forest. Cedars, maples, and oaks competed to reach the sunlight, leaving the forest floor glowing with jade light. The forest smelled of all the sweet, spicy, and damp smells of cedars. Paige loved this spot. Aside from Nesu's garden along the Nile, this was easily the most enchanting place they'd visited thus far. Across the forest floor, ferns and other small plants eked out a living. Here and there birds flitted and called.

"This way." Luxe pointed off to their right.

The earth between the trees was packed and strewn with soft, fallen needles, making their path easy to follow. Paige wasn't falling all over herself for once. They walked on in a pleasant silence, Luxe checking his compass from time to time. Paige's sandals had begun to rub at her feet, and she contemplated asking Luxe for proper shoes. Her kimono hung low enough to cover them for the most part, so she didn't see why she couldn't have sneakers. While she was thinking, Luxe had gotten ahead of her; she ran to catch up and ask before she got blisters.

"Luxe. Wait up," she called.

"Dare ka?" The voice rang through the otherwise peaceful woods like a shot.

Paige let out a little squeak and ran to Luxe.

"Akuryo," a voice in another direction rang out.

"Yokai," the first came back.

Another whiz and thunk in their direction. Luxe grabbed Paige's hand and started to run.

"Can they see us?" Paige asked.

"No. And we're still speaking Latin. They can't understand us either."

Every so often something would come whizzing in their direction, but since they were invisible, the ninjas could only guess at their location by sound. The going got slow as they entered a thicket of bamboo. Luxe pushed through as Paige followed, her heart hammering. They had yet to even see the ninjas. What if they were right next to them?

Suddenly, Luxe tumbled out into a clear spot. Paige fell after him, landing on her knees. The bamboo trunks had parted, but their thick stalks bent inward, creating a green dome.

Luxe gasped and pressed Paige back behind him toward the bamboo. "Well, the *shinobi* won't follow us here," he whispered.

"Why?" Paige asked, even though she wasn't sure she wanted the answer.

"It's a *yokai* house." He pointed across the clearing at a ramshackle wooden house which looked more like a shed. Its thatched roof sagged with age, and a front door full of gaps hung crooked from its frame. "A haunted house. The *shinobi* are too superstitious. They won't come near this place, but then again, we shouldn't have either."

"Right." Paige snorted. "A haunted house. Like I believe . . ."

The front door on the little house slowly opened, leaving a black hole for an entry. Paige caught a blur of movement, and they were surrounded by five individuals with marble-like skin, black hair, and dark eyes. They made the hair on the back of Paige's neck stand up.

"Konbanwa," the one in the center said. The others were all looking at him, so Paige assumed he must be the leader.

"Luxe?" Paige asked.

"Vampires. Shh . . ."

"I thought vampires were Transylvanian," she whispered back. "These guys are Japanese."

"Oh, you speak Latin," the vampire leader observed. His voice was smooth and hypnotic. "Vampires are a species, not an ethnic group, my dear. Much like humans, we have diversity. But . . ." He eyed her suspiciously, and then seemed to change his mind on something. "You are aware you are on our land?" he drawled.

Luxe paled, and Paige swallowed hard on her own fear.

The vampire gave them a toothy grin, flashing needle-sharp fangs. "I am fully within my rights to punish trespassers. You know that as well, correct?"

Luxe pulled himself upright. "Correct, assuming the trespassers were aware of the boundaries of your lands. Being visitors from another timeline, we wouldn't know.

You wouldn't want to start an inter-temporal incident, would you?"

The vampire leader gave them a bored look. "I'm not too worried. The Oda family is far too self-involved to bother punishing me."

Luxe crossed his arms, looking superior. "I'm a Pendragon. The Oda family won't turn a blind eye if you decide to hurt me. We simply stumbled across your land. Let us go, and we'll leave just as quickly."

"How about this?" The vampire sneered. "I'll let you both live. But you can do it as my minions. I'll turn you, and you can serve me."

Paige panted in fear as the five vampires closed the ring around them. She could no longer move away, her back now pressed against the bamboo. What could Luxe do against all five of them? She couldn't help, obviously. She should have insisted he take Nesu's advice and teach her something useful. The lead vampire grabbed Luxe's hand and pulled him toward the yokai house.

"I'll deal with you first. I wasn't born yesterday. It took me a while to sniff the anomaly out, but the little girlie you have with you is using borrowed magic. I know enough about warlocks to know that's a no-no in any family. So I'll dispatch you, and if anyone asks, I'll tell them you had it coming for your crimes." He turned a vicious smile on Paige. "As for her, she'll make a lovely vampire bride. The warlock families would get involved if I married a witch, but they won't care about a stray human. I haven't had the pleasure of a partner since my last wife got herself killed by the Oda for feeding too freely."

Paige watched helplessly as Luxe struggled, the familiar's bond crying out in warning. They were nearly at the house now. Why didn't he make a snake to eat these guys? He looked genuinely scared. She gripped the bamboo behind her, trying not to cry. Only one of the vampires remained within arm's reach of her. She could try running. But the vampires were faster, and the ninja lurked out there somewhere. The bamboo above her rustled in the breeze, and Paige wished with all her might they weren't so thick. Wait—sunlight killed vampires, right?

"Cut, dammit," she whispered futilely at the plant behind her, wishing she knew some spell to chop them down.

A snap rang through the forest followed by another and another. In less than a second sunlight flooded the open area. Five screams pierced the forest and the yokai house went up in flames. Luxe fell to the ground and scrambled out of the way as the vampire who had been dragging him burned, charred, and turned to dust. In moments, six piles of ash were all which remained in the clearing. Five small ones and one big where the house had stood. The breeze picked at the ash, scuttling it away into the forest.

Paige rushed over to Luxe. "Are you okay? I'm not even sure what I did, but I'm glad it happened. I thought . . . I thought we weren't getting out of this one."

"I didn't either." Luxe shuddered and rolled to sit up. "What exactly did you do in the moments before the bamboo collapsed?"

Paige ran through all her thoughts and actions. Before she finished Luxe nodded. "You're still speaking Latin. The word 'cut' plus your desire to level those trees manifested itself as a spell. Good work." He started to reach for her before pulling his hand back, letting his arms flop at his side. "We should see how far off course we wandered." Luxe held up his palm and called up the compass. Once it showed a direction, he stood and led the way back into the ninja-infested forest.

Chapter 12

Luxe pushed his way back through the forest as quietly as he could, until he was sure the ninjas were no longer in the area. He really hoped, since the ninjas seemed to think they belonged to the yokai house, that the warriors might have cleared out when the bamboo collapsed and the house burned. His compass indicated they still had some distance to travel. He made a mental note to research a way to connect the two spells when he got home. This would be a lot easier if tracking the stone to a time and general place could be linked with the close-range compass.

"Luxe?" Paige asked from behind him. "Why didn't you save yourself?"

He stopped and turned so she could see his seriousness. "A vampire's magic negates a warlock's, but only by touch." Somehow, he couldn't bring himself to tell her he'd let himself be caught to stall for time. He hadn't been able to stomach the idea of abandoning her. Had he left, the vampires would certainly have taken their frustration out on her. "*Never* let a vampire touch you. Once they had me, I was screwed."

Paige caught on too quickly for him. "Could you have gotten away before he'd touched you?"

"Yes."

"But you stayed?"

"Yes."

"Could I have gotten away?"

"No." This conversation made him uncomfortable.

"You stayed for me?"

"Yes." For one moment, he imagined her throwing her arms around him and thanking him with affection, but he swiftly shoved that thought aside. Close physical contact wouldn't be appropriate.

Paige turned slightly pink. "Thank you. For staying."

"No, I should be thanking you," Luxe rushed. "I really didn't want to find out how they intended to kill me. Vampires can be particularly cruel to their victims."

They stood in the green light of the forest floor, birds twittering around them, neither of them saying a word. Their silence began to drag on, and Luxe grew more and more uncomfortable. What did she want from him? Why didn't she say anything? Girls always had something to say. When he could stand the pause no longer, he turned on his heel and followed the compass. Better to take the silence on the move than the awkwardness of standing there.

He hadn't gone far when Paige fell behind. He stopped and waited for her to catch up. She limped toward him in obvious pain.

"Are you okay? Did they hurt you?"

Her eyes were wet with tears and she lifted the hem of her kimono. Luxe bit back a gasp. Her feet were bloody.

"What did they do?" He knelt at her feet.

"The vampires didn't do anything, the sandals did."

He looked up at her surprised. "Why didn't you say something? I could have changed your shoes."

"I meant to, before we ran from the ninjas. And by the time we got away from the vampires, they were already torn up."

"But when we left the bamboo grove, you could have said something then."

She gave him a dirty look. "You turned and walked off into the forest. I could barely keep up."

He sighed. "We were both silent. I thought if we had nothing more to discuss we ought to get work done. You could have called after me."

"You could have . . . never mind." Paige started to hobble in the direction he'd been going.

He caught at her kimono. "Don't be sulky. I'll heal your feet and get you different shoes."

"Yes, well. I'd hate to slow you down." Her voice sulked.

What was with women and holding grudges? If only she could deal with her feelings like a man: either speak her mind, or hit him, or something more obvious than pouting. He couldn't imagine how offering to help drew out sulking.

He still had the hem of her kimono in his hand. She looked at his hand on her dress, shot him another dirty look, and gave a jerk and a step forward to free herself. The whole garment unpeeled like an orange, and Paige stood in what looked like an open robe. Luxe took in the sight of her, a tingly warmth spreading through his body. Somehow, despite the revealing garments she'd already worn, the view didn't get old.

Paige tried to wrap herself back up, her face red and angry. "Always going for a free peep, aren't you? How come it's always me getting peeked at?"

Luxe stood, looking at her blankly. "Did you want a peek?"

"No," she shrieked. "I want you to *stop* looking."

A dozen retorts ran through his head, though every one of them just as likely to cause trouble as the next. He couldn't dig himself out of this hole, and he once again elected silence as the best course of action. He made to help her with retying the obi, but she lashed things back together too fast for him to help. She probably wouldn't want him to touch her at this moment anyway, so he shrugged and stepped back. When she finished, he resisted the urge to point out she'd tied it completely wrong. Somehow, he felt that would be counterproductive as well.

"Shall I fix your feet?"

She huffed and lifted her kimono a little.

"Come here and sit down," Luxe ordered.

She sat down right where she stood, and Luxe came over to her, shaking his head. He wasn't sure if he wanted to laugh or scold her. Fixing the popped blisters only required some quick spell-work.

"Pay attention," he instructed her. "This is an easy healing spell, but if you want to know useful magic, this would be important." He held his hand over the wounds and said, *"Curare."* Then he removed his hand. Her eyes widen as the skin knitted itself back together. "All better? Now, what type of shoes do you want?"

"Just athletic shoes." Her voice still held awe as she kept her eyes on her feet. "You and Nesu. You make that look so easy."

"It *is* easy. That's why I wanted you to pay attention. Now if I'm unavailable, or you don't want help, you can fix a wound yourself."

"Shouldn't I practice?"

He couldn't help but laugh out loud. "Who did you want to cut up for practice?"

She blushed. "Oh, yeah. I didn't think of that."

He got her a pair of sneakers and stood, holding a hand out to help her to her feet. The skin on her hand felt so soft when she took his. He nearly kept the hand and pulled her to him. Her very touch was filled with all sorts of imagined promise. Dropping her hand quickly, he resolved not to touch her unless absolutely necessary. He sucked at quashing his crush.

Luxe kept his ears on her, pleased she was now keeping up. Their trek led them steadily uphill. A clear stripe ran through the nearby trees, disappointing him. A road. The only roads in these parts led to the palaces of wealthy *daimyo*. Most likely, the owner of this road also employed the ninjas they'd encountered. If he guarded his palace so carefully, getting to the stone would be much more difficult. And the compass pointed straight up the hill toward the palace.

He stopped and put out a hand for Paige to do the same. "Apparently the stone is inside the palace grounds. Rokkaku isn't part of the warlock Oda family. Even though he's only a human warlord, his soldiers are quite capable of killing us. Especially if he's got more *shinobi* lurking around. At least we'd see the samurai coming. From here on out, be as silent as possible. We're still invisible to humans, but that won't matter if they hear us and fire a weapon in a lucky shot."

"How long do we have to find the stone?"

"This era is a little more dangerous, so I set the return for twenty-four hours. Mid-morning tomorrow. No need to linger and invite more trouble."

"What time do you suppose it is now?"

Luxe looked at the sky. "Dinner time, maybe. Five-ish."

Paige's stomach grumbled, and Luxe chuckled. "We'll get dinner when we're out of the palace grounds safely. We don't have too far, hang in there."

Paige opened her mouth and snapped it shut, then nodded. Luxe took the lead again, going slowly and trying not to make any noise. Unseen hooves vibrated the earth, a low thudding which carried through the ground. Then came the jingling of armor and harnesses. A few moments later, a column of mounted samurai came into view, evening sunlight glinting off their armor. Near the head of the column, behind a personal guard, rode the daimyo, dressed to the nines. Luxe gave a sigh of relief. This would make their task marginally easier. No wonder there had been ninja in the forest. They'd been clearing the way for the lord. With him gone, security on the castle would be a little lighter.

Once the column passed, Luxe figured they were safe enough to use the road for a change. Going uphill on the road instead of through the ferns and around the stones in the forest made for easy passage. Besides, the open road let in more light, making their way easier to see in the dimming daylight. They reached the palace with its huge wooden beams and curving roof lines as the blue of twilight settled over the sky. Other than the forest birds singing sleepy songs, the land had fallen silent.

Being invisible, they slipped easily past the guards, and Luxe followed the compass around the outer wall of the palace. He could smell the cedar cooling from the day's heat. Any pleasant mood the cedar elicited evaporated as he rounded the corner. All thoughts of easily grabbing the rune-stone disappeared, and Luxe groaned out loud before he could stop himself.

"What?" Came Paige's quiet hiss.

"The stone is in there." He pointed to the sprawling Japanese rock garden spread out in front of them.

Bonsai, miniature temples, and bridges sat amongst carefully raked sand. There lay little rivers of stones, which were all about the same size and shape as a rune-stone. The compass could narrow a location down to a small section of the garden, but from there they were going to have to search by hand.

Paige gave a low groan. "How are we ever going to find the stupid rock?"

"You'll know the rune-stone by touch. It will be warm, and you'll be able to feel the magic."

"We have to touch every pebble in here?"

"Not if we wait until morning. Then we can search visually as well, and the compass says the stone is somewhere in the back corner over there." He pointed off to the left. "But where do we stay the night?"

"I don't want to stay out here. It's creepy," Paige said.

"Then you want to break into the palace?"

Paige looked up the looming wall and shivered, shaking her head. Luxe thought for a moment. "Come on. They probably took most of the horses. We'll sleep in the stable."

Paige made a face like she might protest, but after looking again at the palace, she gave a grim nod. He followed the wall around until he found the low building which served as a stable. They settled on the hay loft, and Luxe scrambled up the ladder after Paige. Once there, he magicked up a couple sandwiches and handed one to her. They ate in tired silence, and he made some blankets for sleeping once they finished.

Curled under the blankets, the sound of things scuttling through the hay below him reached Luxe. The knowledge made his skin crawl, but he didn't say anything in case Paige hadn't noticed. He fell asleep with images of giant rats running through his head.

Luxe woke shivering. The night had gotten far too chilly for his liking. Next to him Paige curled in a tiny ball, shivering in her sleep. Luxe made an extra blanket and hesitated. The best way to warm up would be to curl up with Paige, but he'd promised himself he'd stay away. A violent shiver made the decision for him. He threw the blanket over her and curled around her so they could share each other's warmth. After a few minutes, her heat soaked into him and the extra blanket did its job, allowing him into a much more blissful sleep.

~ ~ ~

A burning itch woke Paige. She stretched down to scratch without opening her eyes. Darkness still blanketed the sky, and she wanted to go back to sleep, especially since she was now the warmest she'd been all night. Luxe curled at her back, so she had him to thank. She raked at the itchy spot, but only added pain without diminishing the itch. Then she found another spot and another. She sat up and rubbed at her eyes. Luxe tipped his head back, looking blearily up at her.

"You could sleep a bit longer," he grumbled.

"I can't. I itch all over. It must be the hay."

Luxe shook his head. "It's fleas. We're not alone in the hay."

"*Urgh.*" Paige scrambled out of the hay and brushed herself off. Her stomach turned at the thought of how many creepy crawlies she might have spent the night with.

"You probably have lice now, too." Luxe stretched and sat up.

Paige physically gagged. "Get them off. Now." She gagged again.

"It's part of living in a barn." Luxe shrugged. "Come here, they're easy to get rid of."

Paige looked in disgust at the pile of hay he still sat on. No way would she go back in there. She shook her head and waved Luxe out to her. He crawled out of the hay, chuckling the whole way.

"Your era is way too used to having things unnaturally clean. Not that the nobility in my time aren't pretty good at staying louse- and flea-free. But no one is shocked by them, should they happen to turn up. Bend your head down."

Paige bent her head, and Luxe put his hand on it, muttering a spell. A cool sensation washed across her entire scalp and down her body. Given the horrible things she'd been imagining in her bed, the spell felt better than the best shower.

"All right, you're the only one in your skin." Luxe laughed as he did the same to himself.

"What about the fleas? I still itch." Paige didn't even care that she was whining.

Luxe laughed even harder. "Those aren't the fleas, only the bites."

"Fix them."

"I can't. I have a potion at home which will get rid of them in a flash, but you'll have to wait until we get back to my workroom."

Paige scratched at herself again. Flea bites were a miserable sensation, and she wished they had opted to sleep outdoors despite the cold. Surely Luxe could have magicked up some thermal sleeping bags or something.

"How long 'til we can go home? I really don't like it here."

"This isn't my favorite era either, but the Oda family doesn't rank high enough to get a good pick. In a more peaceful time, this is a very lovely location. We have a little less than five hours, and we ought to get searching for the stone. It could take a while to find."

Paige's heart sank as she remembered the piles in the rock garden. Who made a whole garden of rocks anyway? The word "garden" to her implied a multitude of plants with maybe a stone path as an accent, not mostly rocks with a few stray bonsai.

They climbed down from the hay loft, quietly squeezing past the stable boy as he came in. Luxe brought them to the corner of the garden which the compass had pointed to. In the daylight, everything looked less creepy, except perhaps the palace. The dark holes of the windows left her wondering who or what might be looking out over the garden. She had to keep reminding herself how no humans would be able to see them.

They split the area, working their way from the outside edges toward each other in the middle. Paige created a little system to separate the stones she'd seen from the ones she still had left to look at. The hours ticked by swiftly, and Luxe grew more and more tense with each one that passed. They were nearly together now. She could have reached out and touched his knees. He gave a little yelp and flopped back on his back.

"I found it."

A cry of alarm went up from up on the palace wall. "Luxe. They heard you. I think we need to get out of here."

She made it halfway to her feet when the portal gave its familiar tug. The next moment she connected with the stone floor of Luxe's workroom. She groaned and rolled to her feet. Luxe stood beside her but offered no help. She tried to shoot him a dirty look, but he was too busy checking over the rune-stone.

"We cut that too close," he said.

"And yet we didn't leave nearly soon enough for my taste."

Luxe headed for the door. "I'm going to bathe and get ready for dinner with the court. Will you be joining me?"

Paige looked around at the modern furniture and the books. "If it's all right, I'd like to stay here tonight and wear my normal clothes. If I don't leave, staying should be all right, correct?"

To her irritation, he looked slightly relieved. "As long as you stay in the room, it's fine. I'll come back and check on you before bed. But what about your clothes and dinner?"

"Write out the Latin for the spells, and I'll use the time for practice."

Luxe wrote the spells on a scrap of parchment and told her to enjoy herself on the way out the door. In the peace and quiet, it didn't take Paige long to master the bathtub spell, and she climbed in for a long and luxurious soak.

Paige lay on the sofa in a stupor. She'd stayed in the bath until she'd been lightheaded, then proceeded to stuff herself on exactly the foods she wanted. The sofa had beckoned to her; its soft leather promising a cool place to sort her thoughts. The last week had been a whirl of insanity. It wasn't until she had this time to think that she realized six days had passed since she got sucked through the first portal. In some ways, the time seemed so much longer, and yet the days had passed in such a blur. She hadn't had time to decompress until now.

Luxe emerged from her thoughts in a more favorable light. And now that she had the time, she enjoyed reminiscing over the places she'd been. Their excursions were hardly sightseeing, but who knew she'd see so much of the world? Only . . . how to tell people about her adventures later?

What should she say when asked what she'd done on her trip to Japan? If she told them she ran from ninjas, killed vampires, slept in the palace stables, and tore apart a nobleman's rock garden, they would probably have her committed. Most people visited temples and took pictures of the crazily-dressed people in Tokyo.

The door creaked open, and Luxe poked his head around the door before coming in. "I wanted to check and make sure you were decent."

"Why bother?" she grumbled into the pillow. "It's never stopped you before."

"I've never looked on purpose. Even the gown in Egypt was simply appropriate to the festival and period."

"Convenient for you."

"I never said it wasn't. But I didn't mean to upset you. I'd rather not squabble."

She let out a big sigh. "Me neither. I'm sorry I'm so tense. This week has been completely overwhelming."

Luxe pulled over a chair and flopped into it. "No kidding. I'm so glad the next stone is the tipping point. We've got four out of nine. After the next, it's all downhill from there."

"Depends on what you mean by downhill. So far, getting them back isn't becoming any easier."

"Why don't I track the next before we go to bed? Then we can get started in the morning."

Paige rolled onto her back listlessly. "Nesu gave us four days a piece to find the stones. This last one only took two. Can't we take one day off? I really need a break."

"What if the others take more than four days? We should get the stones back and then play. We can always take a day or two to ourselves if you want to play before we tell my parents."

He spoke to her, but rather than paying direct attention, he'd become very involved in reading the titles of the books on the shelf. Did he need something important?

"I *really* want the down time. Please."

He looked at the door. "All right. One day. Dinner's over, and it's late. Did you want to go up to the guestrooms?"

"I liked the privacy here the other night. Can't we do that again?"

"Sure, I'll make the bed up for you." He used his sparkles to transform the sofa into a bed and made his way to the door. "I'll be back before breakfast."

"You're going to leave me alone?"

He turned a faint shade of pink. "There's really no room for two beds here."

"So." Paige couldn't fathom where this distance came from. "You've spent the last two nights with me. Why is staying suddenly a problem? I can't believe you'd leave me on my own in this creepy castle."

"It's not creepy. This is my home."

"This may be home to you, but to me it's a big eerie castle I don't know my way around. I wouldn't even know how to find you."

Luxe rubbed at the back of his neck uncomfortably. "If you really need me."

"Yes. You promised not to leave me alone, and I'm holding you to it."

Chapter 13

A thud on the door dragged Luxe's eyes open, though they felt like they'd been glued shut. The search for the stones exhausted him. As much as he hated to admit, Paige had a point. A day off might be just the thing. A following thud on the door made him grumble.

"What?" he yelled.

The door opened toward the bed, and Luxe couldn't see who had been knocking. Regardless, Luxe hated the disruption. Paige curled against his chest, but she stirred at the knocking, and his blissful moment swiftly dissolved.

"Hello, little brother." Luxe's stomach sank at the sound of Atlas's voice. His golden hair and broad shoulders appeared as he stepped around the door. "I wondered . . ." He stopped when Paige's head popped up from against Luxe's chest.

A thrill of superior joy jolted through Luxe. *That's right big brother. I've got a girl in my bed. Bet you never thought you'd see that. Ha!* "Go away, Atlas. You're disturbing us." Atlas never had to know nothing romantic happened between them.

Paige rubbed her eyes and looked first at Luxe then at Atlas, who stood with his mouth open, just inside the room. She started to extend a hand in greeting. Luxe struck like a snake: arm around her shoulder and nose in her ear.

"Please . . ." he hissed quietly. "Make me look good."

She slipped her head sideways and gave a little giggle of the sort Luxe had heard in the garden in Egypt. "Luuuxe." Her voice was high and breathy. Sexy. "Stooop. We're being rude to your brother." She crawled across the bed and slid off the end, letting her nightgown ride up her legs. "Good morning. You must be the Atlas I've heard so much about. It's a pleasure." She held a hand out to Atlas for him to kiss. He took it in a very courtly gesture, kissing the back.

"The pleasure is all mine. I'm sorry that I failed to introduce myself. I just never expected to see my younger brother so . . . well entertained . . . at this hour."

"And what hour would that be?" she asked coyly. "Luxe and I had such a crazy night. I have no idea what time it is. All I know is I'm still so exhausted I could sleep for hours."

Luxe was more grateful than he could put in words as shock ran across his brother's face. Paige played this up so well. He had a hard time staying cool while she did this. A nearly irresistible urge to giggle tickled his chest.

"It's nine in the morning, Miss . . .?"

"Paige. Paige Gentry."

"Hmm . . . That's not a surname I recognize. Are you from here?"

"I'm new here. I'm from a small family in the twenty-first century. I meant to explore Europe with my brother this summer. But I got carried away and ended up here. Luxe ran into me and has been showing me around and entertaining me ever since."

Atlas gave a sour laugh. "You can't have been very well entertained then. About the only skill my little brother has worth mentioning is that he can get you home with no problem." He gave a dismissive wave in Luxe's direction. "You don't have to do this to yourself. Find yourself a proper warlock at home. Or I can introduce you to a few."

"Atlas," Luxe broke in. "Say what you came to say and get lost."

"I need you to watch the girls until tomorrow. And I need four of the rune-stones. You've had them long enough. It's our anniversary, and Celia and I want to go to the wedding celebration of Shah Jehan and Mumtaz Mahal."

"You can't possibly need four rune-stones for that." Luxe shook his head. "But if you can't handle making the portal without so much borrowed power, I can do it for you. A little anniversary gift."

"You wouldn't understand the stones' purpose. You're too young, and no amount of lost girlies from other eras will ever give you the skills to need four rune-stones on a date."

Luxe gritted his teeth and fought the urge to throw something heavy at Atlas. "I've got a delicate experiment going. I'll spare two for you."

"Watch the girls for two nights and give me three." Atlas gave an exaggerated sigh. "And just to be nice, I won't tell father you ran off with them without supervision in the first place."

Luxe knew he'd been defeated. "Fine. When do you want to drop them off?"

Atlas stuck his head out in the hall. "Penny, Cricket. Inside, please."

Luxe's nieces appeared at their father's call, blond curls bobbing. To his dismay, they wore matching dresses, and he had no idea who was who. They gave him mirrored grins, which surely hid some monstrous intent. What a disaster. And he had Nesu's time limit pressing down on him. He'd agreed to a day of rest, and watching the girls wasn't exactly restful. And he'd planned on moving on an additional stone tomorrow, but he couldn't very well drag these two along. They were too smart for their own good. They'd find out what he and Paige were up to and ruin everything.

Atlas knelt in front of the girls. "You be good for your Uncle Luxe." They both nodded, bobbing curls. "If he's having trouble, you can help. Or get Miss Paige to help him out. You have your communication crystals in case something really bad happens?"

"Yes, Father," they chirped in unison.

Atlas kissed them both on the top of the head, nodded at Paige and stuck his hand out at Luxe. "The rune-stones."

Luxe wiggled his fingers and three of the stones they'd collected appeared on his palm along with his green sparkles. Atlas snatched them up, turned, and left without another word.

"Urgh," Paige groaned. "That was your brother? He drives unpleasant to a new level."

"Hey. Our father is very pleasant." The twins spoke in unison.

They were on the move, up and onto the now vacant bed, where they immediately began bouncing. They even matched each other while they jumped. Luxe rubbed his face, already exhausted. Would his parents side with him if he tied the girls up for the next two days, as long as he fed them? Suddenly turning kids into mushrooms sounded much more appealing. Paige stood at his side, close enough to whisper to.

"Thanks for that." Luxe leaned in by her ear. "I wish I had a picture of my brother's face. But, I'm sorry it's bit us in the butt. Everything I do lately seems to backfire."

"What do you mean?" Paige asked.

Luxe flushed as her breath stirred the hair at his ear. He stared straight ahead at the bouncing girls, trying to keep himself grounded. "Well, not only can we not go after the next stone, but we're stuck with the twins for two days. And you're going to have to pretend you like me while they're here."

"Huh?"

"I know these girls. They miss nothing. They tell everything. If they catch us lying to my brother, they're going to tell him, and then he's going to ask questions. We don't want him to, for obvious reasons."

"Ah . . ."

"I hate my brother," he hissed through his teeth. "But at least he's self-absorbed, otherwise he might have dug deeper already."

"All I can say is, I think he's mean and wrong. He had no reason to taunt you that way."

"Yeah." Luxe snorted. "And he acted nice because the kids were there."

"That was him being nice?"

Luxe snorted again.

"So, what are we going to do with two kids for two days?" Paige asked.

"Damned if I know."

"Okay, then what are their names?"

"Penny and Cricket."

"Which one is which?"

"Damned if I know." Luxe shrugged.

Paige gave him a nudge with her elbow and made an irritated noise. The twins, bored with bouncing, tumbled off the bed coming to a rest in front of Luxe and Paige, looking at them with bright eyes. One of the two clasped her hands behind her back.

"Are you going to be our new aunt?"

Paige's eyes grew wide and she made a shallow choking noise. "I've only known your Uncle Luxe for a week. Let's not get ahead of ourselves. Why?"

The other twin twined her fingers and pressed her hands to her lap in a very proper gesture. "Daddy says a girl should never sleep with any man but the one she's going to marry." The girl's eyes scanned both Paige's nightgown and Luxe's nightshirt.

Luxe's cheeks grew hot, and Paige swayed slightly before pasting a smile on her face. She cleared her throat a little and bent until she was eye level with the twin.

"Your daddy wasn't talking about sleeping, like with your eyes closed when you dream. That's all Luxe and I did. Like a sleepover."

One twin plucked at her curls. "What's a sleepover?"

The other looked Paige in the eye seriously. "Daddy always says what he means. What other kind of sleeping together could there be?"

Luxe clapped his hands together. "Okay. Moving on." He sprinkled green sparkles over both himself and Paige dressing them in court attire for the day. Then blew green sparkles over the bed, turning it back into the white leather, ultra-modern sofa. "There must be a better way to kill time. How about lessons instead?"

The shrewd twin straightened up and gave him a superior look. "What would you like to learn, Uncle Luxe?"

Paige sniggered, and Luxe bit the inside of his cheek. He'd never wanted to smack a child until that moment. How could she think she'd be teaching him? Not to mention saying something so humiliating in front of Paige. Especially when he'd resolved to show her how responsible and capable he really could be. Paige shot him a slightly worried look and put a gentle hand in the center of his chest. She leaned in, so her lips were at his ear.

"Play along. I'm going to make you the cool uncle." She gave his chest an affectionate scratch with her fingertips. "And relax. They're little kids. They only half know what they're talking about, but actions speak louder than words. Show them how awesome you are. They'll believe."

"Are you two kissing?" they asked in unison.

Paige winked at Luxe. "Delightful, aren't they?" She turned on the girls. "All right, who's Penny?"

The twin to the right raised her hand. Paige snatched the raised hand. "Luxe, a permanent marker." She caught the pen he tossed to her and quickly drew a star on the back of Penny's hand. "Here's how this is going to work girls. You two are going to be angels for us. No tricks, no taunting your Uncle Luxe. In return, he's going to make sure you have the best two days a kid could ask for. How old are you?"

"Seven." They chirped together.

"Luxe, can you make a portal back to my time? Orlando, please. If we're doing this, we're going all the way."

Penny eyed Paige suspiciously. "Why can't you make a portal yourself?"

"Oh, it's just that Luxe is so much better at portals than I am," Paige cooed. "We'll let him do this part."

Luxe shook his head. "My parents would never allow us to take them out. The family doesn't allow time travel for fun until sixteen."

"Wait, so you've never had a family vacation?" Paige gasped.

"What's a family vacation?" Cricket asked her.

"It's where parents take their kids to do something fun and they all enjoy the time together."

Luxe shook his head. "Not really my parents' thing. I doubt an idea like that would ever occur to Atlas either."

Paige crossed her arms and gave Luxe a hard look. "So be a revolutionary. Give the girls a little quality time."

"Please, Uncle Luxe?" They even begged in unison.

"But they have no idea how to behave. They've never left the time period."

"Don't worry." Paige grinned at him. "For what I'm planning, all they have to do is act seven. Trust me, please." She turned a pleading look on him, and he got a funny tickle in his chest.

Had only the twins begged, he would have said no and stuck to it. But something about Paige's wide brown eyes cracked his resolve. "All right." He leveled his eyes on the girls. "You've got to do everything Paige or I say." Luxe gave her an indulgent smile, pulled out his crystal and drew the portal.

Paige put a hand on his shoulder to stop him. "We'd better change here. It's too urban to be discrete and too hot for these clothes."

"Why don't you select the clothes," he said. "You're more familiar with current fashion than I am. You can do the spell while I work on the portal."

~ ~ ~

Paige took a deep breath. Trying magic in front of the twins was trial by fire. She barely had the hang of doing simple spells and she wasn't supposed to let on she couldn't do magic. What if she screwed up? Yet if she didn't do any, it would be just as suspicious. She wiggled her fingers like Luxe always did. To her joy green sparkles appeared. She whispered the spell and blew the sparkles in the direction of the girls. A moment later they were in cute skirts: Penny in bubblegum pink and Cricket in violet, topped off with little white tank tops and sunhats.

"I'm *naked*," Cricket shrieked. "Uncle Luxe, stop her."

"No, no," Paige soothed. "Those clothes are just right for where I come from. Look." She did the spell again and put herself in jean shorts and a teal tank top with a sparkly pink flamingo. "See. In my time, this is okay, and it's very hot where we're going. Your clothes wouldn't work."

"How's this?" Luxe dressed himself in a set of Bermuda shorts, a Hawaiian shirt, and leather, two-strap sandals with black socks.

Paige giggled. "Only if you're closing in on old age." She flicked her fingers at him and dressed him in jean shorts, a pale blue polo and flip-flops. "There, now you look good."

He did, too. They'd been in some crazy get-ups over the last week, but she had to admit, cleaned up and in what she considered normal clothes, he would have turned her head at home. She still thought he had a dreamy look to him: a delicate and artistic handsomeness. He caught her looking at him and quickly shifted his gaze to the portal.

"Everyone ready?" he asked the wall. "Find an adult hand to hold."

Why wouldn't he meet her eyes? He'd been a bit stiff since she'd yelled at him for interrupting her morning with Nesu. In all honesty, she now believed being interrupted that day wasn't such a bad thing. Nesu came off as more of a parent when he'd rescued them, and now she struggled with the age difference. Really, Luxe may have done her a service. Not that she'd ever tell him. She still didn't want him to think meddling was okay.

But she'd have to apologize or be a little nicer or something. He seemed to be stressing out around her. Though, she couldn't really blame him, she'd exacerbated a bigger problem. From the way he talked about his parents and the way his brother had treated him like he was deficient, she could see where any ego he had might be a bit fragile.

This led to a new welling of sympathy. Luxe had mixed up a few things along the way. If you could call making a person your familiar a mix-up. But in general, he didn't seem inept. Maybe he didn't perform well at home because no one ever gave him the chance to shine.

Well, she would let him shine the next two days. They'd bring back his nieces in such a blissful state that the others would take a second glance. She shook away her thoughts. Luxe and Penny had already stepped through the portal.

Paige took Cricket's hand. "Shall we?"

They stepped through together. This time Paige prepared to connect with the ground. Instead, lean arms caught her, and she landed with a thump on Luxe's chest as they all hit the ground. He had somehow managed to catch her *and* keep Cricket on top of the pile. Penny already stood off to the side, giggling at their fall. Cricket scrambled off to join her sister and Paige took a very painful, very sharp little elbow to her sternum in the process.

Luxe yelped in pain. "The pavement is burning me. Get off." He hurried to his feet and brushed himself clean.

"Where did you bring us?" Paige asked.

The four of them stood on a wide expanse of pavement with chain-link fencing all around. A few cars were parked here and there. Off in the distance a single clump of palm trees wavered in the heat. The smell of hot asphalt assaulted Paige's nose.

"You got us stuck in the worst desert ever," Cricket whined.

"You should have done the portal, Paige," Penny told her. "I knew Luxe couldn't do it."

Luxe looked furious, and Paige shook her head at him.

"We're not in a desert," he snapped. "We're not lost. Paige wanted Orlando, Florida. So, we're at the airport in an auxiliary parking lot."

Paige gave him a big, showy hug for the girls. "That's perfect. Now, I need a car."

"You have a driver's license?" Luxe sounded impressed.

"Uh . . . I did at home." To her shock Luxe gave her a pat on the butt.

"You do here, too."

She slid her hand in the back pocket of the cheek which had been patted. Inside, the pocket contained a familiar, slim piece of plastic. Her driver's license. Penny tugged at her arm.

"What's that?" The girl wrinkled her nose. "That's a really bad painting of you."

"It's not a painting, this is called a photograph. And no one ever has a good photograph on their driver's license."

"Is it a rule?" Cricket asked.

Paige laughed. "Yeah, it probably is."

"What kind of car do you want?" Luxe created a small cloud of sparkles.

"I don't know. Something with four doors, AC, and a navigation system."

Luxe blew the sparkles at the parking lot and a black, Honda Civic appeared. "Sorry, I know it's not flashy."

Paige could hardly find her voice. He'd just pulled a car out of a handful of green sparkles. "I meant we should rent one," she choked out.

"Why?" Luxe held keys out to her. "That requires paperwork, and you're not old enough to rent one yet, right?"

"Oh, yeah. I hadn't thought of that. You know an awful lot for having only spent a few years here. I mean, in the future."

Cricket's hand smacked as she hit Luxe's arm. "What is that thing you made, Uncle Luxe? You're not doing black magic, are you?"

Paige pushed the twin toward the car. "It's called a car. They're like a carriage without horses. We're going to use this to travel in."

The twins both stopped, and Penny burst out laughing. "That's a rich joke, Paige. Seriously, what's it for?"

Paige opened the door to the backseat. "Seriously, that *is* what it's for." Paige stuffed them both inside and showed them how to buckle in. She got in the driver's seat and swatted at Luxe's hand as he reached for the stereo.

"Driver gets to pick the music." She started up the car and set the AC to high. The inside rivaled an oven. But Luxe had done well. He'd even conjured up the new car smell. "I'm going to plug in the info on the navigation system. What do you think they want to do first, water park or Disney World?"

Luxe shrugged. "I've never been to either. I really don't even know that much about them."

Paige tapped her lips thoughtfully. "The water park, since the other would be better to start earlier." She pulled up the address on the navigation system and drove off.

Chapter 14

As soon as the car rolled forward, two screams issued from the backseat. Paige braked and peered over the back of her seat. "No screaming. It's really distracting. Everything's fine."

"Does the car move by magic?" Cricket asked nervously.

"No," Luxe answered. "By internal combustion."

"It catches fire?" Penny howled.

"You know what combustion means?" Paige asked, amazed. She shook her head. "Okay, let's just get the crazy train on the road. No noise from the backseat until I say so."

She flipped on the radio, found something nice and poppy, cranked it up, and took off across the lot. She sank back into the fabric of the seat and sighed happily. For the first time in a week she felt in control of her life. How intoxicating.

Paige wiggled her fingers and made herself a pair of sunglasses. She could get used to this magic thing, maybe even the time hopping, if they did it for fun like this. Egypt had been beautiful. She might have really enjoyed herself if she'd been better prepared and they hadn't had to swim with Ammit. She made up her mind to enjoy herself now, since they had the chance to play. As happiness seeped in, she caught the words to the song on the radio and let herself go.

Paige squirmed as all the eyes in the car focused on her. She blushed. "So I sing in the car."

They all still stared.

"Oh, never mind. I guess you had to grow up here. Just go along for the ride."

Paige kept singing as they hit the highway. The twins clutched each other in the backseat. "Is something the matter?" she asked kindly.

"It's *so* fast," Cricket squeaked.

"Everything here goes fast." Paige smiled. "You'll get used to it. But I think you'll enjoy the pace today. I promise not to take you anywhere which will hurt you." She shot a dirty look at Luxe, then flashed him a quick smile so he would know *she* wasn't holding a grudge.

Paige pulled into the parking lot at the water park, found a spot, and ordered everyone out of the car. All three stared open-mouthed at the towering colorful structures.

"So, I take it you've never been to a water park, Luxe?"

"No. What do you do here?" His voice filled with wonder.

"Those are slides but telling you about them doesn't do riding them justice." She pulled them all close. "After this there's no magic here." She wiggled her fingers, creating a big bag. "Our swimsuits," she answered their questioning looks.

Paige led them through the parking lot. When she figured the twins were sufficiently distracted she caught Luxe's shirt. "We're going to need money, and a bunch of it."

"How much?" His tone was unreadable.

"I don't know exactly. Over the two days, a couple thousand for the four of us, probably."

"A couple thousand?" he yelped.

"I thought you had the you-know-what stone. Money shouldn't be an issue, right?"

"I still have to account for what I spend to my family."

"Okay, Luxe." Paige sighed. "But . . . what's it worth

to be the cool, fun uncle? The twins haven't talked about your short-comings at all since we got here. Besides, are you going to tell me Atlas and your parents are all vacationing frugally?"

Luxe's jaw set. "I'll get the money as we need it."

She flashed him a grin. "Good. 'Cause now we need some."

They had reached the gates. Luxe pulled her back. "You're still speaking Latin. You'll want to fix that."

Paige hesitated. Speaking English meant kissing Luxe. But then again, he'd asked her to seem involved with him in order to fake out the twins. So, this was probably for the best anyway.

"Do I have to say anything? Or just . . .?"

His cheeks colored. *"Donum sermonis anglicus."*

"Donum sermonis anglicus," she repeated and pressed her lips to his. "Did it work?" She smiled knowing she'd spoken English.

Luxe ducked quickly away, paying their way in, and the girls simply stared at everything with saucer eyes. Inside the park, Paige whisked Penny and Cricket off to the ladies' room. Getting the girls into their swimsuits took much convincing and a little pleading. They kept insisting the suits were improper. Paige had made one-pieces with lots of ruffles to try to appease them. It wasn't until she pointed out several other children in their suits that she got the twins' cooperation.

Twenty minutes later, she had them in line for a raft ride they could all do together. Paige tried to bite back irritation. The girls still looked dubious as to whether or not this was actually fun, and Luxe looked at any and everything *except* her. Not that she required his constant attention, but a little might be nice.

The ride brought everyone around. By the end, the girls were shrieking with delight and Luxe was as impatient as they were to try every ride, nearly dragging Paige from one to the next. Just when Paige hit her limit, Cricket made a glorious statement.

"I'm hungry, Uncle Luxe."

He looked at Paige and Paige refused to let him lose momentum. "They have food here. Why don't you help the girls pick something from this time you think they'd like, since you have a better idea what they'd eat."

Once they were in line at the concession stand Luxe whispered to Paige, "As if I know what the girls eat. It's not like they come to court dinners at this age."

"Fake it," she hissed. "And while you're faking things, you could fake you like me a little. I've had icicles act less cold toward me. I thought you wanted them to tell your brother we're involved."

Luxe jerked back looking shocked. "But I don't . . . I didn't . . ."

"Never mind," Paige snapped. "I want a cheeseburger and fries when you get up there. I'll meet you back here. I'm going to the restroom."

She flipped her brown hair in his direction sending a few drops at him. The mid-day Florida sun had taken care of the rest of the water even in their short wait in line. In the darker, cooler interior of the bathroom, Paige scanned herself in the mirror. She'd picked a two piece in a tangerine orange she assumed looked good with her hazel eyes. Where had she gone wrong? She had always considered herself as good-looking. She had modest B-cups, but they were properly perky. Her stomach was soft, but flat.

So why did Luxe treat her like she had a contagious disease? Every time she touched him, he flinched. He refused to look at her and had hardly spoken, except to his nieces. In fact, he'd been acting this way for the last couple days.

Paige shook her head at her reflection. Since when did

she even care what Luxe thought? Her involvement in this mess fell solely on him. But whenever she pondered him, she saw him take down the demon in Rome. He'd been nearly as smooth as Nesu doing that, and then when he created the giant snake . . . what a seriously impressive piece of magic.

He'd also had her back in a behind-the-scenes sort of way. Like giving himself over to the vampires for her sake. His actions were a big factor in putting this little outing together. Everything he'd done for her made her see that he didn't deserve the poor reputation within the family. She wanted to show his family what she saw.

Why this neglectful behavior on his part, then? Irritation and rejection bit at her. She never had guys turn her down. She always did the culling, not the other way around. Maybe she just plain held no interest for him. She shouldn't really take it so hard if he didn't want to flirt with her. Everyone was entitled to their own tastes, after all. But the mental monologue in front of the mirror did nothing to ease the sting. She would either have to get over his rejection or get him to look at her.

She used the restroom and put her hair in a messy braid, which looked marginally better than it had down, then headed back to the others. Looking around for them, she caught Luxe's bright hair glinting in the sunlight. On either side of him bobbed two blond, curly heads. Paige stopped. Across from Luxe sat a voluptuous brunette in a tiny pink bikini. Luxe's blush stood out all the way from where she stood, some thirty yards away.

When the brunette reached out and stole a fry off Luxe's plate, Paige snapped. He wouldn't even talk to her, but he'd share his fries with a total stranger? Paige adjusted her top, flopped her braid across her shoulder and pranced over to Luxe. Stopping behind his chair, she bent, running her hands down his chest.

"Luxe—honey. Why don't you get the girls a frozen lemonade, too? I'm sure they'd love it."

Luxe went ridged under her hands, and she bit back a nasty comment. She wouldn't lose her cool. Not in front of Bunny, the playmate without ears. The brunette wore a strange expression, which didn't help Paige's mood.

The woman arched an eyebrow. "Do you know him?" Her tone teased Paige.

"In the biblical sense," Paige snapped back, her voice like a cat issuing a challenge. She draped her arms around Luxe's neck and tucked her chin over his shoulder. "Luxe, where did you find this chick?"

"She found me." His voice was faint, and his whole face and neck were red. "Paige, this is my cousin, Elodie."

Paige grabbed a chair and sat down—hard. "Cousin?" What the hell had all that been for then? And how on Earth had they run into a relative of his here?

Elodie gave Penny and Cricket a quick rub on the head. "We can see the play pool from here. Why don't you girls run along and amuse yourselves while I talk to your Uncle Luxe."

The twins scampered off and Elodie gave Paige a slick smile. "I'm glad to see Luxe with a girl who will stand up for him." She held her hand out for Paige to shake. "Luxe has had many wonderful things to say about you. Good luck in your relationship."

Elodie folded her hands on the table and gave Luxe a serious glare. "Now, I think someone has been a naughty boy. Look what I found while tracking down a few enchanted antiquities for a client." She plunked a small, pale gray stone on the table. "I ran across this in colonial India. Can you explain that, cousin dear?"

Luxe made a choking noise and lost the mouthful of soda he'd just taken.

"Huh? What—how?" Paige gasped.

"She's cute, Luxe, but not very articulate." She gave Paige an incentive grin. "I have a talent in tracking magical objects. A little like Luxe's thing with the time portals. We can't all be like Grandfather Merlin. But Luxe spends too much time focusing on what he *can't* do. I turned what I *can* do into a lucrative hobby." Now her grin went wolfish. "Not to worry. Luxe is my favorite cousin. Since I know how hard the family can be on those of us without fully well-rounded talents, I try to look out for him a little. Which," she focused him in a hard stare, "is why I'm here talking to you and not to your parents. What did you do this time?"

"A really bad thing. I'm not gonna tell you." Luxe stared at the pavement. "If mother and father find out, I don't want the blame to be on anyone else. The mistake is mine and mine alone. But I'm fixing it. Slowly. I've got some help."

"Who?"

"Nesu."

Elodie snorted. "Right. Like Nesu is helping you out of the goodness of his heart. That man is the very definition of unreliable. He'd never commit to anything."

"No." Paige came to Luxe's defense. "Nesu really is helping. Look, I have his communication crystal." She held out the orange stone.

Elodie snatched it off her hand. "Perfect. I've been looking for a way to get a hold of the snake." She squeezed the crystal and then handed it back to Paige. "I've been waiting fifty years to give him a piece of my mind."

Paige gaped at Elodie. Waiting fifty years? She barely looked older than Luxe. Ages were impossible with warlocks. A moment later Nesu's, now familiar, voice came from behind them.

"Yes, this is what I meant by calling me for fun, Paige. You should have . . ."

He'd been walking toward the table and stopped as Elodie stood, glaring at him. Luxe popped up out of his seat, snatched Paige's hand, and hauled her off.

"This might get a little awkward," he whispered.

Paige tested a theory. Luxe stood right behind her, closer than he had been for most of the day, but still not touching her in any way since he'd dropped her hand. She backed up to him until her back touched his chest. Faster than she could call him out on the dodge, he'd side-stepped her. Paige drooped. That cinched it. He was either mad at her or repulsed by her.

"Awkward? Really?" Her reply came out angrier than she intended.

Luxe didn't even seem to notice. "They were set to be married fifty years ago. He got cold feet and disappeared a week before the wedding."

"Okay, that's awkward. Wait, how old is she anyway?"

"Elodie is ninety-seven."

"Damn, I wish I could look like that at ninety-seven." She looked down at herself. Without some sort of procedure, she would never look as hot as Elodie. Even if she could tone her core and slim her thighs, her bust would never naturally look like hers. Some girls had all the luck. "Hell, I'd take looking like that now."

"Looking like how?"

Paige shot Luxe a dirty look. "You know . . . tiny waist, big boobs, thick hair, pretty face. Looking like a model, that's how."

Luxe scanned over her with his eyes and turned pink. "You don't need to change. You're fine."

Oh, that's just fantastic. I'm fine. Paige seethed. *I don't want* fine. *I want gorgeous, beautiful, hot, sexy. I'd even take cute.* "Whatever. So, is it sour grapes?" She nodded her chin in the direction of Nesu and Elodie who were in the midst of a heated, yet remarkably quiet argument.

"I would think so. I mean, he did . . ."

Luxe's voice fell silent and his jaw hung open. Paige turned to see what he was gaping at and saw Nesu snatching Elodie by the shoulders and kissing her passionately. Paige snapped her own mouth shut, turned on her heel and stalked off around the path to the far side of the play pool. Once there, she positioned herself behind a couple of palm trees and a hibiscus bush that blocked her view of the concession stand. A bubble of rage lodged in her throat. She tried to focus on the water and the twins, who were gleefully jumping from one floating lily-pad to the next.

Luxe joined her and gave her a sympathetic look from almost two feet away. "Are you okay?"

She wheeled on him. "No, I'm not okay. I'm madder than f—"

"Shh . . ." Luxe urged. "Small children." He pointed at the pool.

Paige took a deep breath, closed her eyes and tried again. "I'm livid. What was he doing with me before? Someone ought to warn her. Someone ought to slap him. Someone—"

"You want me to?"

"Huh?" Paige paused to blink at him.

"Do you want me to punch him for you? Slapping is a little girly for me, but if it would make you feel better."

Paige ogled him. Was he joking? "No. I can stand up for myself, thanks."

"I never said you couldn't." He shot a look in Nesu's direction. "I kind of wanted an excuse. Hitting him would make *me* feel better."

"Why?" Paige jumped on the distraction. Good thing she hadn't thrown more of her heart, or herself, at Nesu. At least this way she could just be slighted and nothing more.

"I don't want to see you hurt," Luxe answered.

"Yeah, yeah. That whole 'we're connected thing.' My feelings won't hurt you. I wasn't in love with him or anything. I'm only mad about being played."

"It's not that." Luxe now looked intently at a small water sprayer. "It's just . . . I . . . ." He fell silent.

"You just what, Luxe?" she hissed at him.

Now that she'd gotten riled up, the urge to let him have it for his treatment of her welled up. If he were a 'possum, he'd have been on his back, playing dead. She could tell by the expression on his face. But the fear in his eyes didn't stop her.

"I don't want to hear platitudes from you. You've been treating me like a leper for a few days now. You can't even look me in the eye. I'm trying to make the best of being stuck with your nieces, and it's really hard to have fun when you're practically oozing a vibe that says you'd rather be a thousand years from here, without me."

Luxe looked at her with desperation. "No, that's all wrong. I'm having a great time."

"At least one of us is," she snapped, further incensed by the helplessness on his face.

"So help me, I wish you were a demon," Luxe snapped back at her and then flushed deep-red, shaking his head.

"You *what*?" She nearly screamed.

His helpless look intensified. "That came out wrong. It's just . . . I know how to handle a demon. I have a pretty good idea how they're going to act. You, women in general, you move like swallows in flight. One minute you're up, the next you're down, and before I can get my bearing you've changed directions again. I can't keep up, and I can't cope."

"So, this is my fault?"

Luxe looked ready to cry. "No. I meant to make you feel better."

"You want to make me feel better? Than try a little harder to act like you like me. Or at least like I don't repulse you."

"You don't repulse me." Helplessness switched to irritation. "I like you a lot. That's the problem." He bit his lip and turned away suddenly.

Things started to click together for Paige. "Luxe . . . You like me a lot, in what way?"

Luxe shook his head and refused to look at her again.

"It's this kind of stuff which hurts my feelings." Paige deliberately softened her voice. "Look at me, please."

When he turned around he reminded Paige of a lost and scared child. "I really don't want to hurt you," he whispered.

"Then what do you want?"

"I don't know." Luxe shrugged and hung his head. "Things I shouldn't want. Counterproductive things. Things which aren't reciprocated. Not to mention every involvement with a woman seems to be nothing but trouble."

"How many women have ended up trouble for you?"

"Cleo. At least in a sexual way. But I never understand my mother, or my nieces, the girls at school, or you. Interactions with women always go south in some way."

Paige pursed her lips. "Is Cleo the only. . . I'd like to say relationship, but it's more like lover, that you've ever had?" She tried to keep the surprise from her voice.

"I had a couple dates with girls at the human high school. But we only fooled around at parties after they chased me down. I never started anything. They were human. Dating had no future."

"Interactions don't have to have a future for you to enjoy yourself. I knew Nesu and I would never . . . never mind, let's not go there. But still, he and I had fun until twenty minutes ago. You really can't compare all women to Cleo. That's not fair to us. Don't even compare us to your mom. I'm thinking she's a pretty cold lady if she lets the family pick on you the way they do."

"You're *not* like them," Luxe said in a rush. "You're trouble, too, but you're not the cause, and you're helpful in a pinch."

"Thanks. I think." Paige reached for his arm, and he shrunk away.

"Please, don't." He shook his head at her. "You're not interested, and I don't want my hopes to run away with me. Leave me some space until I figure out how to squash these feelings."

He turned and hopped into the pool, tossing Penny up in the air and letting her land in the water. Paige found herself a chair beside the pool and sat, pulling her knees to her chest. What the hell had happened here? Nesu had a lover, and Luxe *liked her,* liked her. This was too much to process.

Chapter 15

"Paige, can we talk for a minute?" Nesu asked, poking his head around the hibiscus.

She scowled up at him. "If you're looking for a second make out session in twenty minutes, I'm not going to help you out. In fact, I'm okay if you want to leave and never come back."

"I can't do that, but I could use the chance to explain." He sat on the chair next to her. "Luxe told you Elodie and I go way back, right?"

Paige nodded and bit down the urge to kick his shins.

Nesu gave her a sad sort of smile. "For what it's worth, I'm sorry. I wasn't trying to lead you on. I never thought I'd see Elodie again. She threw out our communication crystal fifty years ago, and her family won't let me near her. I never got the chance to explain."

Paige snorted her disbelief.

Nesu ignored her. "You see, I really did run off before our wedding. But by the day before the wedding, I'd come to terms with the idea of going back. Marriage is a big deal when you live nearly a millennium, but I finally felt ready. Unfortunately, on my way home I had a run-in with a gang of vampires, thugs really. They thought they'd make a mark for themselves and get some money by ransoming me back to my family. By the time I got out of their clutches, the wedding had passed, and I never got a chance to explain."

Paige shrugged her shoulders and looked away. She really wasn't sure what to say.

"You probably hate me." Nesu sounded and acted

penitent. "I wouldn't entirely blame you. Elodie is willing to give me a second chance. As far as anything between you and I . . . I'm sorry. Though, Elodie says you've moved on. You and Luxe. Don't let that get weird."

"Oh yes, because this isn't weird enough," Paige bit into him. "And no, Luxe and I aren't together. I thought Elodie was hitting on him, and I promised the girls time with their uncle. I said that to clear her off."

"You seem to keep things interesting," Nesu chuckled. "Elodie isn't going to report Luxe to his parents, and she'll trust you to get the stones back within my timeline. As for me, I'll keep my word. Anytime you need me feel free to call. Besides, I promised Elodie I'd keep watch over you two."

"There's no need." Paige pouted. She pulled the crystal out of her bikini top and went to chuck it in the bushes. "We'll do fine on our own."

Nesu caught her hand and pried the crystal out. "Hold on there. What is it with women and tossing out my crystals? I'll let Luxe keep this until you calm down a bit." He gave her a wink and a charming smile. "I had fun. When you're not sulking, you're a sweet lady, and I enjoyed our time together. Good luck with your treasure hunt."

He stood and left without looking back, tossing the crystal to Luxe on his way by. Paige let her head fall back against the lounge chair. She wanted so badly to be mad at Nesu. But she just couldn't. It wasn't like he'd been leading her on. She supposed he could have been lying about his feelings for her, but why bother seeking her out to explain? He could have left and never seen her again. The truth was in the effort.

Looking up at the blue sky between the palm fronds, Paige tried to empty her mind. It didn't work. She needed a diversion. She rounded up Cricket and left for one of the bigger slides. After three slides and lots of giggling over how hairy men were, as Cricket had only seen them covered in umpteen layers, Paige finally felt like herself again. She'd gotten Cricket the frozen lemonade, and they sat in the shade while the girl drank. Without Luxe right there being uncomfortable, she'd nearly forgotten about everything that had happened.

Until Cricket slipped a hand in hers. "I hope you become our aunt." Childish innocence rippled through her voice. "You're fun. I just met you this morning, and I already like you an awful lot, so Uncle Luxe must really love you by now."

Paige squeezed her little hand. "Things are more complicated for adults."

She looked up at Paige with round eyes. "You do love Uncle Luxe, right?"

"I don't know about love, sweetie." Paige sighed. "We'll have to see. I need to get to know your uncle a lot better before I could say that."

"It's because Uncle Luxe isn't much of a warlock, right?" The girl sounded sad, but matter-of-fact.

"No. Actually, we've had a couple adventures together, and I'm quite impressed by him. He's brave and quick thinking. He does his magic as fast and strong as Nesu."

"Are you sure you watched Uncle Luxe? Daddy says he couldn't do a spell to save his life."

"I've seen him use magic to save his life twice, literally."

"Wow, what kind of adventures were you on?" Her eyes were wide.

"Not the kind for young ears," Paige dodged. "But your daddy comes down pretty hard on your uncle. I think if he gave Luxe a chance to do his magic without teasing him, Luxe might do better. Think about it. If someone always told you that you were awful at magic, would you want to do magic in front of them?"

Cricket pondered this for a moment. "I guess not."

"Just because Luxe is grown up doesn't mean words can't hurt his feelings and make him mad. But maybe you girls can help Luxe. Maybe if your daddy sees how much you believe in him, your daddy will start to believe in him, too."

"I guess." She sounded skeptical. "I haven't really seen Uncle Luxe do much magic though."

"Yes, you have. You're forgetting because it's so natural. Who got us here? Made us a car? Got the money to buy all this stuff?"

"Oh, yeah, you're right."

Paige smiled at her. "I'm glad you're having fun. Wait until you see what we get to do tomorrow."

"I want one," Penny shrieked, rushing over to her sister and snatching at the lemonade.

"Cricket, why don't you give Penny the rest of yours?" Paige suggested. "You seem to be done, and I'm sure she can't drink a whole one either."

"No. I want my own." Penny pouted.

"I'll tell you what." Paige tried her best to be soothing. "Next treat, you get to pick and taste first."

"All right." She nabbed the cup and finished the drink.

Though the girls insisted they wanted to stay, Luxe and Paige both agreed they ought to leave. An hour later, both girls were tucked into one of two queen beds, and their hotel room grew quiet. Paige had a surreal sense of being domestic on their way to the room. She and Luxe had tiptoed down the carpeted hall to the room, each with a sleeping seven-year-old slung over their shoulder. They'd laid the girls on the bed, Luxe using magic to put them in pajamas. Then Paige had brushed curls off flushed little faces, an oddly pleasant feeling rippling through her. A bit like playing house.

She flopped down on the other bed. She had to give her parents credit. Being in charge of two small people was exhausting. Even on a day when they did nothing but play. The bed creaked as Luxe sat next to her. Close, but not touching.

"Are you sure about Disney World tomorrow? You know the girls have no idea who any of the characters are, right?"

"I hadn't thought about that." Paige rubbed at her forehead. She'd figured vacations were the easy part of parenting. But planning this gave her a headache, trying to get the details right. "How about Sea World then? It's a giant aquarium. Sea creatures transcend time, don't you think?"

Luxe nodded. "I think that sounds like a better idea. Maybe we can take them to the beach before we go home on the last day. If we use a portal to get there, we ought to have enough time."

"Sounds good." Silence fell, and Paige couldn't think of what to say now. Maybe Nesu's warning carried some weight after all.

Heat radiated off Luxe's leg, and the warmth made her drowsy. She could hardly believe they'd gotten back another stone. That really helped take the pressure off. She wished collecting the stones could go as easily as today. Egypt, Rome, Japan, Orlando. Their trip read like a traveler's dream, and who knew where they'd end up next. If they could stay out of trouble, she might really enjoy herself.

She tried to sit up, but her body wouldn't move. She'd reached the heavy place between sleep and waking. Giving in to the drowsiness, she let the sleep take her over.

~ ~ ~

Luxe tucked Paige under the covers. He wanted to take an extra blanket and sleep on the floor, but then what would the twins tell Atlas? At this point, he didn't want to break their little hearts, either. They really seemed to like Paige, not that he blamed them. He'd had flashes during the day of what life might be like one day, not so long in the future. Atlas and Celia had only been two years older than he was now when they'd found out they were having twins. They'd been married at his age. Twenty was young for a warlock to settle down, but not unheard of.

He lay down on the far side of the bed and tried to sleep. But sleep eluded him. Especially since he'd overheard the conversation between Cricket and Paige. Not only had Paige been awesome with the kids, but she'd defended him so adamantly. She made it so hard not to get more involved. Hearing her come to his defense like that sent warm little shivers through him. Never in his life had he wanted to snatch up a woman and kiss her the way Nesu had with Elodie, except at that moment over the lemonade. Images of Paige continued to flit through his head as he drifted off.

~ ~ ~

Something hit Luxe's head, and stars burst before his eyes. Before he had a chance to wonder what hit him or even where he was, a shrill screaming filled the room.

"Get up."

"Get up!"

"Uncle Luxe?"

"Paige?"

"Where are we going today?"

"Let's go."

"Why are you still sleeping?"

With his brain dampened by sleep, he had no idea which twin shrieked what. Paige sat up, looking bleary eyed and shielding herself from the bouncing girls. Luxe grunted as he took a knee to his back.

"We're not still sleeping," he complained. "No one could be, sharing a room with you two. You're like wild animals."

"Speaking of which," Paige said through a wide yawn, "we changed the plan. We're taking you to Sea World today. It's full of sea animals from around the world and rides and shows. We'll have great fun."

Penny landed on her head. "Then get dressed, Paige. Let's go."

Paige dressed everyone in appropriate outfits for the day. The girls went in matching jean-shorts and citrus-colored tank-tops with little rhinestones glinting on them. Luxe eyed Paige appreciatively. She'd put herself in a pair of tight cream-colored shorts and a flowy floral tank top. The shorts highlighted her thighs, and overall, she looked summery and pretty. He sighed. After yesterday's conversation with her, he at least felt he could openly admire. She would know why he looked, so he didn't need to hide anymore.

The twins were on the move again. As Cricket dragged him past the mirror to the door, he noticed he wore a blue ringer tee with darker blue trim, jean shorts and the same flip flops. Paige kept putting him in blue. Why?

Luxe had gone to an aquarium when he'd been to the twenty-first century before. But it had been nothing compared to Sea World, and he gave himself over to the urge to act the same age as the girls. Finally, they outlasted him. Luxe huffed into a seat, desperate to sit for a minute, but the girls stood with their noses pressed to the glass watching the sharks swim by. They bounced on the balls of their feet in an opposite rhythm from one another.

Luxe gave a quick glance around, and with no one nearby, he held out his hand and let the compass appear.

Where he pulled the dial up didn't really matter, as a human couldn't see the magic anyway. He didn't even really expect to get anything. The compass did short range location. His suspicions proved correct. A dial didn't appear since the compass had nothing to point at. The nearest stone was the one Elodie had brought back.

He really had contrary feelings about that. Perhaps he ought to have been more grateful. After all, he had one less stone to track down now. But it really took something away from the spirit of the journey by having her interfere. Now he couldn't honestly tell his parents he retrieved them himself. He'd been hanging onto that as the only scrap of redemption in this incident.

But, then again, he had Paige. Her presence insured that he wasn't doing this alone from the very beginning. She'd been a bigger help than he wanted to admit. Would he even have gotten past Ammit without her? He might have been in the monster's gut being slowly digested at this very moment.

Paige dropped to the bench next to him. "Should you be playing with that in public?'

He shook his hand to clear the compass. "Don't say it like that. No one can see what you're really talking about."

"Oh." Paige giggled. Then she sighed and tipped her head back against the wall. "I swear." She pointed at the twins. "It's like we gave them double shots of espresso and a bag of sugar for breakfast."

Luxe chuckled. Her description exactly matched what he'd been thinking. "I don't know how my brother keeps up."

"Watching kids is probably better when they're your own," Paige said. "It's not like babies run around like this. You probably have some time to get used to them. At least your nieces aren't bratty."

Luxe let his head drop back, too. "Yeah. Which really surprises me, given their parents. But they still have time to develop bratty tendencies."

"Luxe? Can I be honest?"

He shrugged. Lord only knew where this was going. It didn't sound pleasant.

"I know your brother is a jerk. He only had to say a few sentences for me to figure that out. But I think Elodie is right. You let your family get to you too much. You've only made three real mistakes I've seen. Otherwise, you seem just as capable as the other warlocks I've met. You should stop worrying about what your family thinks and do things for yourself. Like Elodie, you're sure to find your place. Besides, if you respect yourself, your brother and your parents are a lot more likely to respect you, too." She nudged his shoulder with hers. "I'm learning to trust you. They will too."

He closed his eyes, keeping his head tipped back. The words were so tempting to believe. "But my mistakes are huge ones. It's not like I made a pink cloak instead of brown, or steak instead of venison. I lost the source of my family's power. I bound a human to myself. I displayed magic in front of humans. Big magic. You heard Madam Antonius, I deserve big punishment."

Paige's head came to rest against his own. Luxe's heart nearly rammed out of his chest.

"Yes," she continued, "but the second and third are the fallout of you struggling with the first. If you had someone you could trust for help, these things might not have happened. I don't see them as separate mistakes. And you've nearly died numerous times trying to fix this. Is that really not punishment enough?"

"My parents will never see them as one mistake. They'll simply see me making a bad situation worse. And no, it's not enough. The best I can hope for is grudging forgiveness, assuming I get all nine back safe and sound. But forgiveness won't get me out of further punishment."

"Really?"

"Really."

"I'm sorry."

"Thanks." He'd gone completely glum at this point and was entirely unprepared for the twins, who were now rushing at them. The afternoon dragged onwards as he sat in his melancholy. He couldn't seem to perk himself back up.

Chapter 16

Luxe's melancholy continued into the next day. He felt bad but couldn't bring himself to enjoy the beach. Worrying about what his parents might choose as retribution rode him hard. Strangely, knowing that Paige would leave him before his punishment hurt him the most. Lacking her as backup would almost be worse than the consequences themselves.

Paige and the girls were laughing and splashing each other in the sparkling morning surf on South Beach. They'd portalled to Miami to save driving time. The main portal would take them home in about two hours.

Suddenly, the playful shrieks turned to screams. Luxe stared out in horror as one of the twins got squeezed in a giant tentacle. The smell of their magic must have attracted a kraken. Krakens had a massive appetite for anyone with magic, going so far as to crush ships to get at those onboard.

Paige screamed and dragged the remaining twin out of the water. Luxe scrambled up and ran about halfway down the beach before Paige got to him.

"Luxe. It's Penny," Paige screeched.

Luxe closed his eyes to block Paige and Cricket out so he could think of the best way to deal with the creature. His books at home suggested several methods, but once again he had no supplies, so he'd have to use verbal spell-work. First, he had to get the creature out of its element. He made as many green sparkles as he could, ran down to the water, and threw them over a tentacle.

"Per siccum," he yelled.

A moment later, the creature thrashed amongst the palm trees at the top of the beach. The kraken was bigger than he'd anticipated, roughly the size of a small house. Its hide shone a slimy, deep purple with multi-shade green blotches like camouflage. The creature resembled a squid but shorter and rounder, its ten tentacles flailing. One still held the screaming Penny.

Beating the kraken would take mind over matter. Could his imagination and determination best the beast? He closed his eyes again to visualize. Blowing green sparkles in the direction of the kraken he ordered it to bind itself. He opened his eyes and the creature's tentacles had all knotted together. But it was already working to get itself free. He had to come up with a more permanent way to dispatch the creature. He went with the first thing which popped into his head.

He blew a third round of green sparkles over the kraken and yelled, "*Calamari*."

The creature exploded in a burst of sparkles. The next moment something hot hit his arm. He looked down at the breaded ring in surprise. A splat of marinara sauce hit the top of his foot. He ignored the calamari rain, tearing up the beach to where Penny had fallen and lay bleeding. Only two parts of a kraken are dangerous: the big parrot-like beak, which on this beast would have been big enough to cut a car in half, and the suckers. Each sucker had a ridge of daggered spines around it. The spines had cut Penny all over, and she lay in the sand sobbing.

"Paige, help me heal her," Luxe ordered.

Paige jumped in without even having to be reminded of the spell, and between the two of them they quickly healed all the punctures. Luxe made a washcloth and let Paige wipe Penny clean. The moment Paige finished, Cricket leapt on her sister, hugging her and crying. Paige picked a calamari ring off her lap, looked at it and burst into laughter and tears at the same time.

"Luxe, this is so stupid. What were you thinking?"

He plucked a ring off her head and popped it in his mouth. "About lunch." And he dissolved into laughter. too. "You ought to try some. Kraken calamari's not too bad. Who knew?"

Paige nibbled at the ring in her hand. "It's weird, but the creature actually tastes like squid."

The twins looked incredulously between the two of them, and Luxe pulled them both into a hug. "I was so worried about you. Are you girls all right?"

Two sets of arms twined around his neck, and they each buried a face in his shoulder. He hugged them back, surprised at how worried he actually had been. Not only for the trouble he'd get in if anything happened to them, but somewhere in the last three days they had wormed their way into his heart. He genuinely liked the little critters.

Penny gave his cheek a kiss. "Thanks for saving me, Uncle Luxe. I won't doubt you anymore. Paige knew all along. You're an okay warlock after all."

Luxe choked on a laugh. Her little voice was solemn, the vote of confidence touching. But the way she said it in such a grown-up manner tickled him.

"Thanks, Penny." He squeezed her again, and she pushed away.

"Uncle Luxe, you're getting sauce on my new clothes."

He burst out laughing, in large part from relief. The four of them gathered and ate as much of the calamari as they could find which hadn't landed in the sand. With about an hour until the portal opened, the girls sat in the sand burying each other and Paige sidled up beside him.

"You did good. Your solution was ridiculous, but it worked, and that's what really matters, right?"

"Maybe."

"Hey, so what did all the other beach-goers see?"

He looked down the now deserted beach. Double red flags fluttered off the lifeguard stand. "A shark attack."

"How does that work?"

"Illusion. It's why human seldom see things like unicorns, dragons, monsters, that kind of stuff. They're all magical beings, and part of their magic is illusion. It's a natural defense, like camouflage."

"Ah. In that case, I'm so glad all those beach-goers offered to help."

"The lifeguard tried to while you were busy helping me heal Penny. I scrambled his memory to clear him off."

"Ooo . . . so the man can multi-task." Her voice grew playful. "That's an impressive skill on its own. Most guys I know are completely incapable of multi-tasking. If they're focused on sports, forget talking about anything else. If they're working on their car, just walk away. If they're thinking with their pants, good luck. Men have a one-track mind."

"Hey. That's not fair." He grinned at her. "You're only half-right. We tend to focus on one broader topic at a time. But we can handle all the details pertaining to said topic. Girls lose focus far too easily. One simple sentence can derail an entire conversation. In moments, the original subject is lost."

"Hey. *That's* not fair." Paige giggled and sighed. "I guess men and women are pretty much the same no matter when they come from."

"That I will fully agree with. You see the similarities when you time hop. So much changes, and yet people stay so much the same." He found himself leaning toward her. If only the conversation could flow this easily all the time. "So, then, what is your ideal man? Not the jock who'd taken one too many hits to the head with a ball, I hope."

"You must be referring to Justin." She wrinkled her

nose in thought. "I wouldn't say he's my ideal. I just had a crush on him."

"Had?"

Paige blushed. "Well, I don't know. I think I've changed a lot over the last week and a half. I've certainly seen enough to change my perspective. But I think now I'd like to meet someone like my older brother."

"Someone you're related to?" Luxe laughed.

"No." She poked a finger into his shoulder. "My brother has been traveling, and he wants to work abroad. He wants to experience the world in a hands-on way. He has a quiet intelligence. He's modest and fun-loving and adventurous. I'd like someone like that."

"Me, too. Is your brother available?"

Paige snorted with laughter. "The way you seem to hate women, it wouldn't surprise me."

"I don't hate *all* women." He tried to keep his voice casual. "The twins are fine. And there's this one who keeps turning all my preconceptions on their head. I never really thought about my ideals before. I was too busy running away from females. But I'd have to say I'd like a girl like that one: spunky, adventurous, kind, loyal." He gave her a teasing grin. "Know anyone like that?"

Paige's cheeks were a definite pink. "Luxe . . ."

Luxe stood brushing sand and bread-crumbs off his shorts. "Girls, time to go."

The twins pushed aside piles of sand to dig themselves out and scurried over. Luxe looked down at the back of his hand. A countdown had appeared in glowing green numbers. "Three, two, one."

~ ~ ~

Paige landed on something soft. Evidently Luxe had created an air mattress to catch the four of them. The girls were going to begin tumbling on it, but Luxe pulled them off and stood them side by side.

"First you need a cleaning," he scolded. "You're covered in sand, and you smell like an Italian restaurant."

"*Luxe.*" The roar echoed down the hall.

Luxe went white as the door to his workroom crashed open. Atlas stood in the doorway, his face nearly purple with anger.

"Where did you take my girls?"

The girls rushed their father. "Oh, Daddy. We had so much fun."

As they rattled off the story of the last few days Paige observed both Luxe and Atlas. Atlas grew darker and darker and his expression looked like he wanted to draw blood. Luxe had been steadily shrinking toward the back of the room. When the girls got to the part about the kraken Atlas stopped them and threw a handful of aqua sparkles at Luxe. Luxe dodged and the sparkles hit the table behind him, causing all the bottles to explode. The twins screamed and burst into tears. Atlas shot Luxe one last look of pure loathing and grabbed his daughters' wrists to haul them from the room.

"You are *never* to come near any child of mine again." Atlas spat over his shoulder at Luxe.

Paige couldn't take it anymore and darted between Atlas and the door. "I came up with the idea to take the girls out. Luxe said you wouldn't approve and I insisted."

Atlas whirled on her, and she tried not to tremble. Hopefully he wasn't the type to hit a woman.

"Who gave you the right to meddle?" he growled at her. "But regardless, Luxe let them go. He'll never speak to them again. As for you, I warned you to find yourself a proper warlock. You're no longer welcome in my family's castle. Get out."

Paige jutted her chin out and stamped a foot at him. "So, by proper warlock you mean an asshole like you?" The heat of her anger crept up her cheeks. "Of all the witches and warlocks I've met outside my own time, you are by far the most unpleasant. I even like Cleo better than you, and she's horrible. Luxe's problem isn't his ability to use magic, it's the fact that his mother slipped a vampire into the nursery and called it his older brother. I have no idea what makes you hate Luxe, but you're going to teach those two, sweet little girls the same, and I think that's sick."

Atlas raised his hand, and Paige braced herself. At the very least she promised herself she would hold off from crying until the girls left. Luxe darted in and blocked Atlas's blow. He glared at his older brother, holding his wrist so he couldn't strike again. It was the angriest she'd ever seen him.

"You will *not* hit Paige." His tone dared Atlas to argue. "And she stays as my guest for as long as I say she can." He bent to eye level with the girls. "Remember, I will always want to see you, and never let your father tell you I don't love you."

He stood and glared down his brother. "I played with my nieces and protected them as necessary. I'm sorry you disapprove of my methods, but then again, you dumped them on me and didn't leave any instructions. Do what you must do, but the girls are old enough to know and remember if you act fairly. Now, you've insulted me and tried to abuse my guest. It's *you* who needs to get out."

Luxe pulled Paige out of the way and pointed to the door. Atlas stood for a moment, rage and astonishment warring on his face. He finally turned and hauled the girls from the room. Paige reached out and slammed the door after him. She was about to give into her tears when Luxe grabbed her shoulders and kissed her. Not a chaste little peck for switching languages. Not an embarrassed and hesitant first kiss. This was a *make your knees weak, knock you off your feet* passionate kiss.

Paige's first thought had been to pull away, but something about it felt so right, and warmth rushed her body. She grabbed the back of his head, returning his kiss. A funny little voice in her head spoke, the one which always came up with random thoughts to ruin moments. It told her Cleo had taught him some really nice skills. This made her choke on a laugh, and Luxe pulled away looking puzzled.

She gave him a flushed smile and told him her thoughts. They drew an embarrassed chuckle from Luxe as well. After that, she really had no idea what to say, or what to do. He reached out and tucked her hair behind her ear, blushing wildly as he touched her face.

"Um . . . I could say I'm sorry. But I'm not," he said. "I hope you're not either."

Paige blushed and shook her head. She wasn't sorry.

Luxe sighed and plucked at his T-shirt. "I *am* sorry about my brother. I really hope he doesn't treat Celia that way, though I doubt it. Everything about me, including you, seems to enrage him."

"You don't need to apologize for him."

"I guess not. But I do need to thank you." He took her cheeks in his hands and stared into her eyes. "No one has ever believed in me the way you do. I hadn't meant to kiss you. I've been trying so hard to keep my distance. Just the thought of the day I have to break the spell and send you home already hurts. Part of me desperately wishes you really were a cat and I could keep you forever. You've spent the last week saving me in every possible way. I really don't know what I'll do without you."

Discomfort settled over Paige. He looked so sincere and so sad, and she hadn't really thought of their situation in those terms. She'd been so focused on what she'd perceived as a problem, the realities of their adventure ending hadn't occurred to her. She'd be leaving behind Luxe; their new friendship would be forgotten. She'd seen so much of the world, but they weren't going to send her home remembering all her adventures. The loss wouldn't hurt after it happened, but did she really want to forget?

She wrapped her arms around his waist and laid her head on his chest. His heart beat low and steady. "They wouldn't let us be together anyway, would they?"

His cheek dropped to the top of her head. "No. You're a human."

She nodded against the warmth of his chest. "So, let's enjoy what we can."

He lifted his head. "You'd be okay with that?" He sounded surprised.

"Better to have loved and lost, right?" She tried to sound bright, but crying would have been easier. "Besides, it's me who should be asking you if you'll be all right. Your parents are going to put a memory charm on me. I won't even remember you. I hate the thought, but after the spell is done, I guess I won't even know the difference. You on the other hand . . . I mean, I'm sure you'll move on, but still."

He squeezed her to him. "Let me worry about that. Like you said, let's just enjoy what we have. I'd love to say 'let's take a holiday,' but now Atlas is riled up, and we need to find the last stones. Four to go."

"One to two weeks at our current pace," Paige mused. When had the time gotten so short?

Luxe seemed to be thinking the same thing. "I'd normally go have dinner at court, but I don't want to share the time we have left with anyone but you. Shall we eat here?"

Paige smiled at him. "My thoughts exactly."

They blushed through dinner, their feet touching under the table. Luxe turned the couch into a bed again, and Paige snuggled under the covers. Luxe's fingers sought out her own and ran across the back of her hand, up to her wrist and back down again. Drowsiness threatened to overwhelm her when he gave a little pull on her wrist.

"I've curled around you to keep you warm and to drive away your bad dreams. Come curl up for company." He laid his arm out for her head.

Paige hesitated. "Somehow sleeping with you seems different now."

"Don't worry." He yawned. "I think we're both too tired to care about *that*. Besides, I've been watching out for your honor all this time. You really think I'd waste my own efforts? You won't do anything you're not sure of under my watch."

Paige snuggled in against his arm and got a gentle kiss on the back of her neck. She kissed his arm in return. "Goodnight, Luxe."

"Goodnight, Paige."

~ ~ ~

The sound of clinking glass broke Paige's sleep. She reached behind her for Luxe, but he'd gone. He moved around the room mixing one potion or another. Something heavy sat on her chest. They really did have work to do. She slid out from under the covers and padded over to him. Wait, her feet were still warm. In fact, they'd never been cold in this room, even bare.

"Luxe? Does this room have heated floors?"

"Mm . . . enchanted," he answered without looking up.

"What are you working on?"

"Tracking the next stone. If you want a bath, now's the time."

Paige didn't wait to be asked twice this time. She nabbed a bowl off the table and took it to the backside of the bed. The headboard would give her enough privacy. Only two tries later and she had a tub with water, and one further attempt got the water the right temperature. Maybe she could get the hang of this doing magic thing.

Paige tried to hurry in the slippery tub. She didn't want to still need a wash when he wanted to go. But before she'd finished with her feet he called for her. She slipped and slid out of the tub and made herself a towel and some clothes, opting for jeans and a T-shirt since she had no idea where they were going now.

She pulled on socks when a towel dropped over her head and Luxe started scrubbing her hair dry. "Let's get a move on. I want to get out of here."

"What's the hurry?" She took over the towel.

"I overlooked something important. Today is the day my parents return. I want to get clear of the castle and stay clear. I know where all four remaining stones are, and I have a small bag of supplies in case I need to mix a potion. With Atlas angry at me, he's sure to tell my parents about both you and our adventure. Once they start asking questions, there's really no way to hide this. So, we're leaving and not coming back until I can face them."

"Okay. That makes sense. Where are we going then?"

"Our first stop is China in 3033. Then we'll work our way backwards in time: 756 Denmark, 375 Mexico, and finally 10,922 BC Atlantis."

"Atlantis? Really? Which one of the eight ruling families got something that cool?"

Luxe frowned. "None. But I'll give you the history lesson after we get out of here." He pulled her to her feet. "Ready?"

He gave her a quick kiss, then paused and gave her a deeper one. Paige closed her eyes and leaned into him, but he stepped back.

"Mm. Tempting, but we've already stayed here longer than I wanted." He held a hand out to her and this time twined his fingers through hers.

Chapter 17

Paige thought it strange how stepping through the time portal as if it were her front door seemed almost normal now. Once again, she fell after crossing into the opening. Luxe caught her. Without a seven-year-old in tow, he managed to both stop her fall and stay on his feet. He flicked green sparkles over her before setting her on the ground.

Paige wore a long purple skirt of a shimmery, silky type material embroidered with a Chinese floral pattern. A white blouse with metallic blossoms printed all over it wrapped and tied around her waist. Metallic, strappy leather sandals hugged her feet. Luxe had on a loose pair of pants in silvery-gray, gray flip-flop type sandals and a tunic-style top with what looked like two dozen pockets all over. It fastened up his neck in a mandarin collar. The pale blue of the top made his blue eyes stand out, and with his white-blond hair, the overall effect was striking.

Paige only took a moment to look them over, because the city commanded her attention. They'd come out in a park of some sort. A grassy lawn sloped down toward a city unlike any she'd ever seen. Tall, needle-like glass spires jabbed at the sky from all over the city. Not a car drove on the roadways, which now seemed exclusively for foot-traffic. But multi-levels of elevated train tracks crisscrossed between the buildings. On a third level track a train slid by, remarkably silently, and made entirely of chrome, glass, and shining fiberglass. The whole top half was see-through, and the passengers watched their world go by.

"This is the future," she squeaked, squeezing at Luxe's arm again. "I can't believe I'm seeing a thousand years into the future. Is this what the rest of the world looks like?"

Luxe shook his head. "China took over as *the* world super-power about 900 years ago. Within its own borders, it has done what China did for almost four thousand years before: it survived. That granted them stability as the rest of the world fell apart. They eventually had to close their borders to all immigration to save themselves.

"Humanity will flourish for another 725 years, before a solar event renders too many people sterile or incapable of producing viable offspring. From there, it's a slow decline to near-extinction. The human population got too small at that point, and none of the warlock families wanted to take over the time following 4000 AD. Besides, it's not really our place to know everything. So, for our own safety, none of the noble families permit time travel outside 4000 AD. They cut us off in the opposite direction at 20,000 BC."

"What's in 20,000 BC?"

"The start of the very earliest modern civilizations. Much like the human population being too small after 4000 AD, it's too primitive before 20,000."

"You mean warlocks never wanted to see the dinosaurs? What about finding out if theories like snowball earth or Pangea are correct?"

Luxe shook his head. "No. We only travel in times populated by humans."

"So, are warlocks human, since you stick to those times?"

"I don't know. You could ask the scholars in Atlantis. There's any number of historical traditions which explain the existence of warlocks. Each as believable as the next. But there are no ruling warlock families in Atlantis because they have their own magic wielders. They're kind of like our predecessors. They wouldn't take kindly to us trying to rule them."

"What happened to them? I mean, why aren't they around now?"

"They don't use time travel, and Atlantis was destroyed in a cataclysmic geological event. They're extinct."

Paige shook her head, this conversation just got beyond weird. "So, you can go back and have a conversation with a people who are extinct?"

"Yes, but is that really so strange? You're standing here, and you ought to have died almost a thousand years ago."

"I suppose. But, don't warlocks want to know for sure what their origins are?"

"Yes, and no. Like I said, we're aware that too much knowledge can be harmful rather than helpful. Besides, at this point, the myths of our beginnings are to us, what religion is to humans. We simply . . . believe."

"I don't know any of the myths." Paige sat on a sleek metal bench on the hill overlooking the city. "We're not at the castle, so take enough time to tell me the one you believe, at least."

Luxe sat next to her and pulled her against his shoulder. "Okay. Grandpa Merlin said that after doing his own tracing of histories and interviews in antiquity, he came to believe this to be the true origins of the warlock.

"Some 25,000 years ago, when men still wandered with their herds and cities had yet to be invented, a young shepherd stumbled across a *jiniri* at the edge of the desert."

"A what?"

Luxe looked mildly irritated at the interruption. "A *jiniri* is a female *djinn*."

"I'm still lost."

"Uh . . ." He paused in thought. "That's right, your

time calls them genies. I keep forgetting you don't know these terms. Anyway, she was parched and suffering. The young man gave his waterskin to the woman, saving her from agony. With her life force replenished, the man could see she had beauty beyond description, and he immediately fell in love. The *jiniri,* Khalidah, offered the young man a single wish, a boon for saving her from torment. He immediately asked for her hand in marriage.

"Khalidah granted him this favor, and they enjoyed a long life together and had many offspring. Khalidah was a *djinn*, therefore her children were neither *djinn* nor human, but a hybrid: the first warlocks and witches. We inherited some of her magic, and though we didn't inherit her immortality, we did get far longer lifespans than a human. When her partner perished, as he must, she took her children and gave them the island of Atlantis where they could be free to live as their own race. All except her oldest daughter, whom she kept by her side as a companion, and her youngest son, the baby she could not bear to part with.

"Two thousand years after gifting Atlantis to her children, a massive undersea earthquake rocked the Atlantic Ocean. Atlantis crumbled to the sea floor, and Khalidah had only the last two of her children and their descendants. Broken hearted over all those she'd lost, she left Earth to mourn, returning to the home of the *djinn*, a plane of existence between dimensions. There are rumors of ways to summon her back, but as far as I know, no one has ever successfully done that."

"So, you're not human because you're half *djinn*?"

"Supposedly."

"Hmm . . . Well, it's certainly an interesting story."

Luxe stood and stretched. "So are the others. But we don't have time right now. You asked for the one I believe. I trust Grandfather Merlin, and if he believed this version, so do I."

"A week ago, I would have said no way in hell his story could be true. But since I just ate kraken calamari yesterday and escaped from vampires three days before that, why shouldn't *djinn* be real?"

Luxe laughed at her and gave her a squeeze. "See, now you're catching on." He held his palm out in front of him, pulling up the compass. "Let's go get the last stones."

They followed the compass into the city center. Luxe kept guiding Paige around people and poles. She couldn't focus her eyes on where they were going. She stared at flickering signs in windows which seemed to be some sort of projection or hologram technology. Overhead, trains quietly swished by at regular intervals. People chattered happily in a language reminiscent of English but not strictly Chinese either.

In the end, the retrieval went easily. The stone lay under a dumpster in an alleyway. Luxe reached under and grabbed it without incident. Paige stood, studying the dumpster. The receptacle seemed to compact and compost all on its own, with solar panels for lids.

Luxe tucked the stone in a zippered pouch he had strapped to his chest under his shirt. "Want to eat lunch before we go?"

Paige nodded, and her stomach growled at the mention of food. She couldn't wait to try future cuisine. They wandered down the street looking at menus posted outside restaurants. The menus were pictures on a tablet-type screens. You could flip through the pictures by touch or order right there. Luxe told her if she ordered, a table number would appear on the screen. They would answer a quick set of questions and when they arrived at the table, it would be completely ready for them. They finally agreed on a traditional Chinese eatery. The offerings looked something like food she knew, though the ingredients listed were foreign to her.

"Don't they have any meat?" she hissed at Luxe.

Luxe shook his head. "They outlawed raising meat about 700 years ago. Animal farming had too heavy an impact on the environment. Scientists found the capacity to feed humanity nearly doubled when they put the land to use raising cereal grains."

"Oh."

He gave her a wink. "It's not all bad. The food is delicious, and it's a vegetarian's utopia."

They chose their meals and then told the screen that two adults would be dining, with a preference for water and tea with their meal. The number fifteen flashed on the screen and they entered the dimly lit restaurant. Each table had a number printed on it, and sure enough, on table fifteen sat their waters and a steaming pot of tea. They slid into opposite sides of the booth and Paige folded her hands on the table to quell her excitement.

"So . . . Are their colonies on Mars? What did the USA turn into? Did sea levels really rise and drown islands and coastlines? Is China a democracy or what now? Does—"

"Ah, ah, ah." Luxe scolded with a chuckle. "I've probably told you too much already. Given your current situation, I can't really keep everything a secret, but humans aren't meant to know the future. You'll have to ask me something more boring."

"What career do I have?"

"You do a stint in Vegas as an Elvis impersonator. I must say, by the time you're thirty you can grow an impressive set of sideburns. Then after a short career as a card shark, you write your memoir and sell the movie rights for millions. Don't get too excited. You blew your fortune on slots before marrying a redneck and moving into a trailer park. Seven kids later, you're a well-rounded woman. Literally."

Paige stared at him incredulously for a moment before busting out laughing. "You suck at lying."

"Then ask me a question I don't have to lie about. Even if I knew, I wouldn't tell you."

"Could we go see?"

"That's not ethical. Besides, I don't think looking in on you would work. Due to our magic, warlocks only exist wherever they're at. Since you're tied to warlock magic, you don't exist in your old timeline anymore. That's why getting you back is so tricky. Returning you requires repairing time to include you again. I'm nowhere near advanced enough to do that."

"Okay. I have a question you can answer. When is a warlock considered full-grown, and when is your schooling done?"

A door in the wall slid open, and a tray glided out with their food. Luxe passed out dishes while he explained. "We come of age at twenty-one. So, I'm only a few months off. But most of us don't finish with magic tutors until thirty to fifty, and many are still getting their bearings at 150. Of course, Atlas finished with his tutor at twenty-seven, and you can see *that* didn't go to his head."

"So wait, you're still a good ten to thirty years away from being finished with school?"

"Yes."

"Huh, so basically your family is expecting the equivalent of a high school freshman to do brain surgery."

"Something like that." Luxe laughed and pointed a spoon toward a bowl of dark brown broth with chunks of mushrooms, thin white noodles, and green onions. "Try that one and tell me what you think."

Paige sipped it and smacked in surprise. "The soup tastes just like beef."

"They specifically bred vegetables to taste and chew like meat. Mushrooms are a lot more eco-friendly than a herd of cattle. They feed a lot more people, too. New crops pop up every couple days. Needless to say, you'll eat a lot of mushrooms if you stay here."

"That must be terrifying for Cleo." Paige smirked.

Luxe roared with laughter.

When they'd finished, Luxe led them back to the park. The sun stood high, and the park had filled with workers from the city getting fresh air during lunch. The air had a strange quality here: thinner somehow, and with a faint metallic scent, like tin foil.

He pulled a couple of crystals out of his pocket, tossing an orange one to her. "I guess I can give this back to you. Nesu wanted you to have your crystal once you'd calmed down. Can I safely assume you're over all that?"

"I guess so," Paige teased. "Though he *was* a fabulous kisser. Whatever will I do without such worthy entertainment?" Luxe blinked at her with a worried look on his face. "I'm joking, Luxe," she hurried to reassure him. "You were supposed to jump in with some cocky comment about being better than him, and then you were supposed to kiss me to prove it."

Luxe blushed. "Missed that cue, didn't I?"

"It's okay." Paige sighed. "We'll try again some other time. Now where to?"

The shimmering portal had opened in front of them. "756 Denmark. Brace yourself, the Vikings are going to blow you out of the water."

"Vikings?" Paige shuddered as they stepped through.

~ ~ ~

Luxe bent his knees as he landed. He did fine at catching himself on the other side of his portals. They only dropped you about three feet off the ground, but you never got a clear view until you were on it. Landing was all about anticipation, and Paige hadn't been traveling by portal near enough to anticipate correctly. She appeared out of thin air just above him, and he braced for her weight. She anticipated *him* this time and caught at his neck as his arms closed around her.

He set her on the ground and changed clothes for the both of them. Her dress looked very much like the one she'd worn in ancient Rome, but then again, only 400 years had passed since Romans had occupied Europe.

The tube-like, cream-colored dress belted at her waist and a woolen wrap in a rich red-brown covered her shoulders. Paige's hair was tucked under a white head-scarf with ribbon trimmings, and he decked her out in silver and glass-bead jewelry.

His tunic also looked similar to his Roman one, except here he wore thin-cut trousers underneath. A slim sword and dagger hung at his waist. The tap of them against his leg reminded him that Nesu had suggested he give one to Paige. While he had no intention of leaving her alone, their adventures so far hadn't gone according to plan at all.

"Paige, I think Nesu might be right." The words tasted like dirt. He held a newly magicked dagger out to her.

Paige went pale. "I wouldn't know what to do with that."

"The point is to cut someone. Given everything that's happened so far, I think it would be wise for you to have something. You've got plenty of guts. You'd figure out how in a pinch. Don't worry about fancy tricks, just create a distraction to get out of trouble."

"Where do I carry it?" She glanced at her belt.

Luxe shook his head. "A lady wouldn't openly carry. Hold out your arms."

She stood with her arms out and Luxe looked approvingly at her wide sleeves. That would work perfectly. He made a leather strap and started to reach up her shirt. Paige squeaked and slapped his hand away.

"Hey. What do you think you're doing?"

"Strapping a dagger across your chest where you can reach it easily. If I strapped it to your thigh in this dress, you'd have to hike the whole dang thing up to get at the dagger. But on your chest, you can reach straight up your sleeve. May I?"

Paige gave a non-committal grunt, and Luxe went back to what he was doing. He reached one hand up each sleeve tying the strap across her chest. He leaned in and let his hands graze across the skin of her back as he tied the knot.

His imagination began to run away with him, and he shook his head to clear the thoughts, but not before a sigh escaped into her hair. She leaned toward him, their bodies inches from each other. Giving the strap a yank to make sure it was secure, he ran his hands along the length. The strap needed to lay flat, both to be comfortable and to stay unnoticeable. Paige gave a little squeak and squirmed at the same time heat seared his face. He'd bumped a little extra by accident. He swiftly pulled his hands back out.

"I think that'll hold." Despite clearing his throat, his voice came out low and husky.

He went to peck a kiss on her cheek, but she turned to peek up at him at the same time. His lips brushed the corner of her mouth instead. The heat which had hit his cheeks now surged through his whole body. The next moment he kissed her like she was a dessert, as if he could eat her right up. She responded by wrapping her arms around him and pulling him tightly against her body. This time he squeaked. He jumped away, rubbing his ribs.

"Even with a sheath, that dagger can really poke." He ran his fingers through his hair and sighed. "I know this sucks, but it's work time, not play time. My parents could contact the three remaining stones at any time if they were to use the right magic. We need to get them back." He reached out to stroke her cheek. "Hold that thought until tonight, after we've either found the stone or it's too dark to search. We can pick up where we left off."

Paige caught his hand and squeezed. "Lead on."

Chapter 18

Luxe held out his hand and called up the green compass. The dials whirled and came to rest, pointing out over his thumb. He took Paige's hand and started off in that direction. They wandered under the green leaves of the forest, the air around them glowing with a yellow-green light. The tall, straight trunks thrust up from the ground out of thick undergrowth. Luckily, he found a path, something between a small road and a riding trail, leading in the direction they needed to go. The shade kept the air cool and pleasant. On the forest floor the air stood very still, smelling of growing plants and humming with insects.

They walked on in companionable silence for about two miles. Paige appeared to be enjoying the walk through the forest as much as he was. The walk came as close to relaxing as any of their searches could possibly be. The road split ahead of them, reminding Luxe of Robert Frost's "The Road Not Taken." He stopped at the fork, consulted his compass and faced down the green-lit path toward the stone.

"Two roads diverged in a yellow wood.
And sorry I could not travel both . . ." he quoted.

Paige gave his hand a squeeze. *"Two roads diverged in a wood and I—*

I took the one less traveled by,
And that has made all the difference."

As they took Luxe's path, warmth spread through him. Her understanding of him and the feeling it invoked transcended verbal description. This knowledge touched him in a joyful way he couldn't express. The forest had been relaxing before, but suddenly it became a happy place for the two of them.

Paige pulled against his hand. "Do you hear that?"

Luxe stopped and drew his focus back to the present. Sure enough, a soft rustling came from the undergrowth. Luxe pulled Paige close, tucking her slightly behind his back.

"Hello? Who's there?" He spoke Old Norse, and he knew Paige wouldn't understand, but he'd worry about that later, after he'd discovered who they were dealing with.

A party of five men stepped from the undergrowth. All were dressed like him, except they wore mail shirts over their tunics and covered their heads with rounded helmets. The last thing Luxe needed was a tangle with soldiers.

"What business have you upon the lands of Harold the Valorous?" the leader of the soldiers asked.

"We are simply passing through."

"You must request permission for your passage. We shall escort you to the house of our Lord."

The soldiers made a loose diamond around the two of them, and Paige clung to the back of his tunic. "Don't worry. We only have to appeal to their lord for safe passage," he soothed.

"But they're Vikings, right? They aren't going to slaughter us and drink from our skulls, are they?"

"Good Lord, I'm glad they can't understand you. No. That's why I said they'd knock your socks off. Right now, they are the most advanced civilization on the continent. They also have the most progressive society. The women here are free and almost equal citizens. In a little less than 600 years, the Catholic church is going to come through and single handedly ram women into a social class nearly as low as the slaves. And it's going to take them even longer to claw their way out."

"So, no raping and pillaging?"

"You're thinking pirates. But the winners in raids, battles, and wars do that in pretty much any time and regardless of where they're from. These guys aren't trying to conquer us. We're only asking permission to be on their land."

They didn't have to go far before the forest opened, and they were ushered toward a large wooden house in the middle of a meadow. Luxe observed the waving wildflowers and the pastoral views. Viking lords sure knew real estate. He took a quick peek at his compass, not entirely surprised when the hands pointed straight into the Lord's house. Figured. His life would be way too easy if the stone were just laying around in the forest.

Inside, the Lord stood on a small dais in the center of the main room. Wooden walls were gray with age and smoke. A fire burned below an opening in the roof for the smoke to escape. Like nearly all buildings in Europe had for thousands of years, it smelled of smoke, leather, steel, and all sorts of uniquely human scents. The guard escorted them to the center of the room and made a quiet noise to gain his lord's attention. The man looked up, and Luxe was surprised to see a youth not much older than himself. He wore several heavy chains and pedants around his neck and at the center of one sat the rune-stone.

This called for some careful manners and bargaining. Luxe started by giving the lord a low bow. "Greetings. You must be the one they call Harold the Valorous. I am Luxe Pendragon. Your men brought me to your gracious presence so that I might make a request for safe passage through your lands."

"You are well-mannered," Harold observed. He had long blond hair, pulled back and braided with a leather thong, and extremely intelligent steel-blue eyes which he scanned both Luxe and Paige with. "But, I wish to know more about your purpose before I grant your request." He made an obvious show of looking Paige over this time. "I also wish to know more about your companion. Your wife?"

"My kinswoman." Luxe put a hand in the small of her back and pushed her a little forward, toward Harold. "May I introduce the Lady Paige."

Harold stepped off the dais and took Paige's hand, kissing the back of it. "A pleasure."

Paige still couldn't understand, and for a moment Luxe worried she might be offended. But she gave Harold a shy smile before dropping her eyes and curtsying. Thank goodness she made such a quick study.

With an abrupt gesture of his hand Harold had slaves scurrying to set out tables. "Join us for our mid-day meal and tell me about your travels," he ordered.

Harold seemed sociable. Luxe hoped his affability would make this negotiation easier. He started by introducing his family connections. Already the Vikings would be familiar with Britain even if they'd never been there personally. As he thought, Harold nodded with understanding. He left the purpose of their expedition rather vague and then tried to work the conversation around to Harold's necklace.

"You have a very finely wrought chain upon which hangs a rune-stone," Luxe said. "I wish to bring my lord-father home a worthy gift of my travels. Such a necklace would indeed be worthy."

Harold picked up the rune-stone and twisted it lovingly between his finger. "Yes, I'm particularly fond of this piece. I'll give you the name of the smith if you'd like to commission your own."

Luxe shook his head. "I'm afraid I haven't time for that. Our ship departs in a mere fortnight, and we still have much traveling to do before we arrive. Perhaps I could purchase this one from you, and you could have another commissioned at your leisure?"

Harold continued to twist the stone. "This is a *very* unique piece. The stone has a connection with the goddess, of that I'm sure," Harold mused. "As such the stone would demand a very special price, don't you think?"

Luxe set his poker face. Now the bargaining began. This was also why he'd deliberately left Paige speaking English. He didn't want her to say anything to damage negotiations.

Luxe leaned one cheek on his hand and gave Harold a lazy smile. "I'm sure we can arrange something. Name your *special price*." He had access to all the gold the philosopher's stone could make, so he knew he could meet this lord's demands.

"I will give you the necklace you desire in exchange for something I desire. The hand of your kinswoman in marriage."

Luxe's face slipped from his hand. He hadn't seen that coming. Though, looking back on the line of questions over lunch, he supposed he should have. Harold had spent a great deal of time trying to verify their lineage. He'd been checking to see if Paige made a suitable bride all along.

Unfortunately, his shock undercut his eloquence. "Why?" he gasped out.

"I desire connections abroad, and I happen to be in need of a wife, as well. My father passed earlier this year, and as the new lord of these lands, I need to procure an heir. Your kinswoman seems of healthy breeding stock and of noble birth. A marriage to her will connect my house to the houses of Briton, securing ends to both my desires in a single transaction."

Luxe thought furiously. In this day and age, though liberal, a woman's marriage was still arranged. Harold wouldn't find this odd, but such an arrangement would likely send Paige into a funk. Her temper he could soothe, but would Paige be safe if he used her to buy the stone? Most likely.

"I will accept your deal and look forward to many years of trade between our houses," Luxe answered. "Give me a moment to prepare my kinswoman, and your ladies may see to her after."

He took Paige by the shoulders and gave her a serious look. "No matter what I say just smile and nod," he said in English. "I had to make a bargain to secure the stone. But before you freak out, remember the portal is pulling us in about thirty hours. You simply have to play along until then."

Paige gave him a wary nod. "Play along with what?"

"Harold's price for the stone was you. I agreed to give you to him as a wife." She started to protest, and he shook his head. "Smile and nod. It'll take the better part of a week for all the proper preparations to be made. We'll be long gone before they even do the ceremony, and nothing is more prized in a noble wife than her virtue, so you're safe there until after the service. Which won't happen anyway, so . . . Please tell me you're following and can play your part."

"I think so, but what am I supposed to do?"

"Look like a bride-to-be. You're already doing great at looking nervous. His ladies are going to take you away and pamper you, Viking-style, to get you all prepped for the big day. They'll be your chaperones. I won't be able to be alone with you, which sucks, but hey, at least we don't have to fight a disgusting creature this time, right?" He kept her shoulders in his hands, kissed one cheek, the other and a faint brush to the lips. "All right, my kinswoman is prepared. I've given her instructions to honor her family, and she is excited to be a part of the new alliance."

Paige blinked at him incredulously. Probably for the lies. He'd given her Old Norse speech, which she'd need since he wasn't going to be around much. Harold snapped his fingers, and the slaves immediately gathered in front of him.

"Begin the preparations for my nuptials," Harold announced. "See that my bride is readied, and bring the priestesses. We wed at dinner tonight."

Two beefy-looking maids took Paige by the arms and led her off. Paige craned her neck to peer back, panic on her face. Not that he didn't understand. He'd had no idea Harold was in the mood for a rush job. Harold clapped him on the back and dropped the necklace over his shoulders.

"I hope you get as much enjoyment from the necklace as I will from your kinswoman, eh?" He gave a hearty laugh as he walked away, calling his gentlemen to him.

Luxe's stomach went sick. He looked at the curtained doorway which Paige had been led through, and his mind raced over possible solutions which didn't involve fighting. He trailed after Harold. As the bride's kinsman, it should give him nearly family status around the lord. He'd keep an eye on things from this side and just have to hope Paige managed on the other.

~ ~ ~

Paige squirmed, trying to get out of the grasp of the two maids. They certainly had an impressive grip. Most men she knew barely had a grip to match theirs. She had to try to find a way to stall the wedding. She knew Luxe would be working on a way out, too. But just in case he failed, she wasn't going to sit back and wait for the obvious. She'd start with something easy, like playing coy.

"I can't do this tonight," Paige said, squirming against the maids again.

"Don't be nervous," one of the women said. She looked to be in her mid-twenties with an ample bust and wide hips, all of which added to her leverage over Paige. She shot Paige a lascivious grin. "We'd all give a great deal to be in your place tonight. Supposedly, the lord is a very capable lover."

Paige swallowed hard. "I need to pray though. I need to right myself with my gods so I might be a better wife." Hopefully they were religious enough to buy the excuse. "I should be ready tomorrow."

"No need to worry about your gods." The other maid laughed. "As the lord's wife, you'll be worshiping our gods now. Our gods don't require anything special of you. Just please your husband, that will suffice." She slapped Paige on the backside.

Paige scowled at her. She was as solidly built as the other woman with a more common-place face. The maids clearly weren't buying the virtuous maiden routine. Paige tried not to giggle as the next solution popped into her mind.

She'd been pulled into a sleeping chamber. The gray wood walls were decorated with tapestries here. Four other slaves had hauled a huge wooden tub into the room, filled with what looked like milk. The two maids were busy setting out oils and grooming instruments. Paige took the opportunity to wiggle her fingers. Gathering the green sparkles, she held her dress out and let them fall down the top, concentrating on the image she wanted. The garment appeared on her body, and she gave a nervous giggle.

"That's more like it," the prettier maid said. "Enjoy yourself. You're a lucky lady all around today. You've been ordered into a milk bath. Not something offered up very often."

The two maids began to strip Paige for her bath. Two minutes ago, this might have bothered her more, but now she felt like daring them to continue. As the sheath of her dress dropped to the floor, the maids both gasped. The prettier one hurriedly took off the dagger as the plain-faced one went running from the room. Proud triumph surged through Paige. No need for weapons when her best one was her mind.

~ ~ ~

Luxe had been invited to join an archery competition with Harold and his courtiers. Like any male gathering before a wedding, much ribald bantering and displays of testosterone ensued. Luxe had a hard time swallowing the bantering, since they were discussing the woman who was very nearly his girlfriend.

He'd taken a moment while they were preparing the target platforms to check his supplies. He desperately tried to remember a spell to use, because creating a new portal wasn't something he wanted to do. It would screw everything up since he'd directly linked the portals between all four remaining time periods. They still had two stones after this, and he didn't have the supplies to trace the stones again. Getting off track would be bad as he didn't have the exact locations memorized.

As far as the archery went, Luxe held his own. Currently he stood in third place, and he couldn't tell if that pleased or incensed his host. His turn came, and he'd just drawn his bow when a commotion erupted behind him. One of the maids who'd taken Paige away came rushing up to the lord.

She bent her knees, dropping low, and raised her flushed face. "We have a problem, Lord Harold."

"You may speak." He looked a little bored.

"The Lady Paige. She has a peculiar metal undergarment."

"So?" Harold drawled

She frowned and looked around at the gathering. "The item will keep you from performing your duties as husband, and it's locked."

Luxe turned his laugh into a coughing fit. Paige had given herself a chastity belt. That brilliant girl. He wanted to beam with a master's pride at the cunning of his familiar.

Harold suddenly bore down on him, looking furious. "Did you know about this? Did you think to play me for a fool? I don't suppose you have the key?"

Luxe quickly set the bow down. He definitely didn't want to appear armed. "I wouldn't know." He tried to make himself sound imposing. "She's my cousin, not my daughter. Any measures my Uncle has taken to secure her value would not have been discussed with me, and I don't go exploring there myself."

"Are they so backwards in Briton they lock up their daughters?"

Luxe shrugged. "It's a different system, my lord. In Briton, a girl has no more value than her virtue and her father's position. As a father guards his position, so he also guards her virtue. Would you not do the same for your daughter?"

"I won't have any daughters if I cannot get at my wife," Harold roared. He wheeled on the maid. "Shall I summon Ulf the blacksmith or Geir the silversmith? What is the nature of the lock?"

The maid dropped her head. "I wouldn't presume to know enough about metalworking."

"Get them both then." Harold's face had turned a robust red. "And you," he growled at Luxe. "You don't leave my sight. If I find I've been hustled, you'll both pay."

Chapter 19

Paige held her tongue in amused silence as chaos erupted in her prepping room. Once the maid had run off, the other crouched in front of her with a slim knife trying to pick the lock.

"What in the name of the Goddess is this?" she muttered.

"A chastity belt," Paige answered. "My virtue is taken very seriously."

"You don't need your virtue tonight." The maid sighed. "You'll have a husband in short order. No man takes a wife for the wedding. They only want the wedding night. And this is a most firm obstacle to that." The four slaves who had carried in her bath still gabbed loudly in their shock. "You four, see to the rest of the preparations. She'll be married, belt or no. The Lord can worry about this problem in his own way."

The maids pushed Paige into the milk bath. She might have complained, but it felt heavenly. The milk was warm and soothed her skin. The blond maid washed her hair and took to braiding it around her head in a sort of golden-brown crown. Her skin got buffed, her nails polished. While this happened, the other slaves returned with a gorgeous gown of coppery-colored silk, trimmed with gold-embroidered ribbons.

They had pulled Paige from the bath, scrubbed her dry, and dressed her in her petticoat when the door burst open and a small group of men trooped in. Harold led the way, trailed by several other men and Luxe. Behind the backs of the rest of the group, Luxe chanced giving her a wink.

She supposed in such a situation, women of the time might have shrunk away in modesty, but the petticoat covered as much as her winter clothes at home, minus the outerwear. So instead, she gave them her most exasperated look.

"To what do I owe the pleasure of such a visit while I'm dressing? I thought seeing the bride before the wedding brought bad luck."

"I hear there is an impediment, madam," Harold answered stiffly. "I have brought the blacksmith and the jeweler to see what might be done about your uncouth garment."

Paige paled at this. Not only did she dread a bunch of men examining her metal bikini bottom, but didn't blacksmiths heat metal and hit it with hammers? No way was anyone doing that near her girly-bits.

"Lift her skirts," Harold snapped at the maid.

Paige flushed as the maid obeyed. Maybe this wasn't such a great solution after all. The maids hoisted her skirt above her navel, and both smiths crouched to examine the work.

"I can take care of this, my Lord." One of the men announced. He looked up at Paige with sympathetic eyes. "I am Geir the jeweler. I will have you freed shortly, my Lady." He turned to the other men. "Perhaps the Lady would feel more comfortable with a smaller audience. Once she is released . . ." He blushed and made an embarrassed gesture with his hands.

Harold nodded. "You may all leave. I will stay to make sure the job is done properly."

"Wait," Paige cried. "I want my kinsman to stay. If I'm

to be displayed before strangers at least I trust him to keep you honest."

"Fine," Harold grumbled. "Luxe, you may stay as well."

Geir drew a small, slim strip of metal from his tool kit and set to work picking the lock. In moments, he had the clasp open. When the lock clicked, Paige threw Luxe a desperate gaze. He returned it with a horrified gape of his own. But his fingers moved, and he exhaled as he blew green sparkles in her direction.

The maid squealed, and both Geir and Harold gasped as the room went completely dark. The chastity belt hit the floor with a metallic jangle. Paige quickly dropped her own green sparkles on herself. A good pair of granny-panties ought to cover enough. More than the bikini she owned at home. She could live with being seen that way.

"Someone light a torch," Harold growled.

One of the servants, presumably, fumbled around and a small slit of light entered the room as the door opened. A moment later she came back with a fresh torch.

Harold glared at Paige when the light came back. "I know not why you wear such trousers, but at least everything appears to be in order under that monstrosity." He turned and stalked from the room followed by Geir and Luxe. Just before he left the room, Luxe gave her a half-hearted smile, which she knew meant he wasn't done working on this.

Two hours later Paige sat in her wedding dress, feeling normal again yet completely miserable. The hall had been transformed, and the murmur of the guests chatting happily out in the main room drifted in. Her stomach felt full of rocks. She wanted to trust Luxe, but they were cutting it close on time.

The two maids must have heard something she hadn't, because they hauled her to her feet and thrust her out into the hall. She blinked and looked down the aisle, at the end of which her groom waited. Shining faces lined either side, taking in the lucky bride. Suddenly, a strange compassion for all women of antiquity filled Paige. No one cared how she felt about this. Viking women might have been able to inherit and hold jobs and hold clergy positions but still, no one batted an eye at an unwilling bride.

She tried to swallow the lump in her throat, looking around desperately for Luxe. She couldn't find him anywhere. Where had he gone? Though she tried hard not to cry, a tear slipped down her cheek. The aisle was far too short, and walking it went quicker than she had hoped. She stood before Harold and a priest.

The priestess said a prayer in a rolling language she didn't understand. Not that understanding mattered. The prayer was said to a god she didn't know. She said a few other things Paige didn't follow. She simply tried to block the sermon out and come up with a solution. The ceremony must have ended, because Harold led her from the room as the crowd cheered wildly. But they weren't headed outside, they were headed toward the private chambers.

Paige dug her heels in. "No, please. I'm not ready yet."

"Enough with your maidenly shyness," Harold snapped. A few tugs more on his part, and she found herself in a well-appointed bedchamber. He pushed her to sit on the end of the bed and stripped off his outer layers and sword, setting them on a stool beside the bed. Kneeling, he took her hands in his and tried to catch her eye. "I hoped you'd be a more willing wife. Though I'm sure you'll learn. You'll find I'm not a cruel man."

She looked up at his blue eyes and found they held sincerity. That made her tears come faster. So much for the enlightened Vikings. Evidently they did rape, but they just didn't see it as such. He reached up and gently wiped them away with his fingers. He let his hand linger, caressing her cheek, and Paige sobbed. Was this really how her visit to the Vikings would end? Damn Luxe. He promised.

He leaned in and Paige tried frantically to think of a way out. She needed Latin to do a spell, and all she could think of at the moment were curse words in English. Harold's lips came down on hers, and he pressed her gently but firmly until she had no choice but to lay back.

Paige went limp for a moment. She had one idea. She remembered the spell to make her invisible, but she had to get him off first or he'd find her by touch. Shifting, she kicked aside the stool with his sword. It clattered and slid away. Pretending she was only trying to scoot, she shifted again. With no back-up and the entire time period believing she and this man were married, no one would rescue her. Even Luxe had abandoned her. She'd have to save herself.

Harold hiked her skirt up, and since his weight still pressed against her she could tell how much he looked forward to this. She brought her knee up, aiming for the crown jewels. He roared as her knee connected with its target, anger burning on his face. He reached for her throat . . .

Something snapped: the sound of wood breaking. The entire building around them shuddered, then sunlight streamed into the room as the roof crumbled and . . .

Paige let out a bloodcurdling scream at the same time the massive dragon looming above them roared. The thing had to be at least four stories tall and covered in gleaming black scales. Huge bat wings extended from its back and red eyes glared down at them.

Harold scrambled off her and searched for something. Paige assumed he wanted his sword. The dragon reared back its head and let out a noise halfway between a scream and a roar. Paige's veins filled with ice. Before she could do anything, the dragon lunged, and she had a quick view of dagger-like teeth before she slid down the throat.

She landed somewhere dark and soft and let out a long, keening scream. She'd been eaten alive. The dragon would digest her. She really wished the dragon had killed her first, and she slumped waiting for the burning to start as the digestive juices did their job. Instead, her living death-trap began moving with a rhythmic jostling. How long would she be forced to suffer before the end finally came?

~ ~ ~

The black dragon soared over the countryside, admiring the view and feeling very self-satisfied. Luxe gave a contented sigh. Turning oneself into a monster of this proportion was no small feat. Once again . . . if only someone at home could see.

The look on Harold's face as the dragon ate his bride had been priceless, and Luxe almost wished he'd had a camera. Really, Harold had no one to blame but himself. He'd pushed things too fast for Luxe to work subtly. And if he hadn't insisted on the archery competition, Luxe would never have seen the patch of wild snapdragons: a key ingredient in the spell. Finding the rest of what he needed in the surrounding forest had taken him longer than he'd hoped. As a result, he'd almost been too late.

He circled the forest looking for a place to land. The effects of the potion were already beginning to fade. Not that it mattered, he'd flown a distance which would take Harold and his men at least two days to cover on horseback. They were safe.

He landed in a little glade in the forest and hacked a couple times before getting Paige out on the ground. She looked up and him and screamed again, trying to scramble away. The stuff of his gut covered her, so all she did was slip. He'd have to wait to calm her down. Dragons didn't speak. Even a human in dragon form would only snarl and growl. That wouldn't help anything. So, he sat calmly back on his haunches and blinked at her. She finally struggled to her feet and tried to run away. He rounded her up with his spiked tail to keep her close. Any moment now.

A puff of green sparkles and Luxe looked at the glade from his much shorter human viewpoint. Paige screamed again, then stopped and blinked at him unbelievingly. A moment later, she tackled him.

"That was you rescuing me?" she shrieked. "I thought you'd left me. I didn't see you anywhere."

Luxe wrapped his arms around her, ignoring the dragon slime. "I only left to find the ingredients for the spell. I'd seen the most important one outside earlier and was pretty sure I could get the rest. But getting them took longer than I'd hoped, and then I had to mix the potion itself . . . Well, I'm glad I made it in time. And dragon-lore is still secure." He winked at her. "There's nothing a dragon likes to eat more than a virgin on her wedding day."

"Oh, but Luxe, I'm not . . ." Paige flushed. "Never mind. I guess that's not relevant to historical lore."

Luxe loosened his grip. "Really? Was I too late after all? Did he really, you know?"

Paige blushed an even deeper red. "No. I mean. You were on time—barely—but you pulled the rescue off. I, no . . . Not with him. Previously . . . at home."

"No need to be embarrassed. You can take a good guess at what Cleo used me for." He kissed her forehead and gagged. "Let's get you cleaned up."

He magicked her clean, and they exchanged accounts of what happened while they were separated. While they talked, Lux began building a fire, making an air mattress, and setting out dinner. He'd made the fire a magic one, so it would burn indefinitely without having to add wood.

"Um, Luxe?" Paige poked at the chicken on her plate. "I'm a little curious how you managed the spell for turning into a dragon." She cleared her throat. "Not that I don't think you can do impressive magic, but most of it has been spells, not potions. The last big potion you did kinda stuck me as your familiar, and I doubt you're carrying any spell books."

He sighed and set his plate on the ground beside him. "Fair enough. I have the dragon potion memorized. Well, I really ought to have the memory potion memorized, too, but . . ." He rubbed nervously at the bridge of his nose. "Let me explain better. See, Atlas and I have to duel for custody of the stones after I come of age. All warlock families have the potential inheritors do it. That way the most powerful family member gets the safekeeping of them. To practice, my parents forced Atlas and I to do mock duals. I don't know if Atlas was showing off, or seriously trying to eliminate me, but he always went all out. I'd finally had enough. We weren't allowed to use books, only already memorized spells or potions. So, I learned the one to turn myself into a dragon."

Paige wrinkled her nose. "If you're supposed to know the memory spell, why did you screw up so badly?"

Heat from a flush crept across his cheeks. "I mostly know it," he protested. "All wizards have to know that one, in case we do something to call attention to ourselves. We need to erase ourselves from the minds of any humans. But . . ."

"But what?" Some of Paige's previous displeasure had returned to her tone.

"Well, you heard Cleo . . . I only missed a couple ingredients, and they were really close to the ones I mistook them for. Remember, I was *really* nervous. I'd just pulled you out of your time after losing the stones in the first place. Atlas ran off with my spell books, and I buckled under the pressure and distractions."

He scrubbed his hands along his legs. But that isn't a good excuse, and I know it. Another factor played in, as well. This part might sound lame, but the biggest influence is you. When I screwed up, I was still trying to do magic without having you believe in me." He pulled his knees to his chest and tried to hide his face.

"Dear God, Luxe. There's so much both horrifying and flattering in that, I have no idea how to respond."

"If you want me to say I'm sorry I screwed up, I'm not," he blurted, then corrected himself. "I mean, I'm sorry I caused you trouble and anxiety, but I can't say I'd be better off if . . . oh never mind. It's all convoluted."

She gave a little nod. "I get it. Part of me still wants to be furious this happened in the first place. But another part is thrilled at all the places we've gone and things we've seen. It's a lot of clashing emotions all tied into one." A huge sigh deflated her shoulders. "I'm not sure you can separate all of them."

He reached out and grabbed her hand, squeezing. "I'm so glad you understand me."

After the meal, they settled down on the air mattress, and Luxe smiled as Paige snuggled against him. Her hair smelled like flowers, and her skin was so smooth where he stroked her arm. She gave a sigh, dropping one arm lazily across his stomach.

"I really believed tonight would be far different than this. I thought for sure I'd spend it in Harold's arms."

"I could take you back if you're disappointed," Luxe teased between a yawn.

"That's not what I meant, and you know it." She poked a finger between his ribs.

Luxe gave her a little squeeze. "There's no way I'd let you be ravaged by another man."

"Hey. That implies there is a man you'd let me be ravaged by."

"Of course, there is." He stuck his nose in her ear. "Me," he whispered.

She giggled and struggled against his grip. "Be serious, Luxe."

"I am being serious. I would seriously like to ravage you." A huge yawn cracked his face. "Tomorrow." A twinge of guilt hit him as Paige wilted in his grasp.

"Tomorrow?"

"While I'm glad to hear you're disappointed," he chuckled and then continued, "turning yourself into a dragon and flying halfway across a continent with a belly full of damsel-in-distress takes a lot of energy. Tonight, it wouldn't be ravaging so much as being attacked by snuggly bunnies. And while I do love a nice snuggle, in this case I'd rather impress you with the wild beast tomorrow."

Paige's head rocked back over his arm as she laughed. "Every man likes to think he's a beast. I love that your ego wasn't damaged by having to eat your girlfriend in order to save her from another man. And while I've had guys promise to eat me alive before, not one has ever followed through. At least not to that extent."

"Hmm . . . I have to say, young maiden is pretty tasty. Though you're a bit like Chinese food."

"How so?"

"I'm already starving again."

He pulled Paige close and kissed her deeply. She responded warmly, wrapping one leg around him and pulling him close. They kissed and explored each other until he nearly tossed aside the idea of waiting. But still, he pushed her away.

"Tomorrow," he gasped. "This will be better after I rest."

Paige heaved a deep sigh. "But there might only be a handful of tomorrows. And then I'll have to leave."

Luxe sighed himself and pushed Paige further away. "I've thought of that, too. If we're being honest, the time limit actually makes me want to do this less."

"Why?" Paige protested.

"For myself. No matter how brokenhearted you are when our time comes to an end, you still won't remember. But should I go falling in love with you, I'll suffer the broken heart alone. I can only imagine how hard it would be to remember loving you and yet know you remember nothing of me."

Paige tucked her hands behind her head and looked up at the sky. "All I want is to fully enjoy whatever time we do have together. But you really know how to conjure up the cold water, don't'cha?"

He rolled so his back faced her. "Sorry."

He pulled his knees up and tried to block thoughts of Paige out. Maybe agreeing to anything had been a bad idea. As he'd thought, she was nothing but trouble. A different type of trouble from what he'd originally assumed, something far sweeter and more poisonous.

"Luxe?" Paige cut back into his thoughts.

"Mm . . ."

"Is there any way for us to stay together?"

"I already told you. We'd have to ask in Atlantis. I've never heard any mention of anything which would work out for us. I mean, aside from keeping you as my familiar. But we've pulled you from your natural timeline. That's against the rules."

"I've been thinking . . ." Paige started, and Luxe couldn't help but shiver. Somehow, he had a bad feeling about this. "What about Khalidah? Couldn't a *djinn* turn me into a witch? I mean, they're supposed to have incredible magic powers and all, right?"

"I just turned myself into a dragon and ate you. That isn't incredible?"

"That's just it. Your magic *was* incredible. So, if what your Grandfather Merlin supposed is true, and you've only got a portion of her power, surely she'd know how to fix time up so I could stay."

"Wow, Paige. I told you Khalidah's only a belief. It's like trying to figure out how to summon up the angel Gabriel and ask for a favor."

She made a little growling noise in her throat. "You just turned yourself into a dragon. And you think calling up a *djinn* sounds crazy?"

"You don't understand. The texts for summoning her don't even exist in one piece. We'd have to round up the fragments, and even then, her giving warlocks their power is only myth and legend."

"Yes, like Merlin and dragons are myths and legends." She rolled away from him. "But fine. If you're looking for an excuse to be rid of me, I won't stop you."

Suddenly a sleeping bag enclosed him. Paige had further separated herself.

"It's a little cold tonight," she snapped at him.

He pulled the bag up to his ears. "I was thinking the same thing," he retorted.

~ ~ ~

Luxe wanted to lash out at the bird who woke him up way before sunrise. Unwilling to face Paige after their spat last night, he got up and trudged off into the woods. He distracted himself with thoughts of the next stone. They were headed into the heart of the Mayan Empire. This destination actually made him more nervous than most of the civilizations they'd visited thus far. The Maya were incredibly superstitious, and their need for blood sacrifice scared him. Strangers frequently ended up on the chopping block.

He'd never understood why the Canul family had chosen that civilization as their domain. Probably because, at the time the eight noble families had chosen their timelines, the Canul were the lowest ranking family. The time they ruled was largely a period of transition for nearly every civilization on the planet, except the Maya. So maybe the stability drew them in.

Luxe looked up at the sky. The sun rode high already, and he had no idea how the day had gotten so late. He'd need to hustle to be at camp before the portal pulled them in. On the way back, he couldn't remember the undergrowth being so thick. He would never get back to Paige at this rate. Long before he got to her, the portal pulled him into darkness, and he fell hard onto packed dirt.

Before he got his bearings, the air filled with murmuring and chanting. Paige lay in an untidy heap next to him, and they were surrounded by Mayan warriors. Beads and bright colors adorned their loincloths, and they whispered about the newly arrived deities.

Just freakin' fabulous. Not only could he not make them invisible, they were the complete center of attention. He stood and raised his hands and every warrior fell to his knees, pressing his face to the ground. A whole group had seen them do magic. With no other explanation, they'd apparently assumed them to be deities.

Originally, he hadn't planned on making contact with the society here. Or if they had needed to go into a populated area, doing it invisibly. Magic or no magic, they'd stick out like a sore thumb here. They both had light complexions, leaving them no way to sneak around unnoticed.

"Oh, noble warriors." Luxe scowled. He could use magic to speak the language, but he had no idea how a god might sound. Or more specifically, how they would expect their god to sound. "I have come from the heavens in search of an ancient and precious artifact of the gods."

He held out his hand and called up the compass. "The item I seek is in that direction. I will not trouble you as I am in haste to return to the heavens. Please continue what you were doing."

Luxe started off in the direction the compass pointed, straight into the heart of the rainforest.

Chapter 20

Paige jerked her arm away from Luxe when he tried to help her to her feet. She'd planned on reconciling with Luxe, until she'd woken up completely alone. The longer he stayed away, the madder she became. And when the portal had pulled her in alone, she grew furious. He knew she hated being alone in these foreign time periods.

They landed in the rainforest, side by side. But still, Luxe said nothing to her. There wasn't even a pat on the back to let her know things were all right. Then they got surrounded by tribal warriors, and Paige let the sore feelings roil as Luxe stood and said something to the other men.

What was his deal anyway? Had he gotten scared again and run off? That would figure. She had no idea how she'd fooled herself into thinking he might be serious. He'd said he wanted to be with her while they had the chance, but he disappeared right after they started moving that direction.

She swallowed hard on the lump in her throat. If Luxe wasn't interested in going further in their relationship, then . . . she heaved a deep breath . . . that was his decision. At least they only had two more stones to find, then they could part ways. Splitting would probably be best. No matter what she felt for Luxe, she wasn't going to force herself on him. If she stayed, and they managed to find Khalidah, they'd be stuck together for a *very* long time. Better this should happen now, so at least she could still go home to her family.

Paige scowled at Luxe's back as he led them into the rainforest. They entire group of Mayan warriors had joined them. Once again, Luxe neglected to give her the gift of speech. But why would he? Changing language involved kissing her, which he clearly didn't want to do. She grew more and more upset with each passing minute. To the point where tears blurred her vision and her nose threatened to drip, though that might have been sweat. The back of his tunic ran with sweat. They hadn't had a private moment to change their garb. She focused on the sweat stain, letting it piss her off. Why did he have to be so gross?

She had no idea what premise to use this time. They didn't appear to be captives, but somehow, she had the distinct feeling they weren't free either. Luxe stopped abruptly at the foot of a massive tree covered in woody vines. Paige tried to talk herself down from lashing out at him. She'd almost run into him when he'd stopped without warning, and her face had touched that yuck on the back of his tunic.

Her scowl deepened, and Luxe took that moment to blow sparkles into the crevasses of the tree. The effect was instantaneous. Out of every crack poured an insect zoo's worth of creep-crawlies. Ants, spiders, centipedes, and bugs she couldn't even define. Most made her skin crawl. She'd screamed at first, but Luxe had snapped at her to shut up, and her anger returned with a vengeance. Suddenly, she contemplated catching some of the critters to put down the back of his pants later.

Luxe plunged an arm into one of the holes in the trunk of the tree, fishing around until he pulled out a little sand-colored stone. Paige now understood why he'd cleared the tree first. Imagine sticking your hand in one of those holes while everyone was still at home.

The clearing of the tree had an immediate effect on the Mayan warriors as well. When all the critters had issued from the tree, they once again fell into supplication on the dirt. Paige couldn't imagine how they could stand that. Even from her standing height, she could smell the musty, moldy scent of the forest floor. Not that it took any imagination to figure out why anything here smelled. The air held so much heat and humidity that Paige could barely tolerate it. On the way to the stone's location, only her anger at Luxe and the absolute need to refuse his help had kept her going. She wouldn't give him the pleasure of helping her, and she wouldn't give herself false hope if he did.

Luxe said something to call them to their feet and swiftly got into a disagreement with one of them. After a moment, he paled slightly and then set his chin and gestured to the man. The warriors led them off through the jungle once again. This time Luxe followed them, and she followed behind him.

She briefly considered sitting where she was and waiting for the portal to take her to the next location, because now she knew she didn't have to be with him for the portal to pull her. But when that thought ran through her head, the image of the creepy-crawly exodus from the tree quickly followed. She had no doubt that every tree and rock in the jungle housed a similar assortment.

Like stepping from behind a curtain onto a brightly-lit stage, they exited the jungle into a massive clearing. Houses of wood and stone sat in orderly fashion around stone temples and palaces. These reached up to meet the brilliantly blue sky. If the heat had been intense in the forest, it had nothing on being out in the direct sunlight. Beneath her double-layered silk wedding-gown, sweat drops rolled down her stomach and back. She had one moment of an odd chilled sensation before the world went black.

~ ~ ~

A thud behind Luxe drew his attention. Paige lay in a heap on the ground. Luxe lifted her shoulders up, and her head lolled limply over his shoulder, her skin an ashy gray. She felt clammy under his fingers, and Luxe knew she'd overheated in her layers of clothing. For a moment, he hesitated. If he changed her clothes now, he'd once again be using obvious magic in front of people. But if he didn't, she wouldn't take too long to die. He shook his head. These people had already seen them drop out of thin air. They were in the city as gods. Using magic would be natural for a god. Besides, any punishment would be worth Paige's life.

As he wiggled his fingers and sent the green sparkles over her, her clothing switched to an intricately embroidered wrap dress. He switched his own clothing, as well, choosing a garment somewhere between a loincloth and a kilt. He immediately felt better, but Paige remained unconscious.

"The goddess requires shade and water," he demanded of his impromptu escort.

One of the men picked Paige up off the ground, holding her carefully and led Luxe toward a central temple. As they rounded the backside, the man slipped into a nearly invisible entrance. Luxe followed him into the pitch-black hall inside the pyramid. Just when he doubted his decision to trust the warrior, the hall opened into a dimly lit room. The source of light was a strategically placed shaft which directed the sunlight onto what looked like an altar. The warrior pointed toward the altar and left with a bow.

Luxe fought frustration. The warriors pretty much refused to speak to him. He'd tried to have a conversation with one of them, but that had been completely worthless. They insisted on bringing him and Paige back to the city where the high priest would come to take care of his needs. After that the warriors refused to say more. Since they feared displeasing the gods, they would naturally be afraid to do anything without a worthier representative, like a priest or royalty.

Paige couldn't wait for the high priest to ready himself and come to them. Luxe made a cold washcloth appear and began swabbing her down. He gently caressed her face with the cloth.

"I'm sorry, Paige. Why didn't you say you were so miserable? I could have taken care of you sooner." He sighed and ran the cloth down her arms. "I suppose it's partly my fault. I was still upset, and I wasn't paying proper attention to you. I wish I had a way to help you understand."

He pressed a kiss to her limp lips and rubbed his face in frustration. "The idea that you want to stay with me is more thrilling than I can tell you. And if you could stay, I'm sure I'd fall head-over-heels for you. But I can't see how it would be allowed. I'm just not sure what to do since my wishes and the warlock laws are so incompatible. But making you mad was never my intent."

He worked his way to her feet and wiped them with a fresh cloth. Hopefully the cool water on her feet and head would do the trick. As he wiped the bottom of her feet, she gave a jerk and groaned.

"Luxe, why the hell are you tickling me? I feel like crap, and you want to play?" She kicked out at him. "Besides, I'm still mad at you."

"I know." He dropped his hands with a sigh. "I wasn't tickling. I was wiping you down with cold water. You passed out. Heatstroke."

Paige blinked and looked around her. "Where are we?"

"The main temple, I think. They wouldn't speak to me much. They're under the impression we're gods. I thought it best not to argue since they were likely to assume we're demons if we're not gods. Do you know what they do to demons? They'll send us back to Xibalba."

"Where?"

"That's their underworld and realm of monsters. The entrance is through the deepest cenote in the area. They'll toss us in to drown, freeze in the cold water, or get swept up by the underground river."

"Yeah, okay. I'd rather be a god."

"A goddess." He smiled at her. "One who should probably speak the language of her worshipers." He took a step closer and waited for Paige's reaction. She looked stiff but didn't pull away. So, he gave her a quick peck. Part of him wanted to linger, but he didn't want to press his luck.

Paige understood the speech just in time. Moments after he finished the spell, the high priest walked in, bedecked in a rainbow of feathers and sporting a jaguar's pelt over his shoulder. He bowed low to them both and looked at Luxe, excitement shining on his features.

"A visit from the gods wasn't foretold for another five-thousand years. This *is* a surprise. Please excuse our unpreparedness."

"You have my pardon," Luxe said. "After all, even with your best divinations, it is not for man to know every movement of the gods."

"Then, will you be staying to turn this age into a more auspicious one? Until the coming of the next god is forecast? We will build a temple worthy of you."

Luxe shook his head. "Your offer is most kind and will be remembered. However, I have pressing matters to attend to elsewhere in the cosmos."

The high priest fell to his knees pressing his face to the floor. "I will make a sacrifice which will entice you to stay and usher in a new age. Thirteen children in their first year will be sacrificed at dawn." He snapped his fingers and a lesser priest Luxe hadn't notice scurried from the temple.

"No," Luxe shouted in alarm. "I don't want thirteen infants sacrificed. I really can't stay here."

"Another thirteen," the priest barked at a second lesser priest. The high priest crawled toward Luxe's feet, across the floor. "Say the word and it shall be sacrificed in your honor."

"Really. There's no sacrifice necessary. I absolutely cannot stay."

"Perhaps if we add the blood of the young prince—"

"No," Paige said, sliding off the altar and onto her feet.

She flashed Luxe a sly smile, and he stepped back to let her do her thing. Clearly, she had some sort of plan. She turned a honeyed smile on the priest as her hand wandered to her belly.

"My esteemed husband-god cannot possibly stay, regardless of the sacrifice. I am expecting, and our god-child must be born at home in the heavens. You would not ask your god to miss the birth of his first-born son?"

She languished against the altar as Luxe tried not to stare open-mouthed. "My condition is why we came to Earth in the first place. I craved earthly fruits. It's also why I faltered in the heat. Carrying a god is a great burden."

The priest looked up from the floor, focusing on her mid-section, and Paige turned up her nose. "Lunar goddess I might be, but as the wife of a god, my figure will not wax or wane like the moon."

She looked at her fingernails as if bored. "If you wish to please the gods, bring me your finest assortments of fruits. We will return to the heavens tomorrow. If we are pleased with your hospitality, we will bestow a blessing upon you before we leave. Also, since I am nearing the birth of my first child, I'll take pity on the women whose children you would take for the ritual. Spare the children. I wish them to bring joy to their mothers."

The priest scuttled back across the floor. "Fulfilling your desires is our deepest pleasure. Is there anything else you require?"

"I shall decide after I've sampled your fruits." Paige waved a bored hand in a clear dismissal.

When they were alone he crossed the room to Paige and caught her up in a hug, swinging her around. "That was brilliant. I love you." He nearly tripped over her and his face flamed with embarrassment. "I mean . . . you know . . . I love the way you think. And, um . . ."

Paige had pushed herself free and stood scowling at him. "Good God, Luxe. No, I don't know what you mean. You're all over the map. Hot, cold, shy, forward—I'm lost."

He took a deep breath. He was lying to her and to himself, which only spoiled the little time they had left. "You're right. I've been trying to keep my distance, but it's taken all the fun out of the last of our time together. I got over-excited just then, but I do think I'm falling in love with you, and it scares me. I don't want you to go. I can't stand the thought. My heart already hurts, and I can't imagine how I'm going to feel once you're gone. Maybe it sounds cliché, but I'm better when I'm beside you. Look at everything I've done the last two weeks. That's all you."

Paige took a quick swipe at her eyes. "That's not all me. It's all you. You're a fantastic warlock. I can't imagine what you'll be able to do when you finally finish training. In case I don't get another chance to say it, thanks. Thanks for letting me live out my dream and explore the world. I'll always remember . . . I mean . . ." She gave a little sob, and Luxe opened his arms for her.

She took his offer of comfort and lay her face on his shoulder, letting him stroke her hair. The high priest walked in and looked questioningly at Luxe.

He gave a little shrug. "Who knows with pregnant women."

The high priest sent a bowl of fruit on the altar and bowed. "We have arranged a feast for tonight in honor of the blessed event. I do hope it will be to your liking. Shall I send for you?"

"Yes," Luxe answered. "Until then, we are not to be disturbed. I must try to calm her."

"Ah, yes. Well, a pregnant goddess has her whims. Would you like the help of a human midwife, or—?"

"No. After the heat she simply requires rest. She is overwrought."

"I will be back in a few hours then." The high priest excused himself.

"Very good." Luxe had already refocused on Paige.

He made a soft mattress on top of the altar. Luckily, the altar itself was a large square slab of solid stone. It had intricate carvings around the stone sides, but the top was smooth. Paige needed a boost to get up into the bed, and Luxe crawled up beside her. Once again, he held out his arms to her, and she crawled into his embrace.

"Actually, I don't think my explanation hit too far from the truth. Minus the baby part," he clarified. "You're still exhausted from the heat. Let's rest until our feast, shall we?"

She said nothing but settled in against his shoulder.

"Let's put that time to good use," Luxe said. "*You* promised the priest a blessing. And I'm putting you in charge of ideas, since you're in such a creative mood."

Paige opened her mouth to suggest they talk about things between them. He still sounded on the fence, and while the cuddles were nice, she wanted so much more. But she understood him a bit better now. His hesitation didn't stem from a lack of attraction; he simply wanted to protect them both.

They were just going about this from two different points of view. He figured if nothing happened between them, the separation would be easier. She wanted to use every free moment they had left to be together. Neither way was right or wrong, and either way they were both getting hurt.

Paige gave him a smile and went with option "C:" talk about something else and ignore the elephant in the room. "You're the one with all the talent. What can we give them which would be grand enough to count as a blessing from the gods?"

"Hmm . . ." He tapped her nose with his finger. "Hit me with your ideas, and I'll tell you if they're doable."

"Gold."

"Nope. My parents would be pissed."

"Fertility. You know, since I'm having a baby and all."

"Nope. Working through all the ladies would take me way too long."

Paige elbowed him. "I didn't mean you do the job like that. I don't know, some sort of talisman or potion."

"Still a no. There might be a potion, but I don't know it, let alone have the ingredients memorized."

Paige pressed her lips together in thought. "What about crops? Could we ensure a good harvest or something?"

Luxe shook his head. "Again, I don't know the right spell. But that does give me an idea. Since you pulled the moon goddess card, how about rabbits? She has a thing with them in this culture. We can make the area near the city overrun with rabbits, and they can feast."

"A little gorier than I'd like," she said. "But if we have to."

"What do you mean gorier? You saved twenty-six kids and a prince. I think we've done well."

"But all the poor animals we send them will die."

"I didn't hear you complaining while you dined on kraken calamari or dozens of other meat dishes I've seen you eat. Why have a bleeding heart now?"

"I don't know. Maybe because we'd be creating them to be dinner."

"And you don't think the beef farmer's doing the same thing? It's just slower from start to finish."

Paige sighed. "This is depressing. I already said okay. I don't want to talk about sacrifices anymore."

Luxe curled around her. "Then let's nap. Even if the heat didn't drain *you*, I can barely keep my eyes open."

Chapter 21

Paige couldn't tell what time it was when the high priest woke them. Aside from the priest's torch, utter darkness cloaked the altar room. Luxe made a show of helping her to her feet and steadying her, playing up the pregnant goddess bit.

They followed the high priest out the altar room. Paige took Luxe's hand, lacing her finger through his. They were led up a back staircase to the top of a temple, where an altar had been covered with every fruit imaginable. A brightly covered bower of pillows and embroidered hangings had been prepared and now awaited them.

The high priest stepped between the two and took their hands, raising them to the assembled crowds below. "Tonight, we feast the gods. May they be pleased and bestow their blessings upon us."

Then Paige and Luxe sat on the pillows, and slaves began offering them platters of food. Paige carefully took lots of fruit. Not that she minded since she loved fruit anyway. But since they were supposed to be on Earth for her fruit craving, she ought to play it up.

After the fruit came meats. Plate after plate, a sampling of nearly every creature in the forest. Below them the city feasted over bonfires, playing music and dancing in celebration of the unborn god. They served Paige an assortment of fruity wines, and though she meant to keep her head after what had happened in Egypt, this wine packed a punch. She felt very liberated, very fast.

The wine had come at the end of the meal. Luxe, probably prompted by her extra giggling, excused them for the night. As they left, Luxe promised the high priest their blessing at dawn, and then he took her back down the pyramid. Had the stairs been so steep on the way up? He herded her down the hall and into the altar room.

Luxe sat her on the bed he'd made atop the altar and started to leave. Paige caught at his kilt. "Stay, Luxe. Please?"

"You'll be fine here. I'm just going out for a bit."

Paige frowned. "To do what? Avoid me some more?" She giggled. "I think you should stay, and we can have some fun."

"That's exactly why I need to go." Luxe sighed. "You're drunk, that's not how I want you."

Paige sat up straighter and tried to look stern. "I'm not drunk. I'm tipsy, but I'm well aware of what I'm doing." She gave a huge sigh. "Good thing for you, I'm tipsy enough to speak my mind. We're on our way to get the last stone tomorrow. This is our last chance to be together." She pressed her lips tight, and her chin quivered. "I've been thinking about what you said earlier, and I know how you feel. I . . . meant what I said. I don't want to leave you. I didn't use the same words, but I know I feel the same thing. I'm falling for you, too."

Paige held her hands out for Luxe. "Please don't waste the last of what we have. I don't want your memories of our last nights together to be us fighting and distancing ourselves from each other. But if you keep running, that's exactly what they're going to be." She patted the bed beside her. "Come here. Let's enjoy ourselves for real."

Luxe came back and touched his forehead to hers. "Is this really what you want? Or is it the wine talking?"

She tipped her face up and pressed a kiss to his lips. "I asked you for this last night, too."

He ran his hands across the back of her neck and into her hair, pulling her closer. Paige slid her hands across his bare chest and had to admit: she liked kilts. Luxe climbed up on the mattress, pressing her down as he did.

Paige stroked his naked back, caressing his soft, smooth skin as he pressed kisses on her face and neck, wandering lower. Joy and sadness bubbled within her, threatening to ruin what she'd worked so hard to get. With some difficulty, she made herself focus only on the moment, wrapping herself around Luxe as he pushed her dress and his kilt out of the way.

Afterwards, Paige lay there, listening to Luxe's soft breathing beside her. She ran her fingers through his hair and tried not to cry. She didn't want to leave Luxe, and she certainly didn't want to forget this night. The idea that he would get to keep his memories and she would be left with nothing suffocated her. Surprisingly, she found herself wishing she could use time travel to go back and start this again. She'd willingly face Ammit, demons, and vampires just to have the extra time with Luxe. She wanted to do their adventures all over, but without the anger.

She snuggled against his chest, taking Luxe's limp arm and draping it across her. With his sleeping breath, warm on the back of her neck, Paige let all her feelings go and cried herself to sleep.

~ ~ ~

Dust danced in the shaft of sunlight. Outside the day blazed, but the inside was cool, and the air had the sharp, stony smell of a cave. Paige ran her hands across the stone walls of the altar room, pacing circles. They only had minutes until the portal, and she continued to hide from heat.

The feast the previous night had been a spectacle Paige wouldn't soon forget. Or would she? They'd woken before dawn, and she'd initiated another round of sex. She wanted to squeeze in as much of Luxe as she could get before this ended. These moments were all she would have. And even then, not for long. They'd sent the blessing of animals through the city, and the people had rejoiced, but she and Luxe retreated quickly. For a while, Paige had found solace in Luxe's arms and kisses, but even that couldn't keep her agitation at bay.

On what had to be her fiftieth time around her little circle, Luxe caught her hand and held it with a nod. The time had come to get last stone. A moment later, the portal tugged her in.

Suddenly, things went horribly wrong. A force out of their control whirled and ripped her hand from Luxe's. Something slammed into her head, and stars burst in front of her eyes. The world spun, and she sank into darkness.

Blinding lights created rainbows in Paige's vision. She sat, holding her head, only to find herself on some sort of slim, foam futon. Everything in the room shone white. Not that it mattered. The room held only her futon and a single chair shaped like an egg. Where the light came from she had no idea. No fixtures in the room or windows provided a source for the shine.

"Welcome to Atlantis, Paige Gentry."

She looked around for the speaker. A door slid open, and a man walked in. At first, she thought he was Luxe, with his white-blond hair and pale-blue eyes. But this man had many years on Luxe. A loose white tunic covered broad shoulders, and white pants which looked straight out of a yoga studio covered his legs. He went barefoot.

The man nodded in her direction. "I'll be brief, and then you will be sent on your way. We are aware of your purpose in Atlantis. We are aware you know of our heritage. We are also aware of yours, young human. Do not panic.

You will not be harmed, and Luxe already has his rune-stone returned to him."

"Can I go back to him?" She stood. To her surprise she wore an outfit which matched the man's. "Where is Luxe?"

"You will not be returned to the young warlock. He has broken warlock law by turning you into a familiar. By pulling you from your place in time, he threatens the very fabric of existence. We have the knowledge to repair the rip in time and send you home. Are you prepared?"

"Wait. Can't you repair time *and* let me stay with Luxe?"

"We have no jurisdiction to leave you as his familiar. Warlocks police their own laws. We are simply aiding them by providing the knowledge to complete the time repairs."

Panic ran rampant through Paige. She didn't want to leave and forget. "Then, can't you make it so I can stay some other way? Don't you have a potion or a spell to make me just magic enough? I don't need to be able to use magic. I only want to be allowed to see Luxe and remember him."

"We don't have such knowledge. One is born what they are meant to be. We cannot alter facts."

Claws of ice were squeezing her chest. "No. At least let me say goodbye. I want . . ." She gasped a little. "I'm not ready . . . I'll miss him."

He gave her a patronizing look which wasn't unkind. "You were never meant to be with him. But we are not unsympathetic. Your life is, after all, your choice. I have only one other option to provide you with. I can return you to Luxe, and you will both face the CoW of his time. For the hole in time and the loss of his family's heirlooms, his brother will push for execution and win. This process will take some years, and you will have those together.

"Or you can let us clear up this mess here. Return willingly to your time, and in turn spare Luxe's life. With time restored, warlock-kind will never know of his transgressions, and he will live a long life."

Paige scowled at him. "How can you possibly know this?"

"There are other ways of knowing the future besides traveling to it. But our method is not a skill which modern warlocks were meant to know. I will say no more, as that skill must die with us."

"So, you know what happens to Atlantis, and it doesn't bother you? You don't try to save yourselves?"

He gave her a calm and self-assured smile. "Your modern warlocks already know you cannot change the major flow of time. What was meant to be will be. This is something we understand and are at peace with. Not to be crass, but the demise of Atlantis does not affect my own life. Therefore, like most beings, it does not bother me the way you imply. We are all fairly shallow in that respect. Do you need time to consider?"

Paige shook her head as tears dripped. "There's not really anything to consider, is there? I can't let Luxe die." She gave a little sob. "Please, can't I say goodbye?"

The man hooked a hand under her elbow raising her from the futon. "Come, young human. Luxe has already prepared your portal. Your trials will all be over soon. When you arrive home, this will all be forgotten."

"Wait. Luxe made the portal? He agreed to this? He didn't want to see me?"

"Luxe's choices have been revealed to him as yours were to you. This is the course he has chosen as best. You are not meant to know his options, just as he will never know yours. We must all make the best choices we can, based on the information available to us."

Paige jerked her arm back. They were now in a long white hallway. "Hey. That sounds like you're manipulating our decisions."

"Perhaps." The man shrugged.

"*Luxe*," Paige screamed. "Luxe. They're sending me away."

"He cannot hear you. You may not go back to him unless you wish to alter your choice."

Paige slumped against the smooth wall. Her tears ran freely, and her stomach grew sick. Their time together wasn't supposed to end like this. The man stood her on her feet and led her to another white room. This one contained nothing but the shimmering portal. The faint sparkles around the edges were Luxe's particular shade of apple green. Another sob escaped her. Firm hands led her to the portal and pushed her in.

~ ~ ~

Paige jerked awake with a scream. She squeezed her eyes and sobbed. "Luxe. Luxe." Her throat hurt, and warm hands pulled desperately at her, trying to calm her down.

"I think we need to call her parents," a woman's voice spoke from somewhere outside her misery.

"I'll stay with her." The voice belonged to a young male who Paige recognized as if from another lifetime.

Paige cracked one eye. Justin's face, etched with worry, peered at her. "Justin?" she gasped. "Where? What? Huh?"

He ran a hand over her hair. "We were talking at my locker, and you just fell over, asleep. We haven't been able to wake you. You've had everyone scared to death."

Paige jerked upright. "Where am I? *When* am I?"

"Paige, you're at school. It's Monday, April twenty-ninth. School will be out in an hour. You've been asleep all afternoon. What's luxe?"

Paige blinked at him in confusion. Luxe sounded so familiar, but each time she tried to recall details, she might as well try nailing down Jell-O. "I . . . I don't know." Why did she have such a horrible, sick feeling in her chest?

Justin took her hand and glanced around the nurse's office. "I've been trying to ask all day. Paige, will you go out with me?"

Paige stared at Justin. She knew she'd been waiting for this moment. So why was the question so anticlimactic? She stared harder at him. She'd had a crush on Justin for months, but now she couldn't remember why. She had a thing for more delicate, intelligent types. She liked blond hair and blue eyes. Justin didn't fit with her ideal at all.

She grabbed her head and shook it. Something was definitely off. But she knew she couldn't agree to date him, at the moment. She'd better have him wait until she got herself sorted out. She patted his arm.

"Ego paenitet." She stopped abruptly. *"Wakarimasen."* She shook her head again. A funny fluffy feeling had invaded her skull. *"Agriette, nanimente?'*

Justin stared at her as if she'd laid an egg on the cot. She had no idea what she said. The words made sense until they passed her lips. She could even tell the language: Latin, Japanese, Atlantian. Wait, what?

The crushing feeling in her chest swelled again, and she started sobbing. When she finally calmed herself, she was alone. At some point in her little breakdown, Justin had fled.

Paige went home, morose. She couldn't drag herself out of her miserable mood as the last of the school year, prom, and graduation passed her by. She went through the motions on autopilot. She had no explanation for her mood, only the deep-seated feeling that she was missing something. Something which had meant a great deal to her. Her mother, convinced Paige now suffered from depression, threatened that if her unhappiness persisted after she returned from Europe, they were going to seek professional help.

Traveling did help. When she arrived in Barcelona, she felt happy for the first time in weeks. She hauled her brother over the entire city in two days before insisting they visit more. Travel affected her like a drug, boosting her mood by throwing her into an alternate mindset. She couldn't see enough new sights.

Her brother, Owen, happily gave her the history of the sights as she went. They took the train and worked their way eastward through France and into Italy. Paige made him cover everything: clothing styles through history, traditional foods, beginner language books. The details smoothed the edges of the hole in her chest.

Two weeks after she'd arrived in Europe, they stopped in front of the Colosseum. Owen stood behind her, reading a guide book to her as he pointed out the features. Suddenly, everything was real to Paige. She could smell the history, hear it. She gasped and staggered back against Owen. He caught her arm as she started to slide sideways. She shuddered and struggled against his grip.

"The demons will eat us," she shrieked.

As suddenly as the sensation came, it disappeared, and Paige slumped in her brother's grasp. He found a shady spot and propped her against the wall. Wiping her sweaty hair away from her face, he shook his head.

"Mom's wrong. I don't think you're depressed. I think you're sick. What's going on with you? Can't you tell me what feels off, so we can work on fixing it?"

Paige tried to smile at Owen but burst into tears. "I don't know."

That night, when Paige had calmed, they sat on the bed in the hotel room planning their next stops. Paige begged to go north. They would cover some of the countryside and eventually take the Chunnel and end in England. Once again, Paige could hardly wait. Something deep within her told her she ought to be in England. Or at least what she needed to feel better was there.

The weeks of touring northward passed at a slow clip for Paige. Somehow, there had to be a faster way to get around. The feeling that travel could be, or ought to be instantaneous nagged at her. She tried her best to be good company for Owen. After all, he *was* spending his summer taking her sightseeing. She should try to be more fun. But the closer they got to England, the more her stomach buzzed. What she needed had to be there.

She bullied Owen into seeing Windsor Castle first. Somehow the palace didn't look the way she imagined it. She left him examining the architecture and went wandering in the rose garden. She found a little alcove in the hedges which called to her as a good place to sit. She closed her eyes and the impression of a chilly, yet velvet night filled her mind. A blond head with a nose to her ear brought a thrill of desire to her stomach. It didn't matter that they were discussing the most ridiculous things.

"Luxe." She sobbed and slumped to lay on the stone bench. If only she could remember who or what Luxe was and why she so desperately needed it.

Chapter 22

Luxe found himself face to face with two individuals, one man and one woman who were obviously Atlantian. The woman had dark waving hair and sea-green eyes. The man had hair as light as Luxe's own. Luxe put a hand to his head and found he wore bracelets of a metal he wasn't familiar with.

"Hello, Luxe." The woman's voice came low, mellow, and soothing. "Time runs short, so we need you to make a choice."

"What choice?"

Luxe tried wiggling his fingers. As he thought, the cuffs negated his magic. Something else was wrong. His ties to Paige were gone.

"Paige." He started to get up, but the blond man held him down in what looked like an egg-shaped chair.

"Your choices will directly influence Paige, please listen," the woman said. "Here, as a token of good faith."

The woman held the last rune-stone out to Luxe. He took it and waited for her to speak again.

"You have left a hole in the fabric of time by pulling Paige out. You have two choices. We can send her back and undo damage you have created. She will live her predestined life.

"Or you can keep her as you intend to ask your parents for permission to do. Although they will give you permission, the rest of warlock kind will not. We do not have the knowledge to allow you to keep her in any capacity other than as your familiar. Other ruling families will bring the case to the CoW. The ruling returned will be for Paige's extermination, to both break the spell and to deter others from attempting what you have done."

Luxe crossed his arms. "I've heard Atlanteans can read the future."

"This is true," answered the man.

"I also heard Atlanteans use this to their own ends." He scowled at them. "How am I supposed to believe you?"

"The chaos you've created benefits no one," the woman said. "Beyond that, you must use your own intellect or heart and decide."

"Then based on what you say I don't really have a choice. I can have a little more time with Paige while the CoW runs her trial, or I can save her and never see her again."

Both individuals shrugged.

"Send her back," he whispered.

"Please create the portal," the woman ordered as the man left the room.

As soon as Luxe finished the portal, she ushered him from the first room into another which looked identical. "You have all nine stones, I presume?"

"You know too much of my business," Luxe snapped.

"I know what I am meant to know. Please portal back to your own time. Your parents are waiting for you."

Luxe shivered as a chill ran through his body. His parents knew. The time had come to face them. He could almost cry for wanting Paige at his back for this. But he couldn't selfishly keep her only to have her executed.

He drew the portal on the wall. He'd nearly stepped through when someone screamed his name from the hall.

"Paige." He tried to run for her, but the woman caught him.

"Through the portal young man, unless you wish to change your decision."

Luxe let his face drop to the woman's shoulder. "But she needs me," he sobbed. "That tone. It's fear. I need to go to her. I . . . I need her." The woman patted his head, turned him and pushed him through the portal.

Luxe hit the ground with a thud, and rough hands yanked him to his feet. "You're dead," Atlas hissed in his ear.

Luxe couldn't even bring himself to care. Hopefully, Atlas would make his demise quick.

"Atlas. Drop him."

Luxe looked up at the sound of his father's voice. Kyne Pendragon's eyes flashed at his sons. Luxe wanted to crawl into a hole, but Atlas glared back at Kyne with anger in his eyes. Kyne looked exactly like Luxe only older: platinum hair, blue eyes, thin build, intelligent face. Yet somehow, he managed to be threatening all the same.

Luxe's mother Edrea stepped up beside Kyne, her gray eyes snapping. "You boys will *not* fight. It's not the time for that."

She blew a handful of blue-green sparkles over them all. The damp rose garden Luxe had arrived in faded, and they were all in his father's study instead. She silently pointed each of the boys to the two chairs. Kyne moved to stand between them and Edrea took a spot behind the desk, like a displeased headmaster about to scold boys for fighting.

"Luxe."

Luxe cringed. He was in for it now.

"I want to congratulate you on retrieving all nine stones successfully."

His head popped up, and he stared at his mother incredulously. "Huh?"

His mother crossed her arms. "Luxe, you didn't think we'd let you take the philosopher's stone to run experiments without monitoring you, did you?"

Luxe blushed. "I guess not."

"And," his mother continued, "did you really believe we don't keep tabs on our family heirlooms better than that?" She shook her head. "No, we've been tracking you from the very beginning."

Luxe cowered in his chair, and his mother scowled at him. He desperately wished Paige were here now. He got himself out of tight spots so much better with her. Wait, how would this would look to her? Him shrinking in fear. He wouldn't want her to see him like this. He sat himself upright and faced his mother. Whatever the punishment was, he'd take it like a man.

"That's better." His mother smiled at him. "Your father and I were getting worried. You're quickly approaching your coming of age, and yet you still had no backbone. We let you struggle through the attempts to get the stones back to see if you could indeed survive on your own. Had you failed, you would not have made a suitable keeper for the rune-stones. Of course, when we removed the primary level spell books from your workroom, we had no idea what you'd unleash. But all's well that end's well."

"Wait." Luxe slid to the edge of his seat. "How? I mean, I thought Atlas and I had to duel for the stones."

"Atlas is not in line for keeping the stones. He is adopted. You've been timid since you were a small child, and before your adventure, we feared you might never be up to the task of defending our family's source of power. Even though Atlas can only draw a limited portion of the power in the stones, we wondered if we might need to let him have them anyway. The stones would have been safer with him than with you, if you hadn't gained the confidence to protect them."

Luxe stared at Atlas. "Is all this why you hate me so much?"

His brother ignored him, focusing on their mother. "He lost the stones in the first place," Atlas complained. "How suitable can he be?"

Kyne put a heavy hand on his shoulder. "Son, he still has decades of training to receive. We let this happen to prove to us he could handle a big job."

"So, train me," Atlas yelled at him.

"Atlas." Edrea's voice was stern. "You have completed all the training you are capable of. You heard the magic master. If you task your powers any further, you risk damaging yourself." Her smile softened. "We love you, just as you are. You need to learn to love yourself, as well. You may not hold the potential Luxe does, but it does not make you any less my son."

Atlas burst from his chair. "Yes, it does," he roared. "I can't believe a skinny screw-up gets everything, and I get nothing."

Kyne grabbed him and shoved him back into the chair. "You get the rank and privilege which comes with being a Pendragon. Do not speak to your mother so. Nothing has been hurt, save your pride. And if your ego is so easily damaged by truths you already knew, then it's not much in the way of pride."

Luxe's mind whirled. "Am I being punished?"

"I've spoken with Madam Antonius, you are clear."

"But what about everything I've done?"

"Your determination in the face of death several times over was punishment enough, as well as something to be proud of."

He jumped from his chair. "What about Paige?"

Edrea frowned. "What about her? Repairing time would have been difficult for your father and I, even with all the stones. We asked the Atlanteans for help."

Luxe fell back into his chair. "Is she all right? Can I visit her? I never got to say goodbye."

Kyne shook his head. "I'm sorry, my son. She's back where she belongs. Don't meddle."

A lump lodged itself in his chest. "But . . ." He fought for breath. "Everything I did . . . she was the catalyst for it. I can't do this without her. And I . . . I love her." He let his head hang. "At least I was falling in love with her. I tried not to. I knew she had to go home. But . . ." He took a quick swipe at his eyes.

"Oh, Luxe." His mother's voice held pity and a little exasperation. "We'll find you a nice witch to settle down with."

"Leaving aside that there's hardly any my age, I don't want some witch." Luxe begged his mother with his eyes. "Is there really no way for us to be together? We talked about the possibility of calling on Khalidah."

"Djinn are just mythology." Atlas snorted.

"That's what I said," Luxe countered, "but then Paige pointed out dragons and whatnot are mythology for humans, yet they're real to us. Couldn't the same be true of djinn? Grandfather Merlin thought so."

Edrea sighed and rubbed her forehead. "Kyne, what do you think?"

"She's human. The boy's feelings for her hardly matter. Besides, no one has even asked her. To bring her back here means she would be giving up everything she's used to in life. She'd be stuck as his familiar in order to stay. She won't exist amongst humans. It's a big choice for a young girl."

"Please?" Luxe found himself on his feet and breathless. "Couldn't we just ask her? If she wants to stay in her own time we'll leave." He slumped just as quickly. "Oh . . . that's right. They said if she stayed as my familiar the CoW would have her executed."

Kyne looked at his wife. "All part of the test the Atlanteans set up."

"What was?" Luxe asked, glancing between his parents.

Edrea sighed. "You were both given a choice to spare the other. You both took it." She paused, twisting a ring on her finger as she thought. "I'll return to Atlantis. If they will help repair the hole a second time, you may ask. We will reinstate her as your familiar, and your father and I will appeal to the other families on your behalf."

"Would we really have a chance?" Luxe gasped.

"In theory. But the choice to return will have to be hers and hers alone. The CoW won't permit you to take her away. But they might make an exception if she willingly requested to be your familiar."

His mother came around from behind the desk. She took his chin and tipped his face up. "Know this, Luxe. You still have nearly a millennium left to live. She will be bound to you for her entire lifetime. I can't keep requesting the Atlanteans repair holes simply so she can go back and forth. And once her normal human lifeline ends, going back won't ever be an option. You are essentially asking her to marry you."

"But . . ." Luxe stammered.

"Another warlock will not be allowed to marry someone else's familiar. If you expect to be the only man in her life for her entire lifespan . . ." His mother held her hands wide, waiting for Luxe to add it up. "You must understand what you are asking of her and committing to yourself. You are both quite young to make such a decision. Prepare yourself for the possibility she's not ready."

"Wait," Atlas growled. "So, he gets to break the rules *again*? For some girl?"

"Atlas," Edrea's voice carried a warning. "We used the Pendragon name to secure your chosen wife from the Boanerges family, despite their rules against marrying outside a noble family. They overlooked your natural bloodline for us. As a result, you have supremely powerful twin daughters who can draw on the heirlooms of two high ranking families and have free access to nearly 4,000 years of history. We helped you. Why would we not do the same for Luxe?"

"But she's not even a witch," Atlas protested.

"And her humanity will be Luxe's heartbreak to bear. The choice is his. The same as your choices were yours." Edrea started drawing a portal on the wall. "I will let you know what the Atlanteans say about fixing a second hole."

Edrea disappeared and Atlas scowled at Luxe. "Our family would have been better if you hadn't been born." He gave his father a furious look. "See how much trouble he causes?"

"Atlas." Kyne sighed. "This has to stop. Don't make me banish you to some less desirable time period."

Atlas got up and stormed out. Luxe sat blinking at his father, still trying to wrap his head around what had just happened.

"Father?"

"Hmm."

"I . . . I thought everyone disliked me. You and mother never had much faith in me."

"You really had us wondering if you would ever step up and be a warlock, but that doesn't mean we don't like you. You got that from Atlas. We've been on him to curb his attitude for years. It's gotten worse because you're coming of age soon. We put pressure on you to pull out your drive to succeed."

"And Paige did it," Luxe mumbled.

Kyne sat in the chair Atlas had vacated. "The girl's positive influence on you is the only reason your mother and I would consider letting anything with a human continue. But we watched the whole thing. The girl's an asset, no doubt."

The portal on the wall reappeared, and Edrea stepped back through. She gave her son a hard look. "You're lucky the Atlanteans are hopeless romantics."

Luxe leapt from his chair, and his mother caught his hands. "Be careful." She looked at him with sad eyes and ran a hand across his cheek. "There's a good chance one or both of you is going to end up brokenhearted."

"I can go get her now?"

Kyne shook his head and stood. "I'll go."

"Why?" Luxe's excitement drained away.

"Remember, she has to willingly commit herself to servitude. The choice has to come from her head, not her heart. With you sitting in front of her, she's far more likely to do something impulsive." He gave his son a smile. "I'll bring her, as long as she is willing. You have my word."

~ ~ ~

Paige let the tears roll down onto the bench. She could smell wet stone she'd cried so much. The roses hid her from Owen, and he'd wandered off, calling for her. They both had cell phones. She'd call him in a bit when she'd gotten a handle on herself.

The empty feeling grew painful. The last time she remembered feeling this way was when her pet cat had to be put down. She heaved a sigh and rubbed her eyes. Why? How had she ended up in such a state? She hadn't lost anything she could remember. The lack of memory hung her up. In that void the answer swirled, so close, yet so uncatchable.

"Paige Gentry?"

She looked up and her heart nearly stopped. "*Luxe!*"

She leapt off the bench and made it halfway to the man before she stopped. This man appeared closer to her father's age then her own, and she didn't know him. For the first time she knew for sure Luxe was a person. But who was he, and why did she want to see him so badly? Whatever memories this man triggered didn't come with details.

The blond man shook his head, chuckling. "Amazing, you harbor such affection for my son that you've managed to find holes in an Atlantean memory spell."

"Huh?"

His words were English, but nothing he said made sense. He wiggled his fingers and blew in her direction, making Paige back off a bit. Something tickled her nose. Then, like floodgates opening, everything came back to her. She staggered backwards, and the man jumped forward to grab her arm. He stopped her just shy of the thorny rose bushes.

Moving his hand from her arm to her hand, he kissed the back of it in a courtly gesture. "Kyne Pendragon. Pleased to make your acquaintance."

"Kyne Pendragon? Are you related to Luxe?"

"I'm his father."

Her knees gave out, and she fell to her butt on the bench. "This is what I've been searching for weeks to remember. But I don't feel any better. The Atlanteans said I wouldn't be able to see you again. They said if I stayed horrible things would happen to Luxe. That won't happen because you're here, right?"

"*No*. No, no, no." He crouched in front of her. "Luxe is fine and will continue to be. As will you."

Her brain staggered under the completely overwhelming load of memories. She shook her head to clear it.

"Why . . . why do you sound nice? Luxe was always so afraid of his parents."

Kyne took her hand, pulling her to her feet. "A misguided fear instilled by our pushing him to embrace his magic and fueled by his brother's taunting."

She wrinkled her nose and frowned. "Why does Atlas hate him so much?"

"Shall we have a seat? We actually have much to talk about."

Kyne told her about Atlas, Luxe's awakening as a warlock on their adventure, and their option for being reunited. The information whirled around her head like a tornado. Her decision was so monumental.

"But the choice is yours, my dear," Kyne finished.

Paige hesitated. "What if things don't work out between Luxe and I? What if I want to come back?"

"You may return whenever you wish. The Atlanteans have offered their aid. But coming back is a one-time offer. If we return you to human life a second time, you won't be able to return to us for a third."

Paige spotted Owen looking around the other side of the gardens for her. "What about my family?"

"Separating you from your timeline won't hurt them. They won't know you existed in the first place." Paige stopped breathing, and Kyne put a hand on her head. "You don't have to leave. I can return home, and you go back to your life. You won't remember anything, just as before, not even our little chat. I didn't remove your memory spell, I only blocked it for the purpose of this conversation."

Paige shook her head sadly. "I don't want the last few weeks back. I've been miserable because I knew something went missing. I felt like . . . I don't know, like I should have . . . or could have been part of something so much bigger. I've spent the entire trip with my brother searching for Luxe, even though I could barely remember." She shuddered and looked over at Owen. "But to have my own family not know me . . ."

"Would you like for me to return tomorrow? Let you think things through?"

Paige shook her head. "I'm not sure thinking your offer over would make a difference." She sucked air in through her teeth. "I've been miserable back at home. I . . ." a blush hit her cheeks, "I want to be with Luxe. I think." She stared in Owen's direction. "Will my brother be all right?"

"Will you be?"

Paige nodded. "Yeah, I'll give staying with your family a couple of years. I would have to leave my own family to go to college in the fall, anyway." She knew it wasn't the same. She would have been able to call home, and they would, of course, remember her. She heaved a sigh, holding back tears. "Can we go? Before I doubt myself."

"Of course." Kyne put a hand on her shoulders, leading her toward one of the brick walls of the buildings. She could see the drawing crystal in his hand.

"Paige!" Owen had spotted her and ran toward them.

The portal opened. "Let's go, Paige. Don't cause him any extra pain. We need to get the familiar spell back on you so he'll forget."

Paige nodded. The sunny day had become a smear in her vision thanks to the tears. "Owen, I love you," she screamed back at him.

Paige stepped into the portal, and strong, familiar arms caught her.

"Edrea, the potion. I believe her brother is quite distraught."

Without being set on the floor, a woman pressed a vial into Paige's hand, and Kyne ordered her to drink. She did. The icy sensation washed over her and faded. Luxe squeezed her as he pressed his face into her neck.

"I was *so* worried you wouldn't come," he gasped.

She squeezed him back. "I missed you so much. Even with the memory spell, living without you hurt."

"Luxe." A woman with blond hair tucked up under a

French-style hood and piercing gray eyes spoke. "Perhaps you'd like to set the poor girl down and introduce her."

"Oh, yeah." Luxe blushed bright red and set Paige on her feet. "Paige, this is my mom, Edrea Pendragon."

Edrea inclined her head in Paige's direction. "A pleasure."

"Likewise?" Paige couldn't put a finger on it. The woman was intimidating. She could see where it would be easy to believe Atlas if he said she hated you.

The evening followed in a blur of explanations, introductions, and moving in. The Pendragons gave Paige the bedroom adjoining Luxe's and Edrea conjured up a wardrobe of appropriate clothing. Kyne introduced her to the house staff as Luxe's betrothed, since sixteenth-century staff wouldn't understand their relationship any other way. Having a maid to wait on her left Paige mildly uncomfortable.

It wasn't until late that night when most of the household slept and Luxe had joined her in her room that she finally felt comfortable. They sat on the rug in front of the fire, Paige with her nightgown tucked over her knees and Luxe with a cloak wrapped over both their shoulders. Paige sighed and laid her head on Luxe's shoulder, and he dropped his head to rest on hers.

"You're happy now, right?" Luxe asked.

"Yeah." She tipped her head up and kissed under his chin.

He pulled her body closer to his. "Mm . . . So, I never got a chance to ask you, how long are you back for?"

"Are you fishing for if I want to stay forever? Are you proposing?"

Luxe blushed and looked away. "No. I mean, if I needed to. Kind of. I mean . . ."

She giggled and pressed a finger to his lips. "I think I follow. I just wanted to tease you. Your father mentioned

I could choose to go home up to a certain point. But the reality is if I stay long term, we'll pretty much be married. I doubt either of us is ready to decide that yet. So why don't we take a couple of years to see how we feel? Two or three years . . . even four or five. I can pass those off as going to college if we decide we can't stay together."

"Okay." Luxe blushed deeper. "I didn't want you to feel pressured either way."

Paige nestled into his side. "There's no rush. Let's relax and let things go where they go."

Luxe kissed her hair on top of her head. "Perfect. In that case, what would you like to do next?"

"I want to travel and see the world for fun. Let's not find demons, or vampires, or vicious creatures. Instead, let's see . . . everything."

Luxe laid back, stretching out on the rug and pulled Paige with him. "Tomorrow we can start traipsing around history." He kissed her cheek and then her ear. "For tonight, I refuse to let you leave my arms."

"Is that an order?" Paige giggled.

"It is." Luxe chuckled back. "These are the moments which make me so glad you're my familiar. A cat is nice to curl up with. But you . . . Me . . . yow."

Paige, closed her eyes and luxuriated in his snuggling. Her body thrilled with the touch of Luxe's lips on her skin. The anticipation of seeing any event in history she wanted might have been a distraction. But for this moment, she wished time could stand still.

Made in the USA
Lexington, KY
16 August 2019